S0-DJZ-407

DANGER AND DESIRE

Gil's face tightened, and he walked away. He picked up his suit jacket on the way to the door.

"Did I say something wrong?" Maggie was only half joking as she joined him.

"Don't take this lightly, Maggie. Letting your guard down is a very good way to get yourself hurt."

Maggie instantly sobered. "I am taking everything seriously, Gil." She raised her hand to his face, stroked his jaw. "Everything."

Gil held her eyes with his, then he turned his lips briefly into her palm. "Good night. I'll talk to you more tomorrow."

Maggie shut the door behind him, clicked off her porch light, and stood staring at the wood for a moment. She lifted her palm to her own cheek, transferring the imprint of the lasting impression that mattered most to her as Gil drove away.

FLASHPOINT

Tracey Tillis

AN ONYX BOOK

ONYX
Published by the Penguin Group
Penguin Books USA Inc., 375 Hudson Street,
New York, New York 10014, U.S.A.
Penguin Books Ltd, 27 Wrights Lane,
London W8 5TZ, England
Penguin Books Australia Ltd,
Ringwood, Victoria, Australia
Penguin Books Canada Ltd, 10 Alcorn Avenue,
Toronto, Ontario, Canada M4V 3B2
Penguin Books (N.Z.) Ltd, 182-190 Wairau Road,
Auckland 10, New Zealand

Penguin Books Ltd, Registered Offices:
Harmondsworth, Middlesex, England

First published by Onyx, an imprint of Dutton Signet,
a division of Penguin Books USA Inc.

First Printing, February, 1997
10 9 8 7 6 5 4 3 2 1

PUBLISHER'S NOTE
This is a work of fiction. Names, characters, places, and incidents either are
the product of the author's imagination or are used fictitiously, and any
resemblance to actual persons, living or dead, events, or locales is entirely
coincidental.

For V., whose selfless acts of giving
and spirit of faith nurtured the spirit of this story.
Love ya, guy.

Also, my heartfelt thanks
to George and Jackie, for your
commitment to tradition.

Prologue

It was done.

Charlie Denning carefully put the finishing touches to the last page of the document he'd sweated over for the past hour in the hot, steamy Georgia night.

"You gonna rot in hell now, you bastard," he muttered. A violent sneeze shook him, and spittle gusted over the papers. The contemplation of their contents had kept him alive for the thirty years he'd been stuck behind prison walls.

He wiped the papers with a soiled tissue, then he pushed them against the rest of the trash cluttering his writing desk. His eyes settled on a cubbyhole to his right, and he reached inside. The key he had stored there drew him, and he pulled it out, unable to resist.

The metal fit easily inside the keyhole of the locked drawer at his waist. The note was right on top, at his fingertips. He smiled and caressed it, studied the recipient's name he had painstakingly printed there in his tight, spiky scrawl: Magdalaine Thomas.

Wasn't that uppity little miss gonna get a nasty jolt when her sainted daddy, the mighty colored United States senator, came tumblin' down.

Denning's pale, wasted body shook through a long,

phlegmy cough. It may have been a long time coming, but, oh, revenge was gonna be sweet.

" 'And if a man cause a blemish in his neighbor; as he hath done, so shall it be done to him," he murmured. "Breach for breach, eye for eye, tooth for tooth; as he hath caused a blemish in a man, so shall it be done to him *again*.' "

Damn right.

Denning slipped the note back inside the drawer and hesitated in the process of relocking it, thinking. Within the week, he'd mail it to missy Thomas's *New Horizons* magazine. He'd considered sending it to *Newsweek* first, or one of those other political fanzines. But the temptation of sending it to hers, of making her squirm with fear and then futile hope was just too good.

He figured it wouldn't take long after she read his ditty for the blackmail money to start coming. She'd certainly be intrigued enough with what little information he gave her to pay to find out more.

His attention shifted again to the document. What the little girl didn't know was that it was already going to be too late. He'd timed it so that the sweet bomb his document carried would be long gone and into the hands of her media rivals, even a couple of those television rags, a few weeks after she got her note. Those rivals would treat it right, reveal all the juicy details about their national hero just before the next election rolled around.

All that was left for him to do before he mailed the document was to send the note, scare the kid, and wait to enjoy the money that would be his bonus. As he reached for his pen again and a slightly yellowed envelope in which to stuff the papers, he was diverted by a burst of barking.

Buster's damn dog. Maybe he'd just take his

shotgun out back when he finished here, shut it up once and for all. That dumb fuck Buster obviously didn't know what a warning meant. He positioned his pen and started to write. But then a flash of lightning jerked his attention up to the open, unscreened window of the ramshackle room.

If he didn't get his window closed, a good gust of wind and rain was all it would take to gut the remaining innards of this rickety old country shack. He walked over to the warped window, struggled to pull it down, and decided the first thing he was gonna do was use missy's money to upscale his digs from this pig hole he was renting. It pissed him off all over again that he couldn't afford better.

The dog yapped again. "Dammit," he muttered, swinging around to shuffle to the gun he'd propped in a corner. His hand was on it when a noise at the front door brought his head around. A startled "*ah!*" was all he managed before the charging dark shape busted his lock and closed in.

Denning felt the shuddering jab of the knife right before it ripped up into his heart. His finger spasmed around the shotgun trigger, forcing a mighty blast into the air. The reflexive grunt of his killer's curse preceded his own seconds before he died.

Buster's dog started barking in earnest.

. . . The killer stepped back, letting the old man slump to the floor. His eyes darted around the sparse furnishings of the room, intent on what it was he needed to find. And then the upturned edges of the thick document caught his eye.

He ran over to the desk, made a quick scan of the pages, and smiled. The information was rolled into as tight a cylinder as possible and secure in his fist by the time he heard a distant voice beyond the gaping front door.

He just managed to squeeze his body through the warped back screen off Denning's kitchen when the first crack of thunder rattled it.

The killer's escape into the moist, summer darkness was complete, though only seconds old, when Buster arrived at the splintered front door.

Chapter 1

The vultures were circling as if he were already dead.

Maggie Thomas pushed her way through the pool of journalists camped outside the hospital entrance, praying it wasn't so.

Many reporters that night would dramatically note how the great man's daughter, red-eyed and grim, bore little resemblance to the unruffled public image. They would share the sensational speculation that her refusal to offer even minimal comment suggested she had exclusive news about Paul Thomas's condition, and that perhaps the news wasn't good.

All their morbid commentary would matter as little to Maggie then as it did now. Her only thought was to get to her father's side to make peace, if it wasn't too late.

Inside the elevator, she let pieces of her conversation with his surgeon drift across her memory.

". . . There's a change in your father's condition . . . He's grown quite agitated in the last hour . . . insists on seeing you . . . not good . . . I want you here right away . . ."

If only he could have wanted her there two days ago when he'd been capable of communicating, when he'd been gaining strength, apparently stabilizing. If only . . .

"Dammit, Daddy, hang on," Maggie whispered.

She was almost to the nurses' station when one of the women moved forward to meet her.

"Right this way, honey. He was asking for you just before he slipped into the coma."

"Coma?" Maggie stopped walking.

"I'm sorry," the woman said awkwardly. "I thought you knew."

Maggie dropped her head, her gaze blurring against the dull reflection of the white linoleum floor. When they walked on and neared her father's room, a number of people were sitting in the waiting area. Half a dozen others leaned against the walls. Maggie nodded, trying to accept their smiles of encouragement and concern.

Then she was at her father's room, and for one panicked moment she couldn't think at all.

Her slender hand was against the swinging door when the nurse cautioned her.

"Your father's condition is serious enough that I'll have to restrict your visit to five minutes."

"Yes, I understand," Maggie murmured. She braced herself, then stepped inside the room.

Paul Thomas looked old. On the heels of that thought came a worse one He looked frighteningly weak. Utterly incapable of fighting the battle she knew lay ahead.

Maggie moved closer to his bed, and the latter impression was dispelled by the seemingly lifelike blips and monitored readings coming from the support apparatus attached to her father's body.

She dropped her hands to the protective metal railing surrounding his bed. For one wild moment, she was convinced he was going to sit up and tell her this whole thing was a ruse to frighten her into submission.

She sighed, feeling the weight of old frustration. Her father could be dying. Any bitterness held over from the past, any barriers it had erected between them surely signified little now. She was his only child.

She watched him, unable to check the slow tears, unable to stem her horror at his chalky brown skin, at how helpless and still he seemed.

The stillness and defenselessness were the worst. Paul Thomas was not a helpless man. He never had been.

A soft touch at Maggie's shoulder made her jump. "You can come back later tonight," the nurse told her.

Maggie hesitated. Part of her wanted to lean down and kiss her father's lined brow while another part of her feared he'd find some way to rebuff her, even now.

She stood undecided, then she turned and walked away.

"I want to talk to Lai," she told the nurse outside in the corridor. The woman was about to answer when a gruff voice from the distance hailed them.

Maggie turned to see an Asian man of average height, middle-aged, and slightly balding, coming toward them. Lai's soft-soled shoes muffled his quick steps. His slightly crumpled green surgical scrubs added to the low-key effect to put Maggie at some ease.

"Maggie," he said, reaching out to grasp her hands.

"Lai."

"How are you doing?"

"I'm fine. What's his prognosis?"

"I'll give it to you straight. That hit-and-run driver really did a job. The fractures, cuts, and internal injuries we repaired in surgery are holding well. What obviously has us concerned now is the brain trauma he's sustained."

Maggie moved impatiently. "How long is he going to be in a coma?"

"Unfortunately, we can't be sure," Lai said. He nodded absently to another doctor who hurried past them. "To be frank, Maggie, the behavior of head injuries is hell to predict. The long answer is, we'll have to wait until he wakes up before we're in a position to determine possible neurological damage. Aside from that, all I can tell you is that he may wake up any time. It could be a matter of hours or—"

"What?"

"Or"—Lai held her gaze squarely—"it could be a matter of days. Maybe even weeks. It's just too early to say. What I can tell you is that the next twenty-four hours should give us a better indication of which direction things will go."

"I want to stay," Maggie said quietly.

Lai regarded her assessingly. "I'll permit it, but I would suggest that since it's going to probably be a very long night, you leave for a while. Get some rest. Have supper. The nurses on the unit can fix you up in a room for the night after you get back."

He glanced at his watch, reminding Maggie that her father's situation was just one of several dramas demanding his time. When he laid a comforting hand on her shoulder, she was touched to hear him say, "I've always admired your father. Greatly. I'll do my best to get him better for you." Then he was striding away, no doubt already thinking about his next crisis.

Maggie looked back in the direction of her father's room. Only then did she notice the tall, slim figure who had been standing quietly against the wall a few feet away, taking in the exchange. He walked toward her now.

From a distance he seemed familiar. As he drew closer, his unhurried, self-assured stride touched off a flare of awareness that made her heart slow and then pound. She wanted to run, but with full recognition came the resignation that she couldn't.

"Gil," she said when he reached her.

His expression was unreadable.

Maggie had told herself the day he'd left she never wanted to see him again. Until this moment, she never had.

"I didn't know you were back," she said.

"I haven't been for long. Two weeks."

"Why?"

Gil Stewart smiled.

The stark cynicism that twisted his wide, sensual mouth, the hardness that narrowed his eyes, disconcerted Maggie. "I'm surprised you're here," she blurted out.

"Of course I'm here," he answered simply. "What did you think?"

"Do you really want to know?" she countered.

Gil regarded her impassively. "I certainly didn't come back to fight, Maggie. I had a bellyful of that eight years ago. I think we both did."

She glanced behind him toward her father's room. "Well, if you've made your grand entrance for him, you're too late. He doesn't even know you're here."

Gil looked away, saying nothing.

Her words hovered in the air, as hushed as the silence that seemed to isolate them from the surrounding bustle. Moments ticked by, and Maggie had given up on a reply when Gil sighed impatiently. He turned back to her, pinning her gaze with a bitterness that told her perhaps she had not visited hell alone.

"I came back for me, Maggie. This is my home. Indefinite exile finally lost its appeal."

Maggie flinched as if he'd slapped her. She was trying to recover when a stern-featured man of medium height materialized at Gil's side. His cool Nordic blondness contrasted markedly with Gil's bronzed darkness. Yet when his attention settled on her, Maggie could sense his subtle communiqué with Gil. The nature of it was familiar to her, though dimmed with the passage of time and all things she associated with Gil.

She looked questioningly to Gil just as the silent man shoved his hand inside his pants pocket. The gesture pulled aside his suit jacket and exposed the dull glint of a police shield.

"Adam, give us a minute," Gil said.

"Sure, Lieutenant."

The other man was clearly reluctant. Maggie wondered if he wavered because of what even she had very unmistakably understood as a command. So, Gil was still the big, bad cop. And not only that, a cop with some rank. Wherever he'd disappeared to, his career had obviously prospered. Her more urgent awareness right now, however, was of his large, cool hand that had insistently clasped her arm.

Just as firmly, she shrugged out of his grip. Gil looked down at her but let it ride.

"You could use some coffee," he said as they walked. "Let's go to the cafeteria."

"Let's not. We can't have much to discuss."

"I beg to differ. I'd advise you to come along."

Stung by his attitude, Maggie slowed and prepared to let him know it when they were distracted by a disturbance behind them.

"I told you, this isn't a police matter, mister—hey! Get back here!"

A tall, rawboned television reporter, whom Maggie recognized with the irritation of past acquaintance, sidestepped Gil's partner to make a beeline for them. His cameraman was in tow.

Maggie didn't want this. She felt cornered, unprepared, briefly tempted to lean into Gil's strength, support she had once depended upon as her own.

The reporter was intense, abrupt. "Lieutenant Stewart, what's going down? Is Senator Thomas's accident being regarded as deliberate foul play now?"

"I'm here as a friend of the senator, nothing more."

"If that's true, why the surplus of officers stationed around this hospital. Is that just coincidence?" The reporter shoved his microphone in Gil's face. The cameraman's equipment was rolling.

Gil was brusque. "The senator is a very important man. I'm sure you don't need me to explain the wisdom of routine precaution. Come on, Maggie."

This time when Gil took her arm to lead her away, Maggie let him.

"Ms. Thomas!"

Maggie stopped and turned.

"For the record, are you and Stewart back together?"

Maggie's mind went blank. The camera rolled as she struggled for something to say.

"An unexpected turn of events, wouldn't you say, seeing as how it was your magazine that sabotaged his career?"

"Goddammit!" Gil muttered darkly. Maggie couldn't restrain his abrupt turn and controlled charge in the direction of the smirking reporter. The curious crowd that had gathered parted for him.

"Listen," Gil said when he was practically nose to nose with the grinning man, "you've already asked your relevant question, and I've given the relevant answer. Anything beyond that is called harassment by any book. Got it?"

The reporter was still grinning, but he backed up a step. "Yeah, Lieutenant, I got it." He signaled his colleague to stop rolling tape. "Welcome home," he said in a hushed sneer before he trotted off.

Gil caught his partner's eye in the distance and waved him back.

Maggie felt numb by the time they reached the cafeteria and gladly accepted the cup of coffee Gil purchased along with his own. A table toward the back of the room afforded them some privacy from the scattering of others having lunch. Maggie wrapped her hands around her cup and settled back in her chair. The stern, aquiline lines of Gil's handsome face weren't encouraging.

"Why is it that despite what you told that parasite, I get the feeling you're going to conduct this session exactly like a cop?" she asked.

Gil pulled his eyes away from the casual study he'd been making of her. Maggie shivered at the glimmer of heat that faded before he focused on her question.

"You're right," he said. "I lied." He sipped his coffee. "There's been a murder, Maggie. There's evidence that suggests your father may be linked to it."

Pure surprise held Maggie still before she laughed and lifted her cup. "Try again, Gil."

Gil merely watched her, his dark eyes as fathomless as black chips of ice.

Maggie lowered her coffee a bit unsteadily. "You're serious," she said quietly.

"Completely."

"Linked how?"

"Two days ago, a murdered man was discovered. A note was found with his body. He claimed to have something on your father with the power to blow his senatorial reelection bid out of the water."

"Impossible," Maggie stated flatly. "He—"

"Also claimed to have put the details in some letter he was going to mail to a number of high-profile news sources, including yours."

"I never received anything, Gil."

"Are you sure?"

"Absolutely. Any of my staffers would immediately have turned over that kind of information to me."

"Yes, of course. They're a loyal bunch, aren't they?" He lifted his cup to his mouth.

"For God's sake, do you think I'm lying?"

"Well, we both know you're capable of it."

Maggie leaned back against her chair, hating the quick sting of tears. "Damn you for that, Gil Stewart," she whispered.

"You already did once," Gil shot back. More softly, he added, "You have my permission to give it your best shot again. But know one thing. This time I won't lie down quietly. And it still won't change the fact that your father may be in a hell of a mess."

Maggie gathered her purse from the floor and got up to leave.

"Sit down, Maggie."

She looked contemptuously at the strong brown hand that had reached out to grip her wrist. "Let go, Gil."

"Maggie," he intoned with barely suppressed fury.

"I am *not* going to sit here and be manhandled by you," Maggie replied with quiet fury of her own, "physically or emotionally."

Seconds stretched the standoff, then Gil suddenly let her go. He ran a broad hand through his dark, wavy hair, and threw a frustrated look around the room. "I'm . . . sorry," he said on an expelled breath. "I didn't mean to lose my temper."

He didn't look sorry, Maggie thought. In fact, he looked as if he were willing to say whatever it would take to placate her into rejoining the conversation. Obviously, the sooner he had his answers, the sooner he could get as far away from her as possible.

Perversely, Maggie hung back. As she could have anticipated, she thought bitterly, Gil's professionalism calmly reasserted itself. She knew the exact moment when the man gave way to the cop from the way he relaxed, from the way he casually folded his arms across his chest, from the way that impersonal veil she hated dropped smoothly into place to shield his thoughts.

Whatever it takes to get the job done, right Gil . . . ?

"Maggie, did you hear me?"

"What?" she answered distractedly.

"I said we're going to have this conversation. Sit down. Please."

In spite of everything, he was right. They needed to talk. Slowly, Maggie sat back down. And just as slowly, a weariness of spirit infused her.

"What do you want from me, Gil?"

Gil let that go unanswered for what became an uncomfortably long moment, then he leaned across the table and folded his hands.

"I want to know if your father ever talked about an acquaintance or relationship with Charlie Denning, the murdered man. I want you to tell me if you know of anything at all that could threaten his political career."

"You know as well as I do that my father is the most upstanding, law-abiding man there is. Given every-thing, Gil, *everything*, how could you doubt that?"

"I'm questioning, Maggie. I'm a cop, it's my job to

question. I have a note that clearly suggests a dead man believed your father to be involved with something that may have cost this man his life."

"And my father is lying here in this hospital, flirting with death, because he was the innocent victim of someone else who nearly cost him his."

"Are you saying there's someone in particular who may have wanted him hurt?"

"*No*, Gil. I'm merely expressing the absurdity of my father having had the opportunity to be involved in this murder. This man, Denning, died two days ago. My father has been in this hospital for twice that long."

"Your father is a very influential man."

"Meaning he has 'connections?' My God, you sound like something out of a cheap novel. What exactly does this accusatory note say?"

"That your father isn't the civil rights saint you and everyone else believes him to be. That proof of such an allegation was forthcoming to the country. That you could bury it, if you agreed to fork over an appropriate sum of money in exchange for the specifics of the revelation."

"And that's all you have by way of 'evidence' against my father?"

"It exists. It's all we need to establish a valid reason to investigate him. I would think that his daughter would want to be the first in line to find out if any of Denning's assertions are true."

Maggie looked away from Gil. How could they have come to this? Once, they had been everything to each other. Today, all these years later, he was handling her as nothing more than an unpleasant means he was forced to deal with to meet his ends. The pain around her heart was sudden and intense.

"Maggie?" Gil prompted.

"Talk to me about something real, Gil."

"I don't like this situation any better than you do." He drained his cup. "Believe me, once Paul Thomas was every bit as important to me as he is to you."

"Then, how could you believe the worst of him now?" she demanded.

"I told you, I don't have a choice. I'm overseeing a murder investigation. You know that means my first allegiance has to be to the letter of the law."

"No matter who gets hurt, Gil?" His closed expression told her how directly her meaning had hit home.

"You forget, Maggie," Gil murmured, settling back with a smile that didn't even begin to reach his eyes. "Somebody's already been hurt. He's dead."

Chapter 2

Damn Charlie Denning.

The congressman shuffled through the last pages of Denning's document, marveling at the illiterate's comprehensiveness.

"Sir?"

The congressman laid aside the papers and pushed his chair away from his desk. He took the time to tamp down his fury, then looked up at his young assistant, who was leaning inside the open doorway.

"What is it, dear?"

"It's getting late. If you don't need anything else . . ."

She had a predilection for short fitted skirts and long tailored jackets she habitually wore buttoned-up and severe. Her fine-boned features, a study in pale feminine purity, nearly clashed with the short bob of her sleek, mannish black hair. She was a walking contradiction of soft and hard. "I'm fine for the night," he told her. What he needed was something she would never consent to give. And even if she were inclined, experience reminded him he would be incredibly unwise to ask.

"Take off, Sheila." His waved benevolently, dismissing her. "And please, assert yourself more often. I don't want my obsessiveness to drive away the best assistant I've ever had."

"Oh, no, sir," the girl insisted with the impulsive candor he found so refreshing. "The job's no chore. In fact, most of the time I forget it's work." She smiled shyly.

The congressman leaned back in his massive chair, pondering his moves. "Keep up that flattery and you'll have me blushing."

The girl uttered a surprised little laugh. He could swear that it was she who actually blushed. For a space of a few seconds, he casually assessed her and reconsidered the restraint of his earlier thoughts. A halfhearted invitation was hovering on his lips when the red console button linked to his private line started flashing silently.

"I'll see you in the morning," he murmured as he reached for the receiver, all thoughts of clandestine seduction quickly dismissed. He acknowledged his caller after the door clicked smoothly behind the girl.

"When do I get my money?" the assassin demanded coolly.

"When your job is done," the congressman answered with matching ice.

"Correct me if I'm wrong, but wasn't it me who stuck that little shitkicker two nights ago? I *know* it was me who hauled some spectacular ass about five seconds before his neighbor rushed to the scene."

"There's no need for crudity," the congressman commented.

"Then, don't jerk me around. Make your point or the consequences—"

"Listen to me, you son of a bitch, if I choose to have you obliterated back into the obscurity I pulled you from, I can do it!" The necessity for this flunky, the congressman thought, for this *"situation"* was *unten-*

able. "We both know who's doing who the favor here, so you cut the bullshit or I swear to *God* I'll make you eat it."

After a lengthy silence the assassin said simply, "Talk."

Satisfied, the congressman did. "Denning's death was imperative, as critical as I guessed it could become after he was released from prison. However, that little paper he wrote indicates he may have been a bigger wild card than was originally anticipated."

"Meaning?"

"Meaning, though they don't know it, some other players have just moved from the wings into the center of the game."

"And you want them taken out again."

"Yes."

"And they are?"

"In due time."

"I'm still not cheap. You'll have to pay."

"Sir," the congressman said, acutely aware of the irony lacing his reply, "I never thought otherwise."

"Lieutenant, why don't you let me get you a glass of water or something."

Gil looked up at the young nurses aid who had quietly come inside the hospital room, then down at the empty, coffee-stained paper cup sitting on the table beside his elbow.

"That's been gone for a pretty long while now," she urged.

Looking back up, Gil studied the blonde as she waited for his answer. It was her second visit within an hour, and she still wasn't calling him on having sneaked in illegally after hours. "Okay," he conceded, his tone just as hushed as hers. "I'd appreciate that, thanks."

The girl seemed pleased at his acceptance and his smile, which Gil knew hadn't been very much in evidence before now. She walked briskly out of the room.

As she disappeared, Gil's conjured pleasantry faded. He got up a bit stiffly from the dubious comfort of the visitor's chair he'd been slumped in for the past two hours and walked over to the bathroom.

Although he knew Paul Thomas wouldn't know the difference, he closed the door a bit to shield the darkened private room from the bright fluorescent light he turned on.

God. No wonder that kid had been so anxious to play Florence Nightingale.

Gil's eyes drifted over the stubble at his jaw, his loosened tie, which seemed to hang forlornly against his creased shirt, the slight redness of his eyes, the deepened lines of fatigue that hardened his face. He snapped on the cold water, briskly rubbed his hands under the flow, then bent his head slightly to scoop a refreshing bit of it against his skin.

He crumpled the damp paper towel he used briefly and tossed it into the trash can beside the commode.

What was he doing here? It was late, his own soft bed had been beckoning to him for hours, yet here he stayed. He sure as hell hadn't owed Paul Thomas any favors when he'd left town, and he certainly didn't owe him any now.

That last thought brought his eyes back up to the mirror for an uncomfortable moment. Gil muttered an expletive and snapped off the light.

Back outside in the room, a cool plastic pitcher of water and a fresh paper cup were sitting on the table beside his chair. Gil poured a measure and settled back in his seat.

The doctors hadn't said Thomas was going to die. In

fact, they hadn't said much at all, which meant everyone was being forced to watch and wait.

"*He's not moving . . . he won't wake up! Why won't he wake up?*"

"*He's going to be all right, Gil.*"

"*You're lying. Doctors always lie. If he's really okay, why can't you wake him up now so that he can talk to Maggie and me?*"

"*Calm down, son, can't you see you're scaring Maggie? He's sedated, that's all. Sedated . . .*"

Gil raised tired hands to his eyes, rubbed away the memory, scrubbed away the taste of vulnerability that was as pointless now as it had been years ago for that child.

He drained his cup, set it down, and rested his head back against the chair. A moment or two passed before he shut his eyes. His mind drifted.

How the hell could she have grown even more beautiful?

He'd hoped success had hardened her, taken a toll on that dark, svelte fragility that had once bewitched him as thoroughly as any schoolboy who'd lost his heart. Instead, his first startled thought when he'd seen her in the hospital hallway today had been that the news reports over the years hadn't begun to do her justice.

She still got to him, like a slow sock in the gut. And irrationally, here in the deepest darkness of night, that reality made her betrayal even more unforgivable.

Did she hate him? He hoped so, for her sake.

Because God knew he still hated her . . .

"Maggie, say hi to Gil."

"Hello," the girl mumbled.

Paul Thomas explained, "He's my friend."

The way she looked Gil up and down, and then

back at her father told Gil she plainly doubted it. He tucked the basketball under his thin arm, painfully conscious of his shabby appearance.

"How old are you?" Gil demanded of the girl.

"Eight. How old are you?"

"Ten." He turned to Thomas. "She gonna watch?" Gil glared back at the girl—Maggie—not caring if he was rude.

Ever since the morning a few weeks back when Thomas had stayed after his own game to watch Gil and his friends play, Thomas had come back regularly. He'd started singling Gil out for some fierce one-on-one, started coaching him like he was some special kid. Almost, Gil secretly pretended, like he was his own kid. That's the way Gil wanted things to stay.

Maggie looked out over the municipal park and vacant basketball court they were standing on before she turned serenely back to Gil.

Paul Thomas sighed, looking from one to the other.

Days passed before Paul Thomas casually said to Gil one afternoon, "Let's you, Maggie, and I go get some ice cream."

Ever since that first meeting, Maggie had accompanied her father to the park when Thomas met Gil to play ball. Though she always occupied herself during play, Gil continued to resent her, especially when she made a point of dismissing him.

He made a point of ignoring her now, which suited them both just fine.

"We'll go to your house to get permission from your mother," Thomas was saying.

"Mama's pretty sick today. She probably won't like it if visitors show up."

"If she isn't feeling well, she'll probably be glad to see you've got the opportunity to entertain yourself awhile longer."

Gil couldn't think of a comeback quick enough to put Thomas off.

On the way to his house, Gil squirmed in the passenger seat, where he was huddled. He felt Thomas's eyes touch him. The man obviously wanted to ask questions, but realized Gil was too upset to let him.

Gil's house was half of an ugly brick double in a rundown rural neighborhood. The yards fronting most of the houses were tiny and cluttered. Junker cars, scrawny dogs, some chained to trees, and broken-down kitchen chairs littered lawns. Some of those chairs were burdened by impassive, weary-eyed neighbor women, too old or tired to work. Gil could tell what was on their televisions and radios, and he knew Thomas and Maggie could tell, too, because of the sounds that bled through screen doors.

Gil hunkered down farther, as if doing so could make him disappear.

They finally turned onto his street, Blossom Street.

Stupid name, Gil thought. Nothing about his street looked like the happy image its name conjured up. Gil bet Mr. Thomas had probably already realized his mistake coming into this neighborhood when his own was probably as different and wonderful as the one those Brady kids lived in on TV.

Gil's house couldn't have been less like the Brady's. His mother was always short-tempered and tired from working hard to put his food on the table. She was never in the mood to be nice to strangers or even his buddies.

Mr. Thomas had become more than just a buddy, but from the couple of times Gil tried to tell his mother that, he figured it didn't matter much to her. Thomas's name just made her madder than usual.

Thomas pulled into Gil's driveway, carefully maneuvered around a rusting bike Gil had abandoned, and cut his engine. Gil felt those eyes on him again, waiting for him to do something. "Well, come on," Gil mumbled. He got out of the car.

The Thomases were slow to follow. Gil looked back to see them taking in his house, meeting the curious stares of the neighbors. Gil's stomach knotted again as he led them up the driveway to the side door.

They all walked inside the kitchen and were immediately overwhelmed by the unair-conditioned heat of the room. The aromas of simmering vegetables and frying chicken were strong, familiar, and not unpleasant to Gil.

He sneaked a quick glance back at the two behind him, wondering if the smells were too strong for them. Both seemed indifferent. Slightly encouraged, Gil told them, "Ya'll can sit down in here if you want. I'll get Mama."

Just then, his mother came around the corner into the kitchen.

"Mama, this is Mr. Thomas." Gil nodded toward Maggie, who had gone quiet and watchful beside her father. "That's his daughter."

"I know who he is, I've seen him shoutin' down those racists on TV." She nailed Gil with a sharp look. "I thought I told you not to be bringin' no company into this house without me knowin' about it first."

Gil took a step back from his mother.

"Mrs. Stewart, I'm glad to finally meet you." Mr. Thomas extended a hand toward the woman. "It was my idea to come because I wanted to take the kids for ice cream, and I wanted to get your permission first."

Gil felt his mother watch him for one baleful moment before she turned back to Thomas.

To Thomas, Naomi Stewart said, "Did he even think to offer you some water or somethin'? Probably not, he'd be too stupid to think of it. Sit down, I'll get it."

Gil moved out of her way and slid a glance at Maggie. He jumped a little because she was looking right at him.

Thomas said, "You've got quite a ballplayer here, Mrs. Stewart."

"You can get rid of the Mrs. 'cause I ain't got no husband and I ain't never been married."

A flicker of impatience crossed Thomas's face, then smoothed away as he turned to Gil. "Well, you seem to be doing a pretty good job of raising him on your own."

"Ain't nobody else to raise him. I gotta do it don't I?"

A beat passed, then Thomas prompted, "About that ice cream?"

"I'd planned to feed him early and get him over to the sitter's. I been stuck in this house for a solid week, and I got a date tonight that I'm not gonna miss."

"If I agree to let him stay the night with Maggie and me, will that make it okay?" Mr. Thomas asked.

Naomi Stewart looked back over at Gil, seeming to consider it.

Thomas pressed. "I know how hard you must work to take care of your home and your son, Miss Stewart. Let me help you out a little. If Gil stays with me, you'll be able to concentrate on yourself tonight. What do you say?"

"You'd do that for him?"

Thomas shrugged. "No sweat."

Moments passed before Naomi Stewart said grudgingly, "All right. I guess."

Thomas got up and headed for the door. Maggie followed his cue. Gil was already standing there.

"I'll have him back tomorrow morning," Thomas told Gil's mother. "'Gil, why don't you go throw a few clothes together."

Instead, Gil ran to his mother's side and threw his arms around her waist. "Thanks, Mama," he said breathlessly. "Thanks."

His mother grunted lightly and rested her hands on Gil's arms a moment before pushing him away. "Don't you be no trouble, now."

"I won't," Gil promised. He was backing away when he snagged his arm on a glass perched precariously on the edge of the counter by the sink. He tried to grab it in time, but the glass got past him and shattered against the floor. Before anyone knew what was happening, his mother was shaking him.

"You stupid, stupid, little boy!" she screamed. "Why are you always so clumsy! Why are you always so much trouble! You think dishes grow on trees, or the money to buy them does? You stupid, stupid . . .!"

"I'm sorry, Mama," Gil gasped.

"Miss Stewart, please!" Mr. Thomas laid a strong hand on hers, which was clamped on Gil. "It was an accident." While he talked, he pried Gil away from his mother.

When Gil was free, he backed away to the door, where Maggie stood, as if frozen.

"I try so hard to raise him good," Gil heard his mother say. Then she started crying quietly to herself. She dropped onto a kitchen chair and hugged her arms across her thin chest. "I ain't got no help. I'm so tired . . ."

Mr. Thomas touched her shoulder. "It's all right, Miss Stewart, Gil's a good boy. It'll be all right."

She raised her head slowly, the helpless, strained expression in her eyes seeming to say she wanted to believe Thomas. And then, even as Gil watched, a bitter overlay absorbed that tiny bit of softness as effectively as a gray cloud absorbed the warmth of the sun.

"Go on, then," she spat. "Get him out of here. Just get him the hell out."

Gil's eyes teared. And then, in the midst of that embarrassment, Maggie surprised him.

Maggie, who had behaved like a spitting cat whenever she'd been anywhere near him, slowly reached out and curled her hand around his. She kept her wide, condemning eyes on his mother.

Strangely, Gil didn't feel like squirming away from her. He felt soothed, and he felt a powerful need to tighten his own grip . . .

Gil started into consciousness beneath the weight of the heavy hand nudging him awake.

"Hey, Lieutenant, wake up."

He was disoriented for a moment. Gradually, he became aware of Adam, his sergeant, leaning over him, of the white sterile walls surrounding him, of the darkened landscape outside the single window of the hospital room. The man over whom he'd come to watch was as he had been, lying utterly still.

"You okay?"

"Yeah." Gill still felt oddly shaken.

"That was some nightmare, I guess?"

"I guess." Gil leaned forward to stretch. He rubbed the last vestiges of sleep away and was amazed to feel a slight moisture beneath his fingers. That, and a fading tingle in his hand.

Damn.

Chapter 3

Maggie scanned the packed auditorium. It was filled with the electronic and print-media predators she'd summoned.

As a longtime player within the news business, she accepted the necessity of the these pressurized press forums. As the child of a public man, she'd learned to work them with an effortlessness that stood her in good stead during the years she'd carved out a power base of her own.

She'd always counted herself fortunate, for rarely had she found herself on the defensive side of the firing line. However, her father's condition placed her there, albeit on her own corporate turf now.

A hand reached over to cover hers. She looked ruefully at her partner on the hot seat.

Congressman Henry Robb looked as cool as if he were already on the golfing green that awaited him following this dog and pony show. He appeared relaxed and calm. But Maggie knew from lifelong association that this event, orchestrated to clarify the immediate professional course of his colleague and best friend, had his full attention. She knew that as fully as she knew that she, his godchild and daughter of his best friend, had his full support.

"Ladies and gentlemen," Maggie intoned into the mike, "we're ready to begin."

The sudden hush that followed her announcement was quickly disrupted by an opening volley of questions.

Maggie weeded out the most frivolous and settled on one whose essence she wanted to set the tone.

"Ms. Thomas, we've all been given the official hospital reports on the senator's condition," a CNN newsman said. "Is there anything you can add?"

"No. Though he's in a coma, his condition is stable. That's all I know." The veteran reporter was on the verge of a follow-up, which Maggie smoothly evaded by shifting her gaze to another familiar face. "Peter, I believe you're next."

"Hello, Maggie," the reporter acknowledged. "There's been some talk that you'll be stepping into the chief operational shoes at your father's construction firm. Truth or wishful thinking?"

Maggie's smile joined some scattered, good-natured chuckles around the room. There were few who had not followed her longtime opposition to her father's reluctance to diversify the regional business that had established the core of his wealth.

"Pending," Maggie answered at length. "The company's basic maintenance is a chief priority. Concentration on my father's health, I'm sure you'll understand, is absolutely my first."

"Does that include involvement with the investigation into his attempted murder?"

The tension inside the room sharpened. Maggie heard Henry shift beside her. She turned to him and listened, with interest, to what he would say.

"Come on, Jane. There's absolutely no evidence that attempted murder is in any way a part of the senator's misfortune." His smile was gently reproving. "You know that."

"I know that the police are sticking close to the hospital. I know that a ranking officer is right here in this auditorium."

Unsettled, Maggie's eyes scanned the back of the room. Her pulse jumped as she picked out Gil, standing amid a pack of cameramen. He was leaning against the farthermost wall, his cool, unsmiling eyes locked right onto hers.

"No such allegation has been tendered by the police," she heard herself saying. "Therefore, I should think further speculations of the sort you've raised would be premature at least and reckless at best."

"Lieutenant," the reporter bluntly ignored Maggie to address Gil. "Do you support that?"

Maggie held her breath, and Gil held her gaze before he answered. "I am not here as a police officer. Furthermore, I'm not aware of any investigation of the sort you suggest. My presence, as obviously you and your colleagues are wondering, is strictly as a concerned acquaintance."

The reporter looked frankly skeptical, and so Maggie was more than a little grateful when she redirected her attention to the front of the room. Apparently, the woman was going to let Gil's words rest at face value.

Gil read Maggie's relief in the way she absently tucked a long tendril of hair behind her ear. A nervous gesture from the past. She was shoring up her resources. Her subtle determination evoked an old protective twinge in him. Another reflex from the past.

Impatient, he focused on her companion.

Henry Robb was watching him. Gil detected a glint of something in the older man's eyes. A memory surfaced, cousin to the one that had surprised him last night.

Spring 1971. Gil was asleep at the Thomases, in the bedroom next to Maggie's. He was awakened by insistent knocking on Maggie's door. Sleepy-eyed, he got out of bed and shuffled to the hallway to see what was going on.

Mrs. Beaman, the housekeeper, walked into Maggie's room. Gil followed her and peeked in, his long, lanky form silhouetted by the hallway light.

"Get dressed, baby," Mrs. Beaman said, bustling around the room, opening dresser drawers and closets until she had assembled a T-shirt, jeans, and sneakers for Maggie. Then she turned to Gil. "You'd better get dressed, too, young man. We're going to have company."

"Company!" Maggie wailed. "In the middle of the night?" Mrs. Beaman didn't answer, and the look she gave Maggie said it would be better to just get dressed and not waste time asking questions.

After Gil and Maggie were dressed and sitting on the living room sofa with Mrs. Beaman, an insistent knock thudded against the front door. They all jumped before Mrs. Beaman got up to answer it.

Henry Robb stepped inside. He looked as if he'd been in a brawl. His suit jacket was ripped, and he had a nasty cut under his eye.

Mrs. Beaman raised a hand to her mouth. Robb's eyes met hers, Gil saw, just long enough to convey some message that seemed to distress her even more.

Robb walked over to where Gil and Maggie sat. He hunkered down before Maggie and took her hands. "Honey, your daddy's been hurt. Just a little," he added when Maggie gasped. "He's all right."

"What happened to him?" Gil's question hung too heavily inside the room.

Robb flicked him an irritated glance and ignored him. Mrs. Beaman dropped into a nearby chair. She and Gil concentrated on what Robb was saying.

"We were down in Gatty, that little town over east of here." He hesitated and squeezed Maggie's hand. He settled on the rhetorical. "You know what discrimination is. Maggie."

"Yes."

"You know that sometimes your daddy does things to help people who are discriminated against."

"Yes," Maggie's answer was nearly a whisper.

"Well, that's what your daddy and I were doing tonight. Helping some factory workers try to make their boss understand that he was treating them unfairly, that he was discriminating against them because they were black."

"How bad was it, Henry?" Mrs. Beaman's tone was stark.

Robb lifted his eyes to the woman. "Bad enough. Five men got it pretty rough. Two were white, and one of them was the man who attacked Paul."

Maggie started crying softly. It was Gil's cue to move to her side, to slide his arm around her shoulders. Maggie burrowed into his embrace. Gil looked up at Robb. Something in his expression, he saw with satisfaction, caused the man to drop Maggie's hands.

"What happened to that man, the one who hurt Mr. Thomas?" Gil demanded.

"Paul got the best of him. By the time the ambulances arrived, that agitator wasn't moving."

"Good," Gil said darkly.

"Oh, Gil . . ." Mrs. Beaman uttered, but when Gil looked at her, challenging her with eyes that were far too streetwise, far too old, she couldn't muster the enthusiasm to carry through the reprimand.

"I want to go to the hospital," Maggie said, her

small shoulders shaking. Gil pulled her closer, neither of them realizing how the crisis marked a reversal in their relationship. Gil was suddenly the protector, the champion—Maggie, the protected and championed.

"Your father wants me to bring you to him," Robb told Maggie. "My car's outside. You come, too, Gladys."

Gil urged Maggie to take Mrs. Beaman's hand and waited for the woman to lead her to the door. When they were out of earshot, Gil turned back to Robb. "Is there going to be more trouble?"

Robb glanced down at Gil. Gil could just see the faint hostility in the older man's eyes, but he stood his ground.

"Paul's never thought those rednecks or any others would be brave enough to actually attack his home."

Gil waited.

"These are dangerous times, boy," Robb shook his head. "I've already got some men coming to watch the house tonight."

Robb turned away from Gil and started to pull the door open when Gil clasped his arm to venture, "You said he asked for Maggie. Did he ask for me?"

"Why should he have? You're not his kid." Robb pulled away and walked outside.

Thoughtful, Gil followed him out into the night . . .

Gil was just as thoughtful now. He couldn't say why he distrusted Robb. The man had always been the perfect business partner to Thomas, the perfect friend. Many years later, he was an able, aggressive state congressman and respected citizen.

Nevertheless, Gil mused, his eyes held flint.

Henry was just as full of piss as always, the assassin thought approvingly. That was already proving invaluable not only for what needed to be done now, but also for what lay ahead.

The assassin muted the television screen and picked up the videotape at his elbow. He read the transcript and the local public access show it had been taken from so many years ago. Who would have ever imagined the sort of insight it could provide? But then, a lot of interesting possibilities had arisen from among all the things that had transpired lately. His imagination was clicking, and the excitement of it made him impatient for another look.

He leaned forward to push the tape into the VCR that sat inside a cubbyhole next to the television console. He kept the sound down because he didn't need it to contemplate the full beauty of what was playing before his smiling eyes.

There was Gil, Maggie, Thomas, the press, and all the rest of the stunned spectators standing inside the camera-lit halls of the state house. Thomas was playing to the mike in his face, lambasting his young protégé for being the worst sort of racist, one who discriminated to the detriment of his own people.

Gil Stewart was standing with two fellow officers, his face like stone, as he took it all in, listening to himself being publicly portrayed as an unprofessional cop working to see a dangerous suspect go free primarily because that suspect was black.

And there was the lovely and very torn Maggie, clearly aching for her lover's disgrace, but choosing in that critical moment to make the symbolic and literal break with the beleaguered officer. She stood beside her father and even took his hand.

Not even the most oblivious spectator then could have missed the tiny, triumphant smile Robb gave Stewart from the sidelines before Stewart swung away, trying to shoulder his way through the crowd.

That's when one of the two cops who had stood with him followed and called something out. Stewart charged back to confront him.

The assassin didn't need to see the rest. Further details were irrelevant. It was the essence of it all, the dissension that he planned to use to bring to fruition what suited his needs.

Perhaps Gil Stewart should warrant his attention first. A trip to his lair to consider how to set him up when the time was right, was in order.

The conference broke up just shy of an hour. Maggie felt a tension headache coming on. She watched the auditorium crowd slowly disperse, the print reporters scurrying back to their papers, the television people efficiently packing up their cameras and lights.

Henry tapped her shoulder. "Don't worry, dear. Paul is going to pull through this like a champ. You know nothing can keep the man down for long."

Maggie pondered that with more than a little cynicism. "I have faith in that, Henry. If there's one thing about Daddy I've learned to count on, it's his indomitability."

"Good girl." Henry took his hand away, then seemed to think better of it. "Just one word of caution. For the road."

Robb's attention shifted across the auditorium, and Maggie followed it. Gil was walking unhurriedly toward them, not for another confrontation, she hoped. "What?" she murmured, watching him.

"You're your own woman, I know, and a damn savvy one whom I respect completely. But I know you, little girl. You're more vulnerable right now than you're willing to admit, even to yourself."

"Your point?" She looked away from Gil.

"Don't let Stewart take advantage of that vulnerability. Especially, when you two are alone."

Maggie was irritated. "You're off base, Henry, and years too late. As you noted, I can take care of myself."

"If you say so, my dear." Henry nodded as Gil reached them. "Stewart."

Gil gripped Robb's hand. The handshake was civil, but both men kept the contact brief.

"I'll be in touch, Maggie." Robb turned away.

"Will it work?" Gil watched the congressman push through the rear auditorium door.

"What, Gil?" Maggie's voice had a snap she didn't bother to modify. The prospect of Twenty Questions didn't appeal.

"The warning to stay away. I'm guessing that was what that cozy little huddle was about."

Maggie moved around the table. "Grudges get old, Gil, get over it."

"Have you?" he shot back.

Maggie began walking away.

Gil sighed and followed. "I need to talk to you," he said as he caught up, matching his stride to hers.

"About?"

"You know what, Maggie. Cute doesn't suit you."

Maggie stopped. "I thought we said all there was to say yesterday."

He looked into her beautiful and impatient eyes, wondering if "all" would ever be it as far as they were concerned? "I'll treat you to lunch."

Maggie debated. If she didn't acquiesce now, he'd simply push later.

"Come on," she said grudgingly.

"Such graciousness."

Maggie tossed a tight look Gil's way and for the second time left him standing alone.

Gil's smile was bittersweet as he followed her.

* * *

Maggie chose a downtown hotel restaurant. In less than two hours, she was expected elsewhere in the building at another meeting. It was an irony that the endless details of keeping the most intimate of her father's affairs in order had fallen squarely to her during his recovery.

Paul Thomas's daughter was the last person Paul Thomas had been in the habit of trusting for a very long time.

Maggie wondered at Gil's silence as they waited for their orders to arrive. Not inclined to push, she let her attention drift over to the other patrons. Summer tourists, business professionals bridging power meetings, conventioneers. The usual.

"You look good, Maggie."

Gil's compliment surprised her. She noted how he sipped his water, the motion casual. The contemplative look in his eye was anything but.

"I thought this was going to be about Dad, not me." Maggie raised her own glass.

Gil smiled slightly. "You don't want to talk about yourself?"

"What's the point?"

"Eight years is a long time."

"And what, Gil? You missed me?"

Gil gave her a closed look.

"Forget it."

Their orders arrived. Gil decided eating some of his food would be a good idea while he re-centered. But when their waiter left, he veered off track again.

"When we were kids, when we talked about doing big things, did you ever think you really would?"

Maggie considered that.

"To the extent you have, I mean?"

"I was expected to," she shrugged.

Gil guessed she was probably unaware of the nostalgia that softened her eyes, saddened them a little. "That isn't necessarily the same thing, Maggie."

"No. But I didn't know that then."

"What was the turning point?"

The day you left, she thought. "It doesn't matter." She concentrated on her meal.

"That mess with Brooker—" Gil began.

Maggie laid down her fork.

"It certainly didn't take long for his life to collapse while the world moved on."

"All right," Maggie said quietly. "Let's get this over with."

Gil laid down his own fork, unsure of his timing, only sure that he needed to push. "How could you do it, Maggie? After all these years, that's still the part I have trouble with."

"You were wrong, Gil."

"Brooker made a mistake."

"Neither of us are kids anymore, Gil. It was much more complicated than that, and you know it."

"You're right," Gil agreed. He counseled himself to keep this calm. "Surely, by now you've discarded those privileged blinders of yours."

"Sidney Brooker was an unrepentant criminal," Maggie said after an irritated pause. "As the lead investigator working that homicide, you were in a better position than anyone to understand that."

"I was in a better position than anyone to assess his actions against an entire backdrop of circumstances neither you nor other members of the press were privy to, Maggie."

"Whatever those circumstances were, they couldn't have been sufficient to mitigate the fact that Brooker was part of a murder."

"As the chump driver of a getaway car used for a

bullshit robbery he didn't even know had gone bad until his accomplice pulled the trigger?"

"Nevertheless, he still was part of the crime."

"Sidney Brooker was a loser whose life got twisted up in a maze of fraud and petty theft, all part of his misbegotten effort to survive. Everyone's life isn't gilded, Maggie—exercise a little perspective—or is that still too hard?"

"Don't patronize me, Gil." Maggie's intensity was unmistakable, even to some adjacent diners who turned interested glances her way. She moved her chair so that her back was to them.

Gil watched her with a thin smile. "Am I hitting a little too close to home?"

"You're still as inflexible as you ever were," she said, exasperated.

"And you're still as hell-bent to downplay the flaws of a system that always was and still is imperfect."

"The system refused to defend a man who wasn't worthy of it. It did what it should have done, it went after him."

"Yes," Gil agreed bitterly. "It went after him. To the extent of launching a manhunt based on one eyewitness's description of a 'black' driver. To the extent of launching a somewhat less frenzied search for a second suspect, based on another eyewitness's claim of having seen a white trigger man".

"Brooker—"

"I never defended the man, Maggie. I fought to defend the integrity of a due process that was misused by the system that hounded him."

"He was guilty," Maggie insisted.

"To what degree?" Gil countered. "During the entire course of that investigation, Sidney Brooker, *by law*, was entitled to some reasonable presumption of innocence until or unless he was proven guilty. The same presumption that was subtly accorded to the other probable suspect—whose skin wasn't black—when the law dragged its heels looking for him."

"I—"

"*You* and your father were so busy fueling the hysteria of the community against me and the department that you refused to publicly raise that consideration," Gil said heatedly. "You refused to acknowledge what you have to know to be true."

"Which is?"

"Sometimes the flaws in our justice system are more apt to surface if the suspect in question has the wrong ethnicity, income, or creed."

"My heart doesn't bleed for murderers, and Sidney Brooker was culpable."

"Not of pulling the trigger, which he knew nothing about until after the crime had been committed."

"So he claimed."

"So I'm still inclined to believe. I know his kind. I understood his particular brand of desperation years before you ever discovered its existence."

"Daddy reminded me. In fact, I guess that was the real issue at the heart of that whole Brooker episode, wasn't it Gil?"

"Say what you mean, Maggie." He frowned, not liking her tone.

"If it hadn't been Brooker, you would have championed, strictly on principal, the next case involving a suspect who was poor, black, and persuasive."

A muscle ticked in Gil's jaw. "If you're saying I would have voiced an equal objection to similar circumstances where the system's actions toward the accused seemed as race-driven, as process driven, you're goddamned right. I would have." He slumped impatiently back in his chair. "That you, of all people, can wonder at that now—couldn't understand it then—is something I find really hard to believe, Maggie."

"Would you have beaten up a second white cop, Gil?" she went on, doggedly.

Gil's eyes shuttered.

"—Someone else who didn't 'understand'? Someone else who, too, would have been fully within his civil rights, albeit in equally poor taste to voice in front of a TV camera, his opinion of Brooker and your softness on him despite the state's case?"

Gil stared at her for a charged moment.

Maggie stared right back, ignoring her pounding heart.

"You're so naive." Gil checked his watch, giving himself time to push back the temper that threatened to flare after all. "Finish whatever it is you're trying to say so that we can wrap this up."

"I believe you've already said it, Gil." Maggie settled back in her chair, refusing to let him see how deeply his same old contempt of her opinions and judgment still hurt.

Gil's eyes narrowed. "Suppose you clarify that for me."

Maggie shrugged carelessly. "When you're raised in a dump, Stewart, maybe it's just too hard to see past the garbage to the truth."

For a moment, Gil looked stunned.

Appalled at what she had said to him, Maggie instantly reached a hand across the table, as if the futile gesture could take it back.

"*Gil. . . !*" she whispered.

Gil looked down at her unsteady hand. When he raised his eyes back to hers, his were expressionless.

"Please!"

"Go to hell."

Maggie swallowed back tears and stared blindly ahead as Gil got up and left.

Chapter 4

"Stewart, come in."

Gil took a seat inside his captain's office back at police headquarters.

"Carter, as you can see, is already here."

Gil overlooked the rebuke and nodded to Adam. "Sorry. I was following up a point of interest on Thomas."

Captain Berrison Myer asked, "What did 'ya find out?"

Too damn much, Gil thought, still hearing Maggie's stinging words. But not enough, he thought, seeing the remorse he wasn't ready to forgive. "The man's a saint, nothing we didn't already know, right?"

"So?" Myer prodded.

"So it's probably going to take some serious digging to get a line into whatever Denning thought he had."

"Speaking of which," Myer said, steepling his hands beneath his chin, "how is the winsome Ms. Thomas."

"Devoted," Gil said, his eyes going cool. "Is there something else you want to know?"

"If you two would rather be alone," Adam interrupted, rising.

"No need, boy," Myer answered. "Sit down, we're

all friends here. Nothing that's not already public is going to be divulged. Right, Gil?"

"The past was a long time ago, Captain." Gil held his superior's thoughtful gaze until the older man nodded.

"Maggie Thomas handled herself well during that press conference, Stewart." Myer took the time to light one of the thin cigars he favored. He spoke around a puff. "So did you.

"In fact, since I guess up to now there's been no *official* investigation"—he cocked a sardonic eye Gil's way—"I'll have to officially leak this news flash beyond you, me, Carter, and the walls.

"Someone could have been gunning for Thomas, as part of this Denning thing. Or, Denning might have been the victim of some patient enemy biding his time until Denning got out of prison. If the latter is true, Thomas indeed could just have been one unlucky son of a bitch. You two are going to find out which scenario is true."

"Top priority." Gil stated.

"Damned right. You two handle your caseloads however you need to in order to get it done." Myer swiveled around to his single window. It overlooked an uninspired brick building that compromised his view.

Gil and Adam waited patiently while Myer smoked. When that was all he continued to do, they got up, assuming the audience was concluded. Adam was outside the door, Gil close behind, when Myer spoke.

"Gil, you mind?"

Gil caught his partner's eye. "I'll catch up." He pushed the door closed behind him and sat back down.

Myer came straight to the point. "It took guts to come back here. There's a lot of folks, black and white, who weren't sorry to see you go over that Brooker flap. Now you're gonna be associating yourself with a case that could turn out to feature the key players who fanned the fuel of that trouble."

Gil wasn't hearing anything he didn't already know. "Like I said before, sir, the past is done. The officer who ran away was . . . an angry man."

Myer nodded. "I just want to make sure that anger is under control. You're gonna catch some shit when your official assignment to this case goes public. With this possible involvement of Thomas and all . . . scrutiny from some quarters might be rough, even if there aren't any racial overtones this time. Especially, if the good senator turns out not to be as pristine as some folks would like him to be."

"I can handle it," Gil said, making his way over to the door. His hand was on the knob when Myer stalled him, causing Gil to turn around.

"You sure? Because if you have any doubts, any at all, I'll take you off this case now."

He wouldn't tolerate another screwup, Gil read in the slate gray depths of his superior's eyes, eyes that had flattened to the calculating intelligence that was as well renowned as his girth.

"I said" Gil opened the door—"I can handle it. You knew what you were getting when you pulled me onto this case and its implied connection between Denning and the man who may have wanted to see him dead." Gil held his hand against the door, inviting his superior to comment.

Myer frowned. "I don't like *my* motives being questioned, Lieutenant. Despite your unfortunate past, you are quite simply the most experienced officer for the potential scope of this case."

"Yeah. What does that mean?"

"This. Your leaving here may have been precipitous, but you obviously learned some things while you were gone. Your latest doings up North have not gone unnoticed in our law enforcement corridors down here."

Memory with its ever-present shadow tightened Gil's face. "Then my record speaks for itself. If that's not good enough, I guess my word is just going to have to be sufficient."

Myer studied Gil through his cigar smoke, then he smiled. "You still got fire. Always did. Get on out of here." He swiveled back to his window. "Your word is good."

Outside in the corridor, Adam pushed away from the wall, where he'd been sipping a cola. "Everything cool?"

"Yeah," Gil said, "everything's cool."

"In that case, I thought we might make a trip to Thomas's campaign headquarters." They walked. "You know, feel out his friends and associates. Get some sense of the political lay of the land as the Thomas camp views it."

"Trawling's always a good idea," Gil agreed, pushing through the building doors. They headed for the parking lot, and when they reached their car, Gil gestured to Adam before he could get in.

"What?" Adam said over the roof.

"If you've got something on your chest, man, I'd appreciate your getting rid of it now."

Adam looked surprised, then he looked uncomfortable. He scratched his head and climbed inside. Gil opened his own door, got in, and turned the key in the ignition. The two men sat quietly while the car idled.

"I was just a rookie when all that Brooker and *New Horizons* stuff went down," Adam finally said. "I'm not judging anybody. All I knew about the man in the middle of it is what I've seen of him while I've been riding with him." He turned to Gil. "What I see sits fine with me."

Gil was unprepared for the rush of relief he felt. It took him a moment to extend his hand. "All right."

Adam smiled faintly, and gripped it. "Okay. Let's roll."

Gil wasn't surprised that Paul Thomas's campaign headquarters was housed in the most expensive office complex in town. He wasn't even surprised at the stark contrast the office's modest interior made with the overtly plush business operations that neighbored it.

What did surprise him was the youth and freshness of Thomas's small staff. Somehow, he'd expected the Thomas reelection crew to mirror the polished slickness Thomas seemed to have acquired over the years. Instead, jeans, loafers, and a healthy ethnic mix of college-aged adults walked the tastefully appointed corridors of the office.

"Can I help you?"

Gil and Adam walked over to the invisible but clearly understood threshold separating the lobby from the common work areas and offices.

The receptionist who awaited their answer was as young as the rest of her fellow crew. Despite her soft smile, though, she had steady eyes and seemed to Gil more than ready to hurry them along if their answer didn't satisfy.

"Who's in charge, here?" He crossed his arms and leaned against the reception desk.

The girl looked indignant. Gil suspected she was more than ready to take issue with his abruptness. In fact, she seemed to be winding up for a lecture when he pulled his badge and flashed it.

"Oh," she responded, subdued. Her entire attitude

subtly transformed into one more eager to please. "If you two would have a seat, I'll just buzz Sloan." She tapped a line on her phone console.

Adam nodded, but remained standing. Gil took a seat, content to wait and watch.

Moments later, an older black man—in relation to his staff—maybe in his late thirties, walked briskly from the bowels of the office. He was dressed casually, and an agreeable smile was in place.

Adam accepted the hand he offered and introduced himself.

"Pleased to meet you," the man said. "Sloan Michaels, Paul's campaign manager. Are we close to finding the person who did this to him?"

"Your assistance might help get us there," Gil said from his chair. He waited for Michaels to step around Adam to introduce himself.

"Gil Stewart," he said. "Lieutenant."

Michaels smiled faintly. "It's a pleasure."

"Perhaps we can take this to your office." Gil glanced at the listening receptionist.

"Of course." To the girl, Michaels said, "Why don't you get these gentlemen some coffee." He looked at Gil and Adam for confirmation, got no objection, and nodded for the girl to proceed. "Right this way," he invited.

Four offices, two on either side of the corridor, and a glass-encased administrative workstation, comprised the heart of the headquarter's interior. Michaels walked past these and headed for an office to the rear. The space of his single office could have encompassed two. In fact, Gil suspected, from the odd angles and lay of its structure, that was probably what had happened.

Michaels dropped into the chair behind his desk. Gil

and Adam split the visitor's sofa between them, each taking opposite ends.

Conversation was desultory until the coffees had been served, but when Michaels's door closed again, he came to the point. "Officers, anything I can do is done, just tell me how I can help." He propped his hands under his chin and nudged his chair into a gentle swivel.

"The first question is the obvious one," Gil said. He paused, waiting for Michaels's full attention to settle on him, to acknowledge his understanding of the pecking order here. "Paul Thomas must have, as a matter of course, accumulated some serious enemies over time. Do any come to mind?"

Michaels smiled. "You want the laundry list, or the book?"

"My guess is that you're hardly old enough to have read the book let alone produce one. How long have you been Thomas's manager?"

Michaels stiffened, though he responded neutrally. "Three years now. And despite my relative youth, which you've so pointedly noted, my campaign record predating Thomas is impeccable. I know how to win, Lieutenant, and winning isn't conditional with age."

"Duly noted," Gil said mildly. "As for those leads, a few solid names, with some logical justification for each, will be just fine." He gave Michaels a belated smile of his own.

"Well," Michaels said, deflating a little, "that's not something I can compile with any comprehensiveness right off the top of my head. But I can tell you this. Any serious ill will Paul Thomas may have drawn would most likely stem from pure emotion, jealousy, or envy."

"Yes, we know his record," Adam said. "What

we're after, however, probably wouldn't be on that record. Chances are any beefs against him wouldn't have sprung from his nobility."

"I'm not sure I follow," Michaels said.

"Have you had any trouble recently, from people citing grudges, claiming slights?" Adam reached forward to set his mug on the coffee table in front of him.

Michaels's eyes narrowed. "You're saying this thing with Paul is about revenge?"

"We're not saying anything, Mr. Michaels," Gil said. "At this stage we're just looking for productive leads that may point us toward some answers. Politics can be an awfully good place to start if temperaments are involved, and they always are."

"And given Paul's status and our working relationship, you're suggesting I'm probably an awfully good person to make that call," Michaels supplied.

Gil confirmed that with his level regard.

"Well, like I said, I'll have to do some research. As it happens, however, I'm sorry to say I do have something you might be interested in right now." He pulled open his desk drawer and withdrew a handful of letters, bound together by a rubber band.

"Hate mail," Michaels explained. "It's the bane of any politician's existence."

Adam got up to take a closer look.

"When did they start coming in?" Gil asked Michaels from where he sat.

"Not long after the accident. The sickest bastards often wait for something dire to give them the courage to make their moves, even if those moves are only on paper."

"Maybe," Gil said.

"I'm sorry," Michaels said, frowning.

"Maybe those moves stay confined to paper. Maybe not."

Michaels's brow cleared.

"Something else about these letters, Gil," Adam said. He laid down a second and started scanning a third. "The hostility, so far, seems almost exclusively race based."

"Yes," Michaels said. "It's tiresome, occasionally depressing, but not totally unexpected, Officers. Paul carries a lot of history as a very vocal activist in a very old town. He did jail time right along with Dr. King, and today's most visible black leaders still seek his ear."

Adam nodded. "Yes, we're all familiar with certain legacies of the South and Thomas's continued work to counteract them. But we're also talking about a very prominent man whose message has crossed racial boundaries for years. As you pointed out, that commands a lot of respect. What's more, he's repeatedly put his money where his mouth is. He may be an easy target, but he's hardly one whom I think would garner easy antipathy."

"In other words," Gil quietly carried the point, "is it usual for him to get this volume of hate mail? Especially, within such a compressed period of time?"

Michaels thought about it. "No."

"If you don't mind, we'd like to hold on to those letters for a while." Gil got up, and Adam resecured the bundle.

"Certainly, keep them for as long as you need," Michaels said. He came around his desk. "In the meantime, I'll see what I can do about a list."

Gil handed him a business card, and Adam followed suit.

"We'll stay in touch with any developments," Gil said. He offered his hand in parting.

Michaels's smile of farewell was a little guarded but he didn't hesitate to shake. "I'll do the same. Bet on it."

"We are, Mr. Michaels," Adam said.

The three men started down the corridor and emerged into the reception area just as Maggie pushed inside through the outer glass door.

"Gil." She stopped in surprise.

"Maggie." Gil thought she looked a little uncomfortable. He was glad.

"What are you doing here?"

"My job, Maggie." He took some satisfaction at how she bristled. "I could ask the same of you."

"You could," she said brushing past him, "but since he's my father and this is his campaign headquarters, I would think the answer is obvious. Especially in light of what's hit the afternoon papers."

"What?" Sloan demanded.

Maggie stared at him a moment. "You really don't know?"

"No. It isn't good, I guess."

"Sloan?" The receptionist accepted a copy of the daily paper from the delivery boy, who had chosen that opportune moment to arrive. Maggie, Gil, and Adam looked her way as she handed it over to her boss.

Sloan quickly scanned the front page article then murmured a succinct, "Shit." He passed the paper over to Gil. Adam moved in to read the headline over Gil's shoulder:

"INJURED SENATOR LINKED TO MURDER? COVER-UP?
Unnamed sources have alleged that nationally prominent Senator Paul Thomas is the subject of an aborted blackmail scheme, plotted by a murdered ex-convict. That convict, Charles Arthur Denning, sixty-one, was recently found dead in a tiny Georgia town.
Details about the information Denning allegedly

held against Thomas have not been specified. However, sources state evidence that indicates such information did exist and was found at the Denning murder scene . . .

. . . Local police officials, asked to confirm or deny these allegations, have not yet done so . . ."

"It's all innuendo," Maggie murmured. "There aren't more than half a dozen facts here, and those are little more than unsubstantiated suggestion."

Gil handed the paper back to the receptionist. "These days, innuendo is all it takes to get the public going, Maggie. You of all people should know that."

"What are you going to do?" Maggie stood in front of him, ignoring the remark.

"Get back to headquarters, see how much damage has been done."

"What can I do?"

Gil studied her, thinking.

Maggie grasped his forearm, trying to make him talk to her before he walked out the door.

"You can stand by, Maggie," he finally said. Adam was already at the door. Gil disengaged himself to catch up with him. "I'll let you know."

Maggie bit down on her frustration. She was damned if she'd give Gil any satisfaction by showing her annoyance.

Gil knew Maggie wanted more reassurance than he'd offered, but he just didn't have time to allay her worries. The shit Myer had anticipated was posed to hit the proverbial fan.

Besides, he consoled himself, the lady had demonstrated the other day how capable she was of watching out for herself. He felt only the faintest twinge of guilt when Maggie followed him, touched his arm again, then backed away from his chilly look.

"Come on, Gil, let's get out of here," Adam urged. He held open the office door. Gil lagged a bit, unable to resist one last glance at Maggie. She looked as if she wanted to say something.

He turned his back on her and had the satisfaction of hearing her call out to him. The office door closed behind him. This time, he didn't look back.

"Get her in here." Myer paced to his window and stood there with his back to Gil and Adam. "Gil, you, as the lead investigator, and she, his daughter, have to display some solidarity."

Gil looked at Adam, and they leaned against a wall waiting for more.

Myer continued, "That little press conference the other day was the warm-up, it appears. The one I'm going to call won't be the same walk in the park."

Adam interrupted. "Who leaked the news?"

"That's still being determined. But you can be sure when it has been, I'll have his—or her—ass." Myer sighed, turned around, and stepped away from the window. He eyed his officers, hitched a leg up to sit on his desk, and lit a cigar. "Gil, have you seen Maggie Thomas since this thing with the papers?"

"We ran into her at Thomas's headquarters," Gil said. "In fact, she brought the news to our attention there."

Myer smoked. "How's she taking it?"

"Mad as hell. Willing to do whatever it takes to fight the rumor and allegation before it all snowballs into a public mess that's too big to handle."

"She sincere?" Myer studied his cigar.

Gil's eyes narrowed. "I think so."

"Good." He turned to Carter. "I want Gil to go solo on this conference. The immediate association in the public's mind will be one of negativity, remembering that juicy split that was played out for the cameras the last time Gil, Maggie, and Paul Thomas tangled in public."

"With all due respect, sir—" Adam started.

"Yes," Myer said, anticipating him, "it was quite a while ago. But the players in this are big, and some enterprising news celebrity-wanna-be is going to love bringing it all back up, with all its attendant speculations. That's why I want to supplant it with a new image of Gil and Maggie, i.e. the Thomas camp, being in full accord of letting bygones be bygones. By the time that room is cleared, I want that carrion to leave with an aftertaste of nothing substantial that ties the Denning murder to Paul Thomas."

Adam said, "You mean, sir, the official position of this department is going to be—"

"A lie?" Myer stated bluntly. "Nothing so crass, son. You read it in the papers yourself, we've elected to neither confirm or deny. We'll continue to do so."

"I'm not sure I understand."

"Listen, Adam," Gil faced his partner. "We call a meeting with the media, and then we maneuver the situation one step forward. If we do it right, the press takes two steps back. It's known as selective cooperation. If we play it right, it can be effective as hell."

"Amen," Myer muttered.

Adam was quiet for a moment. "What about the bigger boys? The mayor, for instance, the federal connections? Surely, we don't expect that we can be as successfully 'selective' with them as we'll be with the local press? Especially not for as long?"

"We'll jump that log when we come to it," Myer said. "For now, let's just push through one day at a time. Gil, I'll have public relations set something up for tomorrow afternoon. You notify Maggie, get her prepared to go."

"Done."

"All right, then, ya'll are dismissed. Go."

Gil juggled two bags of groceries and used his foot to nudge his car door shut. Maggie had either been out of her office all afternoon, or her secretary was doing a Herculean job of screening her calls. Gil wasn't fazed. He could have pursued it, tracked her down in some other way. But it occurred to him it might be better to give Maggie the rest of the night to think about everything. He'd try her at home in the morning.

In fact, it had occurred to him about an hour ago that seeing as how he wasn't exactly a disinterested party, it might be a good idea for him to use the rest of the evening to do a little of the same.

The moonlight was his only guide through the shrubbery shaded walkway that twined to his condominium, but it was exceptionally bright tonight.

It was enough to illuminate something slightly out of place, just out of the corner of his eye. A movement, a shadow that didn't belong.

With instincts still honed by the Chicago inner city, he set his bags down lightly on the path and melted into a pool of shadow at his back.

He looked around him, refocusing his gaze enough to see more clearly what was both distant and near. There to the right—a shadow moved again. With a silent burst of speed, Gil shot from his hiding place and went after it.

The shadow down the path transformed into a large human shape and responded. It fled.

The darkness deepened within the cove they entered, but it didn't disguise the decision Gil's predator made. He stopped and turned to fight.

Gil immediately considered and discarded the

option of going for the gun concealed beneath his cotton shirt. He didn't want the attention the weapon would draw from his neighbors, and at the moment, his adversary seemed to be armed with nothing worse than fists.

Gil rushed the man.

The man grinned. "I didn't know you were a tank," he muttered.

"What?" Gil slowed less than a foot away, startled. "Who sent you!" When the man just braced himself, still grinning, Gil charged again—realizing too late his opponent's brutally advantageous shift of luck.

Quick as a snake, the man bent down and swept up a length of planking from a pile that adjoined an area of newly landscaped garden beside him. The momentum of his swing worked in deadly tandem with the momentum of Gil's rush. At the last moment, Gil turned to minimize the blow.

The wood smashed into his upper arm. The pain was numbing, and Gil went down. The tears that sprang to his eyes were as involuntary as the grunt of pain that accompanied the blow. Still, Gil made a supreme effort to shake off both, certain the attacker had to be coming in for more. Defensively, he rolled away to make space. But even as he groped for his gun, he realized his attacker was running away.

Using his good arm, Gil pushed to his feet and ran after him.

He was too late.

Frustrated, he stood behind the wrought-iron fence his assailant had just scaled, and watched the man throw himself inside a late model sedan tucked among a row of cars parked across the street.

The altercation had taken only seconds. It had taken Gil only half that long to realize he had been accosted by someone more skilled than some street punk.

His arm still throbbed as he made it back to his groceries, but the pain and returning mobility told him it hadn't been broken.

He quickly walked to his ground-floor unit, got the door unlocked, and shouldered his way inside. The groceries joined a scattering of unpacked boxes and week-old newspapers cluttering his kitchen counter. He grabbed the phone and started punching numbers. The connection he sought was answered on the second ring.

"McLeroy here."

"It's me, Tim. How's our senator?"

"Sleeping like a baby—uh, that was tactless. Sorry."

"Don't worry about it. None of you guys have had any trouble tonight? No unusual visits?"

"No, Lieutenant," McLeroy responded slowly. "Should we have?"

Gil paused, thinking. "No," he eventually said. "Just checking. Good night."

"Night, Lieutenant."

Gil hung the phone up, but his hand hovered. He debated over another number. Pushing emotion aside, he mentally pulled the number from the volume of background he'd read and punched out the numbers. The phone rang once. Twice. Three times. Gil hung up.

He looked down at his watch. It was only eight o'clock on a weeknight. Hardly late enough to justify concern. After-hour business throughout the city was just now beginning to seriously wind up.

There was no hard evidence to suggest she was in danger.

Gil turned his attention back to his recent encounter. His attacker had certainly known who he was. Perhaps he'd surprised the punk, perhaps he'd just wandered into a reconnaissance. After all, this neighborhood wasn't a ghetto, and any punk with reasonable intelligence would hardly have sauntered into it prepared to do blatant mischief, which invited every opportunity of getting caught.

Yes, logic suggested the attack had been defensive, not unsolicited, but probably unplanned. Gil understood he'd already been associated with the Denning investigation and, as such, with the new Thomas quandary. That connection alone could have brought some negative attention his way and his way only. To speculate that Maggie or anyone else was in real danger was a waste of his energy. It was also, on its face, illogical. And these days, Gil trusted implicitly in his logic.

Whatever he could feel, taste, and see with his own eyes was everything to him.

Sheer determination relegated the pain in his shoulder to the same dismissive place he relegated the sentimentality he decided had messed with his mind.

His bags needed unloading. He reached inside the first one and got to work.

Jeff Marrs loved the hush that fell at this particular hour of evening over the elegant homes that distinguished his Georgetown neighborhood.

The mania of the political arena he commented on for the country's top news magazines seemed far away on this beautifully burnished summer night, as far away as the poor, rural Georgia town he'd grown up in. It was a distance he'd cultivated, sweated, starved, and hustled for thirty years to create.

His efforts hadn't always been pretty, but for the most part he didn't regret them.

He jogged, confidently and comfortably, less than two blocks away from the elegant brownstone he'd called home for more than a decade. Once, home had been a tin roof under which meager meals had been available when his parents could afford it. His survival had been a perpetual question.

Education was his escape. In school, he discovered the potential for an entirely different world that lay waiting beyond the cotton fields his family had traditionally sharecropped.

That world became his dream.

Today, his home embodied that dream, all that his political acumen and insights had culled for the ragtag kid from the rural South. Many had aspired to the journalistic hill he ruled, but none had succeeded in toppling him. He was too good, and therefore too valuable to too many people who needed what only he could provide.

Indeed, his life was ideal. He was so pleasantly immersed in the thought that it took him a moment to register the cushioned slap of a runner's feet behind him.

Fellow runners at this time of night were not unusual, and Marrs didn't give it a second thought. That was another thing he loved about this neighborhood, about this life. The automatic assumption here wasn't one of fear and danger, but rather of easy camaraderie and, only if the occasion demanded, civilized strife.

Jeff Marrs glanced over at the man who pulled even with him. The man bobbed his head, his concentration clearly focused on the physical exertion that pushed him beyond Marrs in an impressive display of streamlined grace.

Marrs reached the turnoff that marked his block. The man before him slowed and stopped. Marrs slowed fractionally beside a stand of boxed hedges, more curious than anything as to what the runner was about. He watched the runner finger open the Velcro fastener on his fanny pack.

A sixth sense warned Marrs too late.

The assassin swung his pistol level with Marrs's chest. The muffled explosion, which might have been audible to anyone within a few feet of the men, still would not have been recognizable as a shot that hit Jeff Marrs cleanly in the heart.

Chapter 5

"Oh, my God." Maggie tucked the phone closer to her ear and pushed a hand through her hair. "I can't believe this, Henry. *Murdered?*"

"You'll be expected to make some kind of statement."

"I know."

"You want me close by?"

"No," Maggie answered at length. "I'll handle it. But thanks anyway, I'll stay in touch." She hung up and walked over to her massive office window. Thoughts of her friendship with the dead man blinded her to the panorama outside.

Jeff Marrs had been a friend. First he'd been her father's, then as Maggie had grown mature enough to hold the attention of a lifelong bachelor, he had been her friend as well.

After she'd gone away to college, contact with Jeff had naturally lessened, but they'd renewed the friendship as she'd established her own business, her own life, and her own existence, independent of her father.

Now Jeff was dead. Another statistic, another victim of the sudden, random violence that lurked in too many malevolent shadows everywhere.

Shadows.

Her eye fell on the papers from the file she'd set

aside to take Henry's call. The heading on the top page was direct: Gilbert Stewart.

Her assistant had done a commendable job of accumulating the basic facts. It hadn't taken much effort for her to let imagination color in the gaps.

The two years immediately following Gil's flight from Atlanta were unaccounted for. She thought of the quick hurt she'd put in his eyes at the end of their disastrous lunch, the equally quick overlay of dispassion he'd assumed before walking out. He'd displayed it again at her father's headquarters the day she'd gone there to discuss the campaign with Sloan.

Those two years may have been unaccounted for, but Maggie would lay odds that they hadn't been wasted. Lifelong patterns didn't easily change, and Gil had always had the habit of going off alone to lick his most serious wounds. He'd always come back stronger after those absences.

Whatever Gil had learned over that two-year period may have cost him, but Maggie knew it had toughened him, all the same.

When he'd surfaced, it had been in Chicago and he'd spent the next six years there. He'd worked on the Chicago police force as a detective sergeant for five of those years, all the while accumulating several community service awards and commendations. The last and most impressive, before he'd resigned from the force, had been the promotion to lieutenant.

He'd made an enviable restart after leaving Atlanta, improved on the professional he was. Become the cop's cop. And just at the point where everything he'd always claimed to want seemed within reach, he'd resigned. Given it all up.

To come back home.

Maggie rubbed her eyes and reached for the phone.

"Jerry, deal with my calls for the rest of the afternoon, will you?"

"You taking off?"

"I'm beat."

"Sure thing. I've got it under control."

"Thanks." Maggie hung up, fully satisfied that he did. An early lesson she'd learned from her father had been to surround herself with the best and to pay whatever it took, within reason, to keep them there. Her arrangement with Jerry satisfied each of them on both counts.

She needed to get to the hospital to visit her father. Afterward, she was going to block out some time to deal with matters that were too long overdue. There were two sets of answers she needed. One set was personal and lay in the reflections of a lifetime. The other could be in Chicago. It was time she started looking into both.

She'd start with the easier questions, those wrapped around the enigma surrounding Gil. That meant phone calls, personal contacts, whatever it took to uncover a bit more of his unexplained past.

Maggie had taken her keys from her purse when her private line rang. Impatient, she dropped her purse on her desk, grabbed the receiver, and sat down. "Hello?"

"Maggie?" the caller rasped.

"Yes. How can I help you?" Maggie frowned at the muffled voice.

The caller didn't respond.

"How can I help you?" Maggie tried again.

The phone clicked gently, and the dial tone droned through.

"What the hell?" Maggie wondered softly. She replaced the receiver. She'd only given her direct number to her closest friends and business associates. That person hadn't sounded like either.

And yet, the caller seemed to know her. Disturbed, Maggie picked up her purse and left the office.

The hand that replaced the receiver shook slightly. Maggie Thomas had sounded so pleasant. So trusting.

And she was in such danger. Or was she?

Jeff Marrs was dead, but there was still no real justification for panic. And yet . . .

Conversations had transpired. Action may have been undertaken. Perhaps Jeff Marrs's death was proof of that.

The boy shifted the box of cinnamon rolls more securely in the crook of his arm and rang the doorbell. He yawned. It was barely dawn. Two rings later, after getting no response, he raised his fist to knock on the door.

What he didn't figure on was the door being yanked open and the muzzle of a very deadly looking pistol being shoved into his face.

"Jesus!" The boy jumped back.

"Who are you?" Gil demanded.

"Ponce's Bakery! Delivery!"

Gil waited.

"Listen, I'm just delivering this, mister, like I was told. Look at the slip." He dug inside his jeans pocket, withdrew an order form, and held it out to Gil. "This is you, and this is this address, right?"

Gil read the paper, belatedly remembering that a step onto his front porch would bring his weapon into full neighborly sight. He angled his body to shield his weapon. "This verifies that an order was placed. I never called one in."

"I know," the boy insisted. "The customer called it in last night wanting us to deliver here at your home."

Gil took in the box, the stunned disbelief that had frozen the boy's features, his own nearly naked state, save for the low-slung pajama bottoms and jumpy nerves he wore. He lowered his gun, irreverently tempted to laugh.

"Mister, I can come back." The boy backed away some more.

"Give it here," Gil said, relaxing. "I won't hurt you. What do you need?"

"Nothing. It's already paid for."

Gil nodded. With little left to say, he looked down at the box in one hand, his gun in the other, then back at the boy. "Thanks."

"Yeah," the boy muttered. "Last damn time I make a morning run without making sure the client is up."

Gil caught the boy's words as they floated back to him. A slight smile broke through after all.

Inside the kitchen, he rustled around in his utensil drawer until he found a sharp knife. He slit the string on the box and peeked beneath the lid. Plain white icing, adorned four fluffy rolls. An envelope, bearing the bakery's logo, was propped in the corner. One word was printed on it.

Pax.

Gil lifted the envelope and scooped off the icing that had smeared on it with the top of his finger. He tasted the sugar then pulled out the note inside.

We got off to a horrible start.
    Maggie

Gil didn't have sufficient time to consider a response because for the second time that morning, his front doorbell rang.

He wasn't really surprised at his visitor this time.

"Well," Maggie said, "I'm glad to see that I, at least, don't rate a gun in the face."

Gil didn't return her smile. "Where the hell were you so that you could watch?"

Maggie sobered. "Over there." She gestured toward something sleek and silver parked across the street. "May I come in?" She moved tentatively toward him.

Gil stepped aside.

Maggie released a breath and for the first time in eight years moved inside Gil's personal space. Immediately, she was curious about this place he'd chosen to live.

At the moment, it was bare bones. Still, Maggie could see that structurally it was lovely. Lots of windows, especially those off the dining room and kitchen that were mullioned, admitted a warm splash of early-morning light. The condo was small, but much had been done to instill the illusion of airiness. Interesting angles and clever walls helped one room's space to flow smoothly into another.

Beyond Gil's back patio door, elaborately shrubbed and flowered landscaping provided a potent sense of country-garden tranquillity and seclusion. Maggie knew, with professional familiarity, he and the other owners of this community paid dearly for it.

In silence, she made her way over to his living room sofa.

Gil watched her make the visual rounds. He could practically hear her thinking, and his lips twisted with curiosity. Had he passed inspection? "You've already supplied breakfast," he told her as he grabbed a plate from the cupboard. "I can provide the milk, coffee, whatever. Or did you want something more?"

Maggie deflated a little at his sarcasm. "My message means what it says, Gil. One of the first things you said to me when you came back was that you hadn't come back to fight. Well, I'm telling you the same thing now."

Gil was slow taking down a second plate. He set it carefully on the counter and faced her across the width of the kitchen, across the distance of days, the distance of their lives. She looked sincere. And tense. He fished around in the drawer for napkins, found them, and gave Maggie one. "Your peace offering is accepted. I guess I'm just wondering what it's really about."

Maggie pushed up from the sofa and walked slowly over to the breakfast bar. She selected a plate and pulled up a bar stool.

Gil remained standing. He studied her bent head and waited for her to make her next move. He'd taken one bite, then another, by the time she did.

"I don't want to live with this bitterness any longer," she said, her voice low. "I don't want you to go on thinking the awful things I said to you have no effect on me. They do." She looked straight into his eyes. "I'm sorry."

"About what, Maggie? The fact that you said them, or the fact that they don't have the power to destroy anymore?"

"Dammit," Maggie whispered. Her plate clattered to the counter. She dropped her head.

Gil's own appetite faded. Without thinking, he reached out a hand and watched it hover, unseen, over the softness of her hair. And even as he considered it, a tiny voice deep inside reminded him that her remorse was her own. He pulled back.

"I'm sorry I came," Maggie said suddenly, leaving the stool and walking over to the sofa to sweep up her purse in a rush. "I won't keep you from work, or bother you any longer."

Gil was around the counter before Maggie made it to the door.

"Maggie!" He grasped her shoulders, felt a shudder go through her, and accepted with some obscure sense of resignation that his whispered entreaty was not so much for her comfort as it was for his own. "Don't go like this," he told her.

"Why not, Gil?" she demanded, turning in his arms. "When does this tearing at each other end?"

I don't know, he wanted to honestly tell her. With the warmth of her so close, with the memory of all the joy they had been to and for each other, he honestly couldn't say. But explaining that conflict wasn't something he could manage now. Not when the beauty and scent of her was so tempting, so vividly remembered. So near.

Maggie sensed the kiss coming, knew that she should turn back around, just walk away. But the strength to do it seemed suddenly too elusive for her. The reality of the gentle-eyed, hard-bodied temptation who held her, who tantalized her with a memory of desire, was too real.

At the first touch of Gil's lips, Maggie sighed. At the first taste of him, she opened her mouth to deepen the contact. This simple joining had been lost for so long. Too long. She trembled.

Gil's hands left her shoulders to trace a delicate tactile path along her arms, down to her wrists.

She moved in closer.

Gil sighed.

Maggie didn't need his gentle clasp to prompt her to wrap him in her arms. But she reveled in it all the same. The warm smoothness of his naked back was better than memory. The moist skill with which he could adjust the angle of a kiss, the temperature of her desire, still had the power to make her weak. It frightened her.

"No, Gil," she breathed pulling back, trying to move away from his arms.

"Yes," he contradicted just as softly, drawing her back.

Her second denial was aborted as Gil lowered his head and, with a butterfly touch, touched his tongue to her trembling lips. He wondered, hazily, if she would give him what he wanted.

She did. Overwhelmed by the seductive pleasure of his touch, Maggie acquiesced, parting her lips again. His kiss changed tenor. She gasped against his mouth, mingling her startled breath with the warmth of his.

Gil pulled her even closer against his body, against the strength of his muscled thighs, and succumbed to a helpless little shudder of his own.

No, Maggie thought dimly. This time when she found the determination to move away, she pulled completely out of Gil's arms, desperate to convince them both that she meant it.

"We can't do this, Gil," she said, breathlessly. "You know we can't . . ." She twisted the strap of her purse futilely around her hand, begging him with a look to let her go.

Gil stepped back, running a hand through his hair. He saw that Maggie was reeling. He felt as if he were coming out of a trance of his own. What the *hell* was he doing? And then he realized that Maggie was backing away, backing away from the anger he knew was hardening his face, not understanding that more of it was directed at himself than could ever be directed at her.

"I should never have come," she murmured once more. She faced him unflinchingly, her movements and eyes clear, before she turned around and headed for the door.

Whether the reprimand was for him or herself, Gil supposed he'd never know. He could only stand where she left him and watch her walk away.

Chapter 6

Myer had been right. The conference wasn't a walk in the park, but the difficulty for him, Gil mused, lay not in the barrage of questions he and Maggie fielded. Those had been anticipated.

The real difficulty for Gil lay in dealing with the surprise he felt at many of the quiet, self-possessed responses Maggie gave.

"Ms. Thomas, do you really believe someone tried to murder your father?" one print reporter demanded.

"The investigation Lieutenant Stewart is heading will determine that," Maggie answered.

"Maggie, do you believe your father is capable of something that would make someone want to murder him?"

Maggie smiled at the field reporter. "Mr.—Powers, is it?—I'm sure my father, along with about a thousand other public figures, garners at least a dozen people each day who claim to 'know' something potentially damaging about them. I put as much faith in that as I would in any unsubstantiated hearsay. As for the possibility of my father engaging in questionable behavior? I don't have to remind anyone here of Paul Thomas's political record, social contributions, or personal philanthropy."

"So you're saying you don't believe he could be guilty of anything."

"Mr. Powers, I believe what I've just said is quite clear. Mr. Crowly," she urged, turning to a more junior television reporter.

And so it went, Gil noted. Her poise and distant certainty never faltered. In fact, Gil thought, her answers portrayed a man she thought greatly worthy of admiration as a leader and respect as a father, but not obsessive love, unlike the sentiments of the young daughter Gil had left behind eight years ago.

Thirty minutes into the session, Gil made a point of looking at his watch and leaned into the mike. "Ladies and gentlemen, let's wrap this up. We'll take two more questions." He pointed to his left. "Yes?"

A newswoman spoke from the pack at the rear of the precinct auditorium. "Do you have any suspects in Denning's murder yet?"

"No, but we're in the process of following up on some very promising leads," Gil said.

"Such as?"

"In the interest of not compromising our investigation, I'll have to ask you to stand by on that."

"Have any of those leads connected Charlie Denning to Paul Thomas, even indirectly?"

"No," Gil said levelly. "So far, our investigation into both Denning's murder and Paul Thomas's accident is taking us down different paths, despite the implications suggested by the dead man's note."

"Would you tell us if those paths converged?" Another reporter asked.

Gil, Maggie, and many of the listening reporters looked to the back of the room, seeking the new source of the latest question. The challenge and the insinuation had been very clear in her voice.

"Ms.—?"

"Patricia Melrose." She named a local station as her network affiliate.

"Ms. Melrose, I believe Ms. Thomas and I have been as forthright and candid as we can be in our answers this afternoon. Given that, I don't fully understand your question."

"Perhaps the police would consider clouding the progress on this case as being in their best interest. Perhaps, for understandable reasons, Ms. Thomas would agree."

"I resent your insinuation that I'm lying, that my presence here is anything less than sincere, Ms. Melrose," Maggie said, leaning forward. "Were I a cynic, I could venture that your doing so promotes an interest in network ratings, and that perhaps your own motivation is equally as—how did you put it— cloudy?"

Some smiles were exchanged around the room. One or two reporters directed their looks Patricia Melrose's way but she didn't smile back.

Inwardly, Gil did. "Thank you, ladies and gentlemen," he said. "That's all." He turned his mike away and pushed back his chair. Maggie did the same. As according to the pre-conference plan, they both left the auditorium through an exit near which they'd strategically seated themselves.

In the corridor, Maggie dug her car keys out of her purse. "What do we do now?"

Gil walked her to the door. He shoved his hands inside his pockets and said, "We don't do anything for the time being. You sit tight, stay alert, and I'll let you know."

Maggie settled her purse strap on her shoulder

and shot Gil a look that told him to get real. "You're telling me to be a good little girl and to let you handle everything."

Impatient, Gil said, "Don't cop an attitude, Maggie. Tracking down murderers is my specialty, not yours. Contrary to what you seem to think, you can't control everything."

"Gil, I never meant to suggest that I could," Maggie said wearily. "You just can't honestly expect me to sit around and twiddle my thumbs when Daddy's in danger."

Gil nodded to a passing officer who gave him and Maggie an interested glance. Gil stepped around Maggie so that she was shielded from other prying eyes that might come their way. "Let's not fight." His voice was low.

In another life, Maggie might have characterized his tone as intimate. She watched his eyes, knowing that the truth of the matter was eight years of separation carried a lot of baggage, too much for one night to overcome. "I'm not fighting with you. I'm just trying to get you to see where I'm coming from."

"I do, Maggie." Gil stepped back a little, respecting the wariness in her eyes. "You've stated the facts. The additional fact is this, I don't want you hurt. The best way I know to ensure that for the time being is to keep you from putting yourself in a line of fire. That means I have to know what you're doing and where you're going to be."

That stopped Maggie, because while his words embodied a cop's logic, the expression in his eyes was very personal. She looked down at the floor, feeling his nearness, savoring the protection he was giving her, not caring for the moment if he was reluctant to do so or not. "I'm sorry. I don't want to hassle you, I just hate feeling useless."

"You won't be useless," Gil murmured, moving close again, bending down a little so that his mouth was at her ear, so that he could draw the essence of her close. The scent of her, enhanced by the light, floral perfume she wore, enveloped his senses. The remembered softness of her skin, the beauty of her that had grown more vivid with time suffused his mind.

"When the time is right for you to do more, I'll let you know," he said. "Until then, you've got to be patient, Maggie."

"And let you do your job." Maggie wanted to tell him she understood. But all she could do was feel him. Want him. She ducked her head a bit and brushed against him, then moved past.

Gil stood there slightly rattled by the sudden emotion that had gripped him. He took a calming breath, held it, and let it out slowly. Remembering to act like a cop was the only way he was going to be able to handle the job he had to do. "I understand you've got a charity benefit this evening."

From whom, Maggie wondered as she paused, although she wasn't really surprised that he would know. "What about it?"

"Maybe I'll see you there."

Maggie tried to figure his game. "I don't remember issuing you an invitation."

"That's okay. Eight-thirty, right?"

Which told Maggie he was back to the purely professional. Distant. Safe. There was, she doubted, little she could do to keep him away from the party, and all at once, she was tired of trying. "I'll see you there, then."

* * *

"Man, she's a piece of work." Adam snagged another hors d'oeuvre from a passing tray, one of several circulating among the ostentatiously rich and famous overcrowding the hotel ballroom. "No offense," he told Gil belatedly, "in light of your past, et cetera, et cetera."

"None taken." Gil polished off a finger sandwich then chased it down with the glass of carbonated water he'd been nursing. "You're absolutely right. As any one of the hundred men who've been milling around her tonight would probably agree."

Adam looked askance at Gil, considered his partner's not so casual observation. "There still something there, Stewart?"

A passing waitress gave Gil an admiring smile. Gil acknowledged her attractiveness, the compliment, and smiled casually back. "Something," he said to Adam. "But it's not what you're thinking."

"Yeah." Adam wandered away.

Gil followed his progress with a look.

Across the room, Maggie observed Gil's exchange with Adam over the shoulder of a particularly long-winded colleague who had her trapped against a canapé table.

"Excuse me, Nathan," she murmured with an apologetic smile and set her glass down behind her. She drifted away, ignoring *New Horizons* prized foreign correspondent trying to bite back his annoyance at his boss's polite brush-off. She headed for Gil.

There was a time when she wouldn't have had the nerve to do that, to risk disapproval for the sake of her own comfort. However, life, she reflected, had a way of mellowing that sort of reticence, especially when the ones feeding upon it had little regard for it. These days, it felt quite good to burst a pompous bubble whenever it presented itself, and Nathan's look of out-raged astonishment was especially priceless.

"What's the joke?" Gil wanted to know when she reached him.

"Just an observation." Gil nodded in response, seemingly without much interest, and looked past her to the band winding up for a post-break set. Clearly, he wasn't feeling inclined to pursue it, so she used the pause to her advantage and studied him. He was tense.

"So, what do you see?" Gil said, still watching the band.

"I'm not sure."

"Guess."

"Someone I've hurt very badly." She surprised herself.

Gil turned, looking for the sincerity in her eyes.

"Someone who deserved better, and who had every right to expect it," Maggie continued, compelled to ever more honesty by the depth of what was in Gil's eyes.

Gil felt something shift deep inside. Dammit, he didn't want to be vulnerable to her, was furious that a word from her was all it took to show him he still could be.

"Forget it."

Maggie shrugged and looked away.

He'd hurt her, Gil thought. Or, maybe her con-science was kicking her. God knew, ever since they'd laid eyes on each other they'd both demonstrated the knack of being able to zero right in on each other's hot spots.

Maybe some things couldn't change.

Then again, he remembered the kiss they'd shared. He heard himself say, "Can we get away from here?"

Maggie was shaking her head. "I have obligations."

"No, I don't mean the function, I mean the crush." The impromptu idea that had occurred to him gained momentum as he talked. "Is there somewhere we can disappear to? Just for a while?"

Maggie thought about it. "Come on," she said, weaving her way through traffic to head for a side door.

Gil set his glass down and followed. Just before he got outside, he caught Adam's eye across the room. Adam shook his head and turned back to the conversation he was having.

Gil knew what Adam was thinking, and he had neither the time nor the inclination to remind his partner he was wrong.

Maggie was waiting in the lobby. As Gil closed the distance between them, he admired all over again the elegant picture she made.

Many women might have chosen to wear the style of dress Maggie had chosen. Its flowing ankle-length lines, its dramatic Doleman sleeves, its tasteful cleavage would look deceptively accommodating on the rack. But few would transform the garment with the sensual simplicity that Maggie's elegant figure and style did.

The dress was a classic statement of subtlety and poise.

So was she.

Maggie read the look in Gil's eye. She remembered it well, regretted, again, that both of them had gravitated to such different places in their lives that took them so far away from all they'd thought had mattered.

"So, where to?" Gil asked quietly when he reached her. He traced the delicate angles of her face, the deep, exotically tilted eyes that were locked on his. "Where?" he breathed.

Maggie looked away, fighting a sudden breathlessness. This hadn't been the reaction she'd wanted or anticipated. "There's a lounge downstairs," she suggested, and found herself stopped by Gil's strong, warm hand that clasped her own. She kept her back to him.

Gil moved closer, slid his hand along her arm until it rested softly at her shoulder, until the warmth of her was tantalizingly close to his chest.

"I've got a better idea," he murmured above her ear. For the life of him, he was unable to *move*. But then, he realized Maggie wasn't pulling away, either.

"What?" She still didn't move.

Gently, Gil turned her around. The question in her eyes was one he couldn't even begin to answer, but the importance of this moment was something neither of them seemed inclined to deny.

"Will you trust me?"

"Where do you want to go?" Maggie countered.

"Away. Just for a while."

Maggie was uncertain.

"Will you trust me?" he asked her again.

Maggie looked down at their joined hands, felt the touch of Gil's cool fingertips as he tilted up her chin. He looked straight into her eyes and smiled, the curve of his mouth touched with an old recklessness Maggie remembered.

"Come on," he said.

Maggie took a mental breath and held on tight as Gil squeezed her hand and led her away.

She was surprised when they left the building. They collected his car, and he drove them west through a series of neighborhoods that gradually deteriorated.

"Where are we going, Gil?"

"Scared?"

"Curious."

He didn't answer.

"So it's a big secret, then." "

"No, Maggie." Gil stopped teasing. "Back there at the hotel, I thought . . . I just wanted you to see something."

Maggie studied his profile beneath the rhythmic spill of the streetlights that sped along beside them. Gil's tone suddenly seemed less than certain, and she didn't want to destroy the mood that had brought her here, his gentleness she'd missed so deep in her heart for so long.

"It's okay," she said softly. When he looked her way, as if to see if she really meant it, she murmured, "Lead on."

Gil did.

Eventually, he exited the expressway and cruised along for about ten minutes before he turned onto an unpaved thoroughfare. Street, Maggie thought, was too generous a description.

Houses were sparse, especially those that were occupied. Boarded and or obviously abandoned dwellings easily outnumbered their neighbors, two to one.

Beneath the deceptive moon, one could stretch one's imagination to impose an almost primeval ambiance on the area. A lush profusion of wildflowers overgrew many grassy alleyways and roadside stretches.

But Maggie knew any fancy imaginings would burn away with the dawn. The unrelenting sun would expose the true poverty of the area and its dust, which had long since usurped any lingering glory.

Here and there, groups of men loitered aimlessly beside parked cars. Some swapped bottles as easily as the lies Maggie could imagine they exchanged. Others sat huddled beneath muted dome lights inside their parked cars. What they were passing around, Maggie could only imagine, though she supposed her scenario would be pretty accurate.

Automatically, Maggie touched her door handle to make sure it was locked. Gil chuckled. She ignored him.

Another half mile or so passed. At some point shortly after, Maggie could swear she heard music in the distance, party music that was very loud and a little heavy on the bass. The party site was confirmed by a lighted, massive stone building that soon appeared ahead.

In stark contrast to its surroundings, the building was an artistic statement of grace, natural stone, and glass. It rested on a beautifully blacktopped lot filled with cars whose owners had obviously gathered to celebrate something.

Gil found a space and cut the engine. "Don't look so apprehensive, Maggie. It's perfectly safe." They got out, and Gil met her around the hood to take her arm.

"In any event," he added, "I'm a cop. And I'm armed."

Maggie tossed him a sanguine smile. Gil laughed and briefly pulled her close.

At the entrance, since Gil still didn't seem inclined to fill her in, Maggie scanned the stone inset above the huge double doors. And faltered. Gil's strong hand tightened on her arm, steadying her as he looked up, too.

"Brooker Community Center?" Somehow, Maggie felt duped. "This has to do with Sidney Brooker?"

Gil merely watched her closely and opened the door to usher her inside.

Light, noise, and laughter spilled out to greet them. The few guests who turned took absent notice of them before turning back to their conversations. One member of the crowd, a stunning black woman of about sixty, spotted them and separated herself to come their way.

"Gil!" She clasped Gil's arms and bussed his cheek. "You made it. I thought you couldn't." She turned her interest to Maggie. "And who's this?"

"My friend, Maggie. Maggie, I'd like you to meet Helen Brooker."

The woman waited for Gil to elaborate. But when Gil didn't, she hardly missed a beat.

"Glad you could come, Maggie. You like my son's place?"

Maggie looked to Gil, at a loss.

"It's her son's achievement tonight that we're celebrating, the inauguration of this community center he designed. He and his backers finally compiled the last bit of funding they needed to finish it."

"Mrs. Brooker, it's lovely," Maggie said, feeling increasingly uncomfortable. "You must be very proud."

"I am, yes," Helen said. She seemed distracted. "Sorry if I'm being rude, but have we met somewhere before?"

"No," Maggie said smoothly, "I don't think so." She rarely had to deal with the occasional hassle of being recognized by her readership since she did her job, for the most part, behind the scenes. That circumstance was only broken on special occasions, which was why she honestly couldn't sift through eight years of memory to pull up a recollection of this woman. The realization made her feel vaguely ashamed.

Helen Brooker looked doubtful but not particularly inclined to push. "Well, I'm sure you're right. I wouldn't have forgotten so lovely a friend of Gil's."

Maggie smiled and tried not to mind the quick once-over that followed the compliment. She could see the dollar signs on her dress adding up in her hostess's head, the quick comparison of her party attire to her hostess's own. But oddly, Maggie wasn't offended or even annoyed because she felt a genuine warmth in the woman's smile and knew the scrutiny was from honest admiration, not spite.

"Gil, why don't you show Maggie around. I'll see if I can track down Eddie."

"Sure."

Maggie pulled back when Gil took her arm again. "Why did you bring me here? What does all of this mean?"

Gil regarded her quite seriously. "It means just what I said earlier. There are things here I thought you should see."

Short of making a scene, Maggie didn't think that she had many options other than following where Gil led.

He walked her to a winding staircase whose flowing lines were artfully designed so that the tiered column appeared to sweep unsupported to a second-floor mezzanine.

At the top, Maggie could see several framed drawings, some in charcoal, others in watercolors. All were distinguished by a primitive style that was, nonetheless, filled with heart and artistic grace.

The subjects were children. Some were playing games on a school playground. Some were engaged in chores at home. All were oblivious to—or perhaps resigned to—the downtrodden backdrops against which they lived and played.

Even as Maggie registered that thought, she realized something else.

There was a feel to each of the works that said their subjects' spirits were anything but downtrodden. These children's faces expressed a joy that overcame the harshness of their physical lives. It was a look of purity, peculiar to the innocence of childhood, and it touched her.

She looked at the signature scrawled at the bottom of each of the illustrations. Sidney Brooker.

Maggie looked up at Gil, and he nodded.

Maggie couldn't pinpoint why she suddenly felt close to tears. She managed to say, "Why?" But Gil was turning away to acknowledge the man who slapped a hand to his shoulder. Maggie raised a finger to the corner of her eye, hoping that Gil hadn't noticed the moisture she wiped away.

"Eddie, hi." Gil smiled. "This is great."

"Thanks. My only regret is that my father can't be here to see it."

"How is he?" Gil asked.

"Hanging on, man. That's all he can do in prison." To Maggie, Eddie said, "Mama said you were fine, and she didn't lie."

Maggie shook the hand he extended.

"Edward T. Brooker, architect and master builder of this little establishment. I'm honored you've come to visit."

"Maggie." She introduced herself then waited uncomfortably, as she had with his mother, for Eddie to display some curiosity about her surname.

"Pleased to meet you, although it's my bad luck it's got to be on Gil's time."

Maggie smiled, relieved. Relative anonymity definitely had its advantages. "Thank you."

Eddie turned to the wall beside them. "I saw you admiring Daddy's drawings. They're something, aren't they?"

"Yes," Maggie said. "When did he do them?"

A shadow crossed Eddie's face. "A long time ago. When I was a child."

Maggie let Gil take her hand. "Doesn't your father paint anymore?" She dreaded the son's answer.

"Sometimes." Eddie's voice was detached. "It's— difficult for him these days. Painting's not a hobby he can as easily indulge."

Maggie understood why, but because she could hardly let on, she said, "That's a shame."

Eddie didn't respond.

Maggie was driven to add, "He's quite a talent."

"Yes." Eddie turned away from the art and took her and Gil down the corridor. "A few years ago, my father fell on hard times. His life took a dramatic turn away from my mother's and mine. But before that happened, he gave me a vision, and that vision gave me my life."

"What do you mean?" Maggie guessed how uncomfortable his answer was going to make her feel.

"Here, let's get something to eat first." They'd come to a long buffet table laden with enough caloric goodies to make Maggie's mouth water.

Chicken hot wings, barbecue tips, cole slaw, assorted salads, chilled fruit, and hot buttered rolls were in abundance. An ornate silver steamer filled with Swedish meatballs sat adjacent to another that held a mound of fluffy wild rice. Three huge platters of sliced beef, turkey, and cheeses rounded out the treats.

Maggie thought of the decorative, sedate salads she'd featured at her own party, and eagerly picked up a plate. She selected a variety of foods, and after her two companions had likewise arranged their own plates, she followed them to an empty table in a relatively secluded corner.

"You were telling us about your father," Gil prompted, once they'd all taken some time to start eating.

"An extraordinary man." Eddie dabbed his mouth with a napkin. "At least, in my opinion. A lot of other people probably wouldn't agree with me."

"Why not?" Maggie asked.

"Because he made a lot of mistakes. Don't get me wrong, I'm not excusing him. But no matter what he made of his life, I'll always have my memories of a man I know at heart just wanted to make his family's life better."

"Those illustrations?" Maggie prompted.

Eddie laughed spontaneously.

Maggie smiled at the infectiousness of it, in spite of herself.

"They were my bedtime stories. Even when I was a kid, I suspected Daddy wasn't an ordinary dad. He had a way of telling a wicked tale about somebody or something that made me suspect that perhaps some of the telling was from firsthand experience.

"I guess it didn't matter, though, because the one thing I always remember him telling me was that he was proud I was his kid. Lots of people thought Daddy was a loser, but he knew how to hope, and he passed his hope on to me."

"This center shows that," Gil stated, and pushed his plate to the side of the table.

Eddie was a little slow to answer. "As the manifestation of what he wanted for me, yes. This center is that."

"And what did he want, Eddie?" Maggie's attention drifted briefly to Gil. She wondered at the pensive look in his eyes.

"Freedom," Eddie said. "Freedom from the shackles of this neighborhood's despair. An education for me, so that I could escape it on my own terms. And autonomy, so I could give back to the neighborhood, so that those who couldn't leave it could at least live here with some recaptured pride and sense of purpose."

"And because of that you built this center for the children," Gil said.

"Yes. Like I've been saying, my daddy didn't give me and Mama much by way of physical comfort. But he always gave me hope, and that was my motivation as a child to strive for something more."

Maggie felt Gil watching her. What did he expect her to say?

"Well," Eddie scooted his chair away from the table. "I've droned on for way too long about myself. I think a bar run is in order. Either of you want anything?"

"No," Gil said.

"I wouldn't mind a juice," Maggie said.

"Done." Eddie sauntered off.

"Well, hell, Gil, if this trip was meant to cheer me up, I wonder what you've planned for an encore."

"I'm not playing, Maggie. I just wanted you to hear a few things, see firsthand some of what I've tried to express to you."

Maggie toyed with a roll on her plate. She thought of everything she'd just learned, wondered if she had really been as closed-minded as Gil was implying.

She looked around and saw that Eddie had been waylaid by a very pretty woman. "What I'm wondering is how you could ever have fallen for the sort of snob you think I am."

Gil pondered that, looking inward for the truth in her observation. Her analysis, he finally decided, was a little harsh. "You weren't a snob, Maggie. And I wasn't that kind of fool. What we both were"—he hesitated—"was very young."

"Yes." And somehow, at this moment Maggie was feeling very old. She pushed her plate away restlessly.

"I think I probably should be getting back to my own shindig, if you don't mind."

Gil had wanted to open her eyes a little. He hadn't wanted this melancholy, this sadness. Perhaps it was he who had been hopelessly naive in believing it could be avoided.

"Come on," he said pushing back his chair, "let's go find Eddie so that we can make our exit."

"You just got here," Eddie insisted when they tracked him down. At least stay and enjoy some of the dancing. I'm paying this band a fortune, and I want to see that they earn their take."

"Counter deal," Gil offered. "Why don't you join us for dinner sometime soon. My treat."

Maggie wondered a bit at the "us," at the impetus behind the invitation, but said nothing and quietly awaited Eddie's answer.

"You got it, man," Eddie replied. He said to Maggie, "I'm not one to easily pass up a winning combination of free food and the company of beautiful women."

"It was a pleasure, Eddie," Maggie thanked him. "And congratulations, again. Your father would have every right to be proud."

Someone attracted Eddie's attention, and he left.

For a long time while Gil drove back to the hotel, Maggie sat thinking.

Exactly where in the past had she grown complacent to let the social conveniences her father's money could buy, the diffused racial inequities its abundance could assure, insulate her from the struggles of poor blacks like the Brookers? Their lifestyles were not as refined as hers, and their aspirations, by some conservative standards, were not as high. But their chosen lack of visibility didn't deserve anyone's contempt or to be mistaken as a lack of heart for what was right, or even, as in Eddie's case, noble.

Gil, always quick to call her on her indifference in the past, had been just as quick tonight. And here she sat, stewing and uncomfortable, as any contrite racist would be.

Eventually, she couldn't take the silence that filled the car any longer.

"You must hate us very much." She concentrated on her folded hands, then out at the passing buildings of the downtown cityscape.

Gil was startled to hear the words that so closely paralleled his own thoughts of a few short days ago. Eddie's speech had affected him, too, in ways he hadn't anticipated. He thought of how it might take some time to sort it all out. One thing, however, had become disturbingly clear. "I don't hate you, Maggie," he told her. "We've shared too much."

Maggie's stomach fluttered.

"I feel the same, Gil . . ." She shrugged, uncertain of how to go on.

"Perhaps there isn't much more either of us can say right now. Let's just let it rest."

Maggie silently agreed. Her heart felt strangely heavy and strangely full. She thought maybe the emotion riding her, riding them both was truly too fragile to dissect just now.

They drove on without conversation. When Gil pulled up beside the hotel garage, he waved away the valet.

"I'm going on home, Maggie."

Maggie accepted that, still searching for something to say, still needing to end the evening with something more substantial than speculations and regrets.

As if he sensed that need, Gil reached over and took one of Maggie's hands. He contemplated it and his own thoughts for a few hushed moments. Then he lifted her palm to his lips.

Maggie sighed. Again, the tears weren't far away.

Gil raised very dark eyes to hers, exposing the turmoil that turned his voice husky. "Good night, Maggie."

He looked as if he wanted to add something else. Maggie waited a bit breathlessly for it.

Gil only shook his head, then let her hand go.

"Good night," he repeated.

Maggie watched him lean back, saw him turn from her, knew that cool cop's detachment had eased back into his eyes. With a conflicted heart, she too turned and opened her door. The parting click of it closing was still loud in her ears after Gil drove away.

Chapter 7

Gil wanted distance, and Maggie was more than willing to oblige. Two letters into her morning mail, however, she knew she wasn't going to be able to do that.

She sat down in her breakfast nook with her coffee and reread the words that made little sense to her.

Thomas may die. Marrs shouldn't have, but maybe it was already too late for him. Maybe it's already too late for you.

A threat? Maybe. A warning? Most definitely. She reached behind her to grab the phone extension from the wall, and dialed. She was quickly patched through to Gil and was grateful she didn't have to touch on the particulars of her request to the operator.

"Maggie, what's wrong?"

A little hesitancy, she thought, but not enough to override his professionalism. "I've received some correspondence I think you should know about. It has to do with Jeff Marrs."

"I'm coming over." Gil hung up.

Maggie looked at the receiver before she hung up, too. She wondered how much of last night was going to be something Gil regretted.

She found out roughly fifteen minutes later. She

opened the door, met Gil's somber eyes, then stepped aside to let him in.

Gil took a slow, comprehensive look around, then got down to business. "Let's see the letter."

"Sure," Maggie said, as terse as he. "It's in the kitchen."

"Where?" He followed her into the cozy nook.

"On the table. Sit down, I'll pour you some coffee."

She brought two mugs over to the table and sat while Gil read the note. When he finished, he laid the single-spaced sheet aside, picked up his mug, and concentrated on the lush flower garden outside the picture window.

"Well?" Maggie watched him sip his coffee.

"What's the connection?" Gil mused softly.

"They were lifelong friends," Maggie offered.

"And what else?" Gil turned his attention from the garden, and his intent expression settled on her. "I don't remember seeing Marrs around when we were kids."

Maggie noted how easily Gil had referred to the past and wondered if he did. "He was never a frequent visitor. I only saw him sporadically before I went away to college. I saw him even more infrequently after that. He always seemed to be more of Daddy's past than of his present."

Thoughtful, Gil said, "Go on."

Maggie shrugged. "There isn't much I can add beyond that. They met in college, I think. They stayed in touch afterward, and for all I know seemed to remain good friends. That's really it."

Gil made a mental footnote. Murder and a link of friendship suggested that probably wasn't all. "Did your father ever talk about those early days? Stories from school, post-college affiliations? Anything?"

Maggie thought about it. "Nothing that really stands out, Gil. Although—"

"What?"

"Right before I left to go to college, Daddy told me about some campus prank he and some other guys played on a fellow freshman. He mentioned Jeff and others being in on it with him. The thing that stands out about it is that he talked about the others as if they were particularly close, like a special club or clique or something."

"What was necessarily odd about that? Lots of pack friendships form in college."

"That's what stuck with me. He talked as if this particular group of friendships didn't last, even though they were obviously important to him all through school. The only contact he seemed to seriously maintain afterward was with Jeff."

"Still, do you remember anything about any of the others? Who they were? Their names?"

Maggie shook her head. "It was all so long ago." She sighed. "Do you really think this note could have been sent by the person who killed Jeff?"

"You seem skeptical."

"It's just ... everything is becoming too complicated, too ugly. What's to say this note isn't the work of some prankster. I mean, so soon after that call—"

Gil frowned. "What call?"

Maggie told him about the call she'd gotten at her office.

Gil listened intently. "No other calls like it before or since?"

"No."

Gil watched her, but he didn't really see her. He didn't like what his instincts were telling him.

"You're thinking the caller could have been the same person who sent this note?"

"Maybe." Gil was noncommittal. He returned his gaze to Maggie's garden.

"But you don't believe that," Maggie urged.

"Maybe," he said again.

"What? Are you going to talk to me?"

"I don't like the feel of this." Gil pushed away from the table. "I don't like the fact that whatever is going on seems to have taken a turn to directly involve you." He carried his mug over to the sink, set it inside, then settled both hands against the rim of the counter.

Maggie was sobered by the depth of emotion Gill seemed to be struggling with. She didn't consciously plan to walk over to him, to touch him again, not this soon. But before she knew it, she found herself doing so.

"Gil, what is it?" She rested her hand on his shoulder.

He shrugged away from her touch. Then abruptly, he left her completely, putting distance between them.

"What?" she insisted.

"Can I trust you? If I'm going to do this right, I've got to know if I can trust you." He watched her closely.

He was waiting for her to answer in the negative, Maggie guessed, maybe hoping she would. She felt an old rush of regret, mixed with a little shame. She hated it, hated most of all the fact that she partially deserved it.

"Can we ever get beyond the past, Gil? I need to." She dropped her head tiredly. "It's been too long."

"But you chose him, not me."

The hurt underscoring Gil's quiet observation pierced Maggie to the heart. But she was afraid to let him see, afraid to give him the kind of control that sort of vulnerability would allow him to take.

"Let me tell you something," she said instead. "I did

some hard thinking way before that encounter with the Brookers last night. After everything blew apart, I considered the fact that Dad had been too harsh, that I had been too judgmental right along with him."

"And?"

"And I confronted him with my doubts after you left. He was furious."

Gil hadn't expected this, hadn't expected this to be behind part of that sadness he'd already glimpsed in Maggie. But he knew it was. "Go on," he said carefully.

Maggie sat back down at the table, uncomfortable with the distance Gil kept between them, grateful all the same for the support it gave her.

"He said you were carrying around too much anger inside you, too much bitterness to ever be able to really believe in a middle road. He said the proof was in how you'd let your emotions get in the way of your judgment about Brooker's guilt. He said the boy he'd helped raise had become a man he couldn't trust."

Gil had suspected all Maggie revealed to be true, guessed it to have become a defining vision for her father. But hearing the confirmation still hurt.

"And what about you, Maggie?"

"I lost my father's trust the day you walked out. I'm ashamed to admit it was only then that I started to really question the strength of the stand he took against you.

"That was the day I told him that even though he disagreed with your judgment, and that I shared some of his views, maybe the way we'd publicly treated you had been wrong."

Maggie paused, and Gil sensed she wanted him to intervene to give her time to collect herself in the wake of all she'd said. But he didn't because what she was allowing herself to reveal was too important to him.

"It's why, though, everything has come to this, or maybe because of it, I need to take the opportunity this Denning enigma has presented to find out one way or the other if there's some hidden past in Daddy's life," Maggie finished.

Her words hit Gil like tiny painful pellets. He walked back over to the table and sat only because he needed to. It took him a moment to be able to look at her. When he did, he wasn't entirely surprised to see that her eyes were moist. But the barrier he'd lived with for so long stayed firmly around his heart.

"So you went to bat for me, after all," he finally said. "It was too late, Maggie."

"I know," she whispered. "It was all so complicated, Gil, with Dad, with us. It was the best I could do."

"Yes." It had been. Always. "So you want to help me to"—he smiled humorlessly—"expedite this investigation now. Well, that's understandable. But, before you commit yourself, I want you to think about something, and I don't expect an answer now."

"What's the question, Gil?"

"How far are you willing to go? How high can you let the price go that might be demanded in lieu of your winning back your father's acceptance?"

Maggie searched for words, felt Gil waiting. Gil had been like a son to her father once. However, Paul Thomas was her father and that link was an elemental one. Gil might think he appreciated it but he would never be able to fully understand.

Given that, Maggie's turmoil deepened, because she knew in all honesty that if she searched her soul, she didn't know what that answer would be.

Gil reached over and covered her hand with his. "I loved you once, Maggie." He hesitated, wanting to be as honest as he could. "I can't tell you, in all sincerity what those feelings have become now. But neither can I lie and tell you I don't care."

Maggie's tears spilled over. For him. For her. For what they had lost, for what they had shared, because she felt the same way, too. She turned her hand palm up, and curled her fingers around his. She was grateful for the strength in his grip. For the briefest moment, she remembered how easily for her that strength had once given way to gentleness, to comforting reassurance, to a soothing caress, a passionate touch.

When the memory grew too poignant, Maggie slowly broke the contact and raised her hand to wipe away a tear. "Then, let's just deal with what we can for now, Gil. Our immediate concern is clear. Someone's out to hurt Daddy. And now, based on that letter, the revenge or whatever it is that's at work seems to have expanded to involve me."

Gil looked deep into her eyes for long, long moments, fighting back his own emotion, trying to gauge where they stood. He felt an inexpressible loss. But with the trembling smile Maggie was able to offer, he felt an incredible weight lift, too.

He took a cleansing breath. "Okay. I'm thinking you're probably privy to some relevant connection between your father and Jeff Marrs, even if you don't know it. Marrs was syndicated with your magazine. Had his contact with your father all these years been marked by any political conflict?"

"Not that I know of, and like I said before, their closeness was only as constant as the distance between Georgia and Washington could keep them."

"Did Marrs ever talk to you about your father in terms of anything nonprofessional? Did he ever bring up anything that suggested some extra dimension outside an ordinary friendship?"

"No," Maggie answered, thinking. She could hear Jeff's regret over the break between her and her father, but there was little else that involved him beyond that. "No," she repeated.

"Your father's political views have always been fairly liberal," Gil said, thinking. "Marrs always struck me as being a bit closer to the right, or at least the center, than your father is. Did that cause friction?"

"Despite his liberalism, Dad was always remarkably adept at living and letting live." Realizing how Gil would take what she'd just said, she lifted her gaze to his and smiled humorlessly at his rueful look.

"Most of the time, hm?" Gil voiced.

"Yes, most of the time."

"So," Gil continued, "if they didn't clash politically, and their friendship was still intact, what was it they shared that could have linked them as victims now?"

"Listen, let me pull some more clips of his columns. Maybe there's something there that I'm overlooking."

"All right. In the meantime, stay alert. And if anything at all feels out of place or seems threatening to you, call me. Or call Adam Carter, my partner." He reached inside his suit jacket and pulled out a notebook. He wrote down the appropriate numbers, tore the sheet off, and handed it to her. "Day or night."

"Thanks," Maggie said, glancing down at the paper. She thought about how to best phrase what else she wanted to know.

Gil read the question in her hesitation and as he walked to the door said, "Don't worry, I've decided to take the initial watch. That means you'll see me hanging around, for the time being."

Maggie looked up at that, unsure of how to interpret his careful explanation. Feeling her way, she said, "I'm glad. I'd be lying if I told you I didn't feel better being guarded by someone I know."

Gil shrugged.

Maggie saw that he wasn't going to help her so she gathered her courage to ask the truly tricky question whose answer she badly needed to know. "Can we be friends again, Gil?"

Gil pulled his sunglasses from inside his jacket and put them on. "Let's take it one day at a time, Maggie."

She expelled a breath and replied thoughtfully, "That's fair." When she saw Gil visibly relax, she found the impetus to follow an impulse. "We could start today."

Gil tilted his glasses down. He watched her over their rim and leaned against her kitchen door.

"I have a charity ball I have to attend tonight." She conjured a slight smile. "You could be my date."

Gil pushed his glasses back up. He considered his duty and knew he really had little choice."

"I could," he agreed.

Maggie relaxed then felt foolish a moment later when schoolgirl butterflies assailed her as Gil stood where he was, watching her.

"What time?" he asked quietly.

"Eight-thirty should be fine." She hesitated again. "Gil?"

"Hm?"

"What do you think about Daddy? You don't believe Denning could have been alluding to anything real?"

"Eight years ago, I didn't believe your father could have turned on me and what we had together like he did."

Maggie had no answer to that.

Gil watched her stricken expression and relented. "I honestly don't know, Maggie. The problem is, we don't know what it is Denning claimed to have had. If we can get a handle on that, the rest will be easier."

"Good." Maggie dragged a hand through her hair. "I just want to know, that's all."

Before he had time to second guess himself, Gil walked back over to Maggie, hunkered down, and took her chilled hands in his. Maggie looked up with what was clearly surprise. And then her surprise was overlaid with gratitude and maybe, he thought, something more.

"We'll get to the bottom of this, Maggie—I need to know, too, not just for the sake of this case, but for me. He squeezed her hand, looking away. "And maybe for us as well."

Maggie's lips parted.

Gil trapped whatever she started to say against his fingers. "I'll see you later."

"Okay," Maggie whispered after the door closed behind him. "I'll see you then."

Gil passed several day-shift officers who were leaving to go home as he made his way through the precinct corridors back to his squad room. Technically, he should have been joining the departing crew. Realistically, there was always one more thing that needed taking care of before he felt comfortable calling it a day.

The presence of Thomas on his front burner had created a recent backlog of little things. His "date" with Maggie tonight was going to create even more. He headed to his desk to get a few of them done.

He wasn't surprised to see Adam lighting the late-night oil. One of the reasons they were getting along so well was because of their shared understanding that the best results often dictated that they let it burn.

"A call came in about a half hour ago that I think we should check out," Adam said, swiveling around in his chair.

Gil stopped at his partner's desk and took a look around the squad room. The day was still hot, the air-conditioning was down, ties were loosened, and the few voices still inside the room were clipped. "Who from?"

"Denning's neighbor. Seems he may have remembered something he forgot to tell us when he was questioned the first time."

"Like what?"

"A better description of Denning's assailant."

Gil juggled his keys. "Let's go."

Buster Mullens pulled his door open, interrupting what would have been Gil's third knock.

"Ya'll came," he said. "Come on in."

Adam went first. Gil started to follow and almost fell when the fattest, wettest-mouthed hound dog God ever created waddled out of nowhere right under his foot.

"Clyde, you get down, boy!" Buster ordered.

Buster could have saved his breath, Gil thought. Clyde didn't look as if he'd had the energy to get up to anything in years.

Inside, Gil took a look around. Buster's living room consisted of a sprung chair, a sprung sofa, a threadbare rag rug, and a rusting refrigerator propped in the corner of what he'd obviously designated the official dining area. Two windows admitted light into the cabin's single room, at least what light managed to crawl between the cracks and tears of Buster's drawn yellowed window shades.

Gil watched Adam look from the chair to the sofa before rejecting the chair. Briefly curious as to what had weighted that decision, Gil also selected the sofa.

"Buster," he said, "my partner tells me you've been

thinking about the night Denning was murdered. You've remembered more?"

"Yeah, yeah. Hey, let me get ya'll a beer. Sit tight."

Gil glanced over at Adam, saw him casually thumbing through a stack of magazines on the cloth-draped crate that served as Buster's coffee table. The corner of a *Hustler* magazine caught Gil's eye, as did two *Playboys*, all strategically placed beneath some outdated *Field and Streams*.

Adam's mouth twitched and so did Gil's when Clyde walked over to them, nosed the magazines with a garlic-scented "woof," and offered what could only be described as a very giddy doggy smile.

"Here ya'll go." Gil and Adam looked up at Buster, who handed them their beers. "You can take those if you want," he added, nodding affably at the magazines. "We already seen 'em."

Deciding not to ponder the ease with which Clyde had been included in "we," Gil picked up where he'd left off.

"There was something else you want to tell us about Denning's murderer?"

Buster nodded and dropped into the vacant chair. He popped the top of his beer and took a swallow. "It was a man," he pronounced.

Gil and Adam waited.

Buster took another swallow and settled back with great satisfaction.

"And?" Adam prompted.

"And I bet that's somethin' ya'll didn't know before." Buster grinned.

Gil squelched his irritation, knowing it wasn't worth the energy. "Can you add a few details to that description, Mr. Mullens?"

"Only if you call me Buster." He chuckled again. "The man was kind of tall, skinny. Looked like he was wearing black, although that could have been the night shadin' him. It was really dark, nasty." He finished his beer and set the can down at his feet.

Adam said, "During our initial interview, you told us you didn't see anybody at all when you arrived at Denning's house. How is it you remember seeing this man now?"

"To tell the truth, I thought I saw somethin' then, but with all the excitement and the ruckus Clyde was puttin' up, I just wasn't sure until I got to thinkin' on it."

"And now you're sure," Gil said.

"Yep, I am."

Gil got up. So did Adam. "Anything else?" Gil asked.

Buster squinted his eyes in concentration. "Yeah," he finally said.

"What?"

"Sucker sure could run."

Adam let out a frustrated breath and walked around Gil to the entrance of the shack.

"I say somethin' to rile him?" Buster peered at the open door Adam had left behind him.

"You did fine, Mr. Mullens," Gil assured him. He reached inside his jacket. "I know I've already given you my card, but here's another one just in case. You remember anything else, just let me know."

"Sure thing," Buster said, scratching his chin, "I'll tell you what, you're real sharp. Thought so the first time I saw you. You've got some real impressive manners, too." He winked. "Fellahs like you ain't nothin' but a credit to your race. Remember that."

"Thanks," Gil said very seriously. "I will."

Back in the car, Adams said, "What else did that yokel have to say?"

"Nothing," Gil said smiling. He smiled a little wider

as he realized he wouldn't have been able to a few years ago. The change felt good.

"This sure was a waste of time," Adam said.

"Hey. We know we're probably looking for a man now."

"A sucker who can run *real* fast."

"I don't know about you, but I'm betting we have this case solved tomorrow."

"Shit."

"There's something else." Gil told Adam about Maggie's letter.

"She needs to be watched," Adam said.

"Yeah, I know. But I don't want this newest connection with her to surface in public yet, not until we can get a better handle on the reason for it."

"Yeah, I agree with that. But the danger of the threat shouldn't be ignored, Gil."

Gil heard the scrutiny, understood the question. "Let's keep it contained between ourselves and the captain. The both of us should be able to take care of providing an adequate lookout for now."

They rode in companionable silence awhile longer. A few blocks from the station, Adam turned his face to the window, studying the passing streets. "With Paul Thomas out of commission, it seems to me our best bet at gaining a little insight probably lies with his daughter."

Gil glanced at Adam briefly, then turned his attention back to the road.

"Daughters and sons," Adam mused. "Same as wives and husbands, all of them the first to hide family secrets and the last to reveal them."

"She doesn't know anything, Adam."

"How do you know? Did she tell you so?"

Gil hit the turn signal and pulled the car into a smooth, tight right. "Yes."

"And you believe her." Adam's tone said clearly he was poised to do anything but.

"Look, man—"

"You look. She could be in this thing deep. I'm just worried you'll get sucked too far down into those baby browns of hers to know it."

A sharp denial hovered on Gil's tongue. That denial was made all the sharper by his memories of what had transpired with Maggie this morning.

Adam sighed. "Listen, I just don't want to see you blindsided."

Again, Gil heard beneath his friend's words.

"Maybe she's being honest, Gil. But maybe she isn't."

And maybe, Gil thought, it was time for him to start being brutally honest with himself. Adam was right. A residual attraction to her he hadn't anticipated could make it fatally hard for him to recognize the difference.

"The lesson she taught me was clear, Adam. I can handle her. Nothing's going to get on top of me again."

Adam studied his friend for a few moments, then looked back out the window as they pulled into the station lot. "Like I said, I'm just looking out for you, man."

That makes two of us, Gil thought. Because sure as hell, the most important part of the lesson he'd been dealt was to at all costs look out for himself.

Chapter 8

A plan started to gel in the killer's mind during his second pass by Maggie's house.

Plenty of shrubs, plenty of trees, and there was lots of shade in the daylight. More importantly, there was lots of shadow at night. If the order came, he'd be able to take her out easily.

The ultra exclusiveness of her neighborhood wasn't a deterrent. There were special ways to create invisibility, and the killer was first and foremost a specialist.

Satisfied by his third pass, the killer smoothly drove away, still trying to figure why she might need to die.

In theory, anything was possible, he supposed. But he couldn't honestly conceive a plausible set of circumstances that would have Paul Thomas's golden child turning on her father.

Of course, he wasn't paid to debate the probabilities surrounding what he did. Others had always laid the groundwork and figured the odds, and in that respect, this job was no different.

He was on standby for now, and the point was that he would be ready if the order came. Any consideration beyond that would literally be a distraction he couldn't afford.

He braked at a stop sign and caught the eye of a thin

young woman on the adjacent corner. She held the
leash of her energetic spaniel in one hand, the handle
of her child's stroller in the other. The killer nodded,
and the woman smiled shyly.

The killer's smile was chillingly humorless as he
drove away.

Gil told himself he was making a mistake all the
way to her house. He was still telling himself that
when he parked in the rutted drive, got out of his car,
and walked up the drive to see the woman he'd
lost significant contact with for the better part of
eight years.

He still had the key, but it stayed in his pocket.
Somehow it seemed more appropriate to ring her bell.

Gil took one look at the expression that seeped
across Naomi Stewart's face when she opened the
door and knew he'd been right. This was a mistake.

"Hello, Mama."

She looked him over, her expression still impassive. "Gil."

"Can I come in?"

Naomi continued to look at him, seemed to reach
some decision, and stepped back to let him by. Gil
avoided her eyes and told himself she hadn't looked
through him when he walked past her.

He stood in the foyer, delaying the move into the
living room, into a house that still held too many
ambiguous memories, even now. There was laughter
and sporadic joy, but overall there was a mother's
strained bitterness. The man recognized it more
clearly than the child who had been her son.

Even so, the hard and the easy parts of that past
were exclusively his. For reasons he didn't understand
he'd suddenly needed it tonight, after all these years,

whether it was foolish or not. He'd needed to come home.

"Where's Noah?"

"At work. He got hired on at that new packing plant on the westside."

Gil took a seat on a living room sofa that was unfamiliar to him. So was the new husband. He'd learned of Noah's existence during one of the two phone conversations he'd shared with his mother after he'd left Atlanta. She hadn't been too inclined toward expansiveness then, and he'd taken the cue and followed her lead.

So now that he was here, he fished around for something to say. "You doing okay? You look well."

Naomi took an armchair across from him. She reached inside her housecoat pocket, pulled out a pack of cigarettes and a lighter. She put one between her unsmiling lips and lit it. "What do you want, Gil?"

"Oh, Mama." Gil sighed. He wanted to get right back up and leave, but he wasn't a boy now. The man who sat in stony awkwardness before his mother told himself he owed it to them both to find a way to stay.

"You didn't waste any time getting hooked back up with those Thomases, did you?" Naomi took a deep pull on her cigarette.

"The Denning case isn't about Paul Thomas. I'm sure you've been following the media closely enough to know that."

"I know you can't lie to your mama. Thomas is involved or you wouldn't be trying to sidestep me so neatly. What's she got to do with it?"

"She?"

"The one who cut you off at the knees the last time. I suppose she's trying to wrap you up all over again so you'll go easy on her daddy."

Gil shook his head, frustrated. "This isn't about Maggie and me."

"It's gonna be, you just wait and see. You got a weakness for that girl, although I never knew why. She was a spoiled little witch when you met her, and she's just an older one now. And richer, with lots more to lose."

Gil was still wading through his own doubts. He hadn't come here to talk about Maggie and their past, and he wasn't going to. "I can't stay long, is there anything you want me to do for you before I leave? Anything you need?"

"Noah gives me what I need. You didn't seem too worried about it all those years when you were gone. I don't need anything from you, Gil."

It hurt. Gil dropped his eyes to the scarred coffee table where his mother impatiently tapped out her cigarette in a cheap ceramic ashtray. "Mama, I don't want us to be enemies. I came here to tell you I'm sorry for not staying close. I want us to do better with each other." He lifted his eyes back to hers. "Can we do better, Mama?"

Naomi's face shuttered and she got up, pulling her bathrobe closer around her. "I got to get Noah's dinner on." She hesitated on her way to the kitchen, then turned. "You want to stay?"

Gil's mouth twisted with frustrated regret. "I can't, not tonight. I've got to work."

Naomi's expression turned cynical. "Yeah, it was always somethin', wasn't it. First it was school. Then it was taggin' along after that man, Thomas, taggin' along wherever he snapped his fingers askin' you to go, just like you were his son or somethin'."

"Mama—"

"Then it was hangin' around that girl of his, like she was the juiciest fruit on earth and you always had to have a bite. What's this work you have to do? Does it concern her?"

"Yes." Gil felt the first twinges of anger. Would he always have to justify himself, his life, to the one person, maybe the only one whose acceptance was supposed to be unconditional?

Naomi laughed harshly. "How hard do you have to get kicked, boy?" She turned away from him and started back to the kitchen. "Go on, then. I'll see you when I see you."

Gil watched her narrow back until it disappeared beyond the kitchen's swinging door. He examined the emptiness he felt inside. It wasn't new and he was older now, but age didn't make accepting it any easier. He walked to the front door and wrapped his fingers around the knob. After one last look around, he opened the door.

Maggie stood in her front doorway, smiling at Gil's promptness. Wow, she thought, giving him and the elegant fit of his black tux an involuntary once over. "You look great." She continued to smile at the way Gil glanced down at himself, seemingly distracted.

"Thanks. So do you."

Maggie's smile turned reflective. "I wasn't fishing, Gil. Come on in, I'll just get my bag and then we'll go."

Gil walked inside behind her, admiring the way the midnight blue of her silk gown flowed and clung exactly where the designer who had dreamed it up had surely designed it to flow and cling. The fabric was so dark, it appeared to be black. The way it clung to her small breasts while leaving her creamy shoulders bare only enhanced the illusion of understated drama.

He suddenly thought of his mother's suspicions

about Maggie, her speculations about him and his motives, about the foolishness that once had almost ruined his life.

Maggie swept back inside the room. "Okay, I'm ready." Abruptly, she stood where she was, looking at Gil. "What?"

Gil cleared his expression. It must have been formidable to cause her to look so apprehensive. "Nothing." He opened her door and stepped aside so that she could precede him.

"Where to?" He asked her once they were settled inside his car.

"Is something wrong?"

Gil looked her way. "Why?"

"You seem touchy all of a sudden."

Gil started the car, saying nothing.

"We're going to Tom White's home, I'll give you directions."

"Another politico. Why the good congressman?"

"He's a close friend and supporter of my father. This shindig's been on his books for a long time."

"And he's not going to postpone it?"

"No. Tom's making a public point. Going on with the fund-raiser demonstrates that despite Daddy's condition, Tom's committed to keeping the faith for a speedy recovery and my father's continued senatorial bid. He's hoping others will follow his example."

"Your father's a popular guy, I'm sure it'll work."

Maggie listened for Gil's sarcasm and could only detect the smallest trace. She was relieved. She and Gil had made some real strides over the last few days. She didn't want to disturb the truce they'd reached, especially tonight.

She only hoped what she was planning was the right thing.

* * *

The mansion was ablaze with lights, cars, and an aura of money that hung over the grounds like a perfumed haze. Maggie was amused when an actual butler greeted them at the door, and she raised a brow Gil's way when the butler wasn't looking to see if he shared the laugh. His mouth quirked, and she knew he did.

"Maggie!" Congressman White loped down the curving staircase before them and pulled Maggie into an effusive embrace.

"Tom, how are you?" Maggie stepped out of the congressman's arms, then turned to introduce Gil. "Gilbert Stewart—"

"Of the Atlanta police force," White supplied. "Lieutenant, isn't it? I saw you quite recently on television."

"Yes." Gil gripped the congressman's hand. "Good to meet you."

"Um." White nodded, looking contemplative. "Are you in the process of rounding up a list of suspects, Lieutenant, a roundup that includes me?"

"Not at all, sir. I'm more or less here as Maggie's escort tonight."

The congressman studied Gil a bit. "More? Or less?"

Gil laughed. "Let's just say I have no intention of disrupting the party."

"Well, you're a friend of Maggie's, and that certainly makes you welcome in my home. Though, I must confess, I've never been the subject of a police vigil before. It could make one a bit nervous."

"Don't be." Gil smiled and selected a fluted glass of club soda from a passing waiter. "I do have a legitimate interest in the festivities here. I'm sure it's no secret to you that Paul Thomas and I have a history that goes beyond professional bounds."

"Yes, young man. But all that's a bit heavy to get

into now, don't you agree? Please, you and Maggie make yourselves at home, enjoy the party. I'm sure you'll find some interesting people here you'll enjoy meeting." He turned to Maggie and lifted her hand to his lips. "My dear."

Gil's mouth twisted as the gangly, white-haired senator hurried away.

Maggie caught the look. "Flamboyancy is just his way, Gil." They moved farther into the living room, nodding here and there to acquaintances who passed by.

"Coupled with a little pre-party libation? That flush of his was nearly as red as his cummerbund."

Maggie chuckled. "He's really quite harmless. Besides, it's his party. There are worse places he could choose to get a little tight."

"Um."

"There's Sloan."

Gil followed Maggie's gaze across the room. Sloan Michaels was having what appeared to be a very exclusive exchange with a very lovely companion.

"Who's the woman?" Gil asked.

"His wife. He manages to trot her out occasionally, either as a display for those interested or a reminder to himself. I still haven't quite figured it out."

"Doesn't Mrs. Michaels have a voice?"

"You bet. It's an unfailingly perfect echo of her husband's. Monica," Maggie greeted the subject of her observations as the woman caught her eye, waved, and approached.

"Maggie, you look beautiful, as always," Monica Michaels bussed Maggie's cheek. She turned to Gil, and the look in her eye sharpened to one of curiosity and clear interest. "I don't believe we've met?"

"He's a cop, dear." Sloan inserted as he walked up beside her. "Lieutenant Gil Stewart. He's investigating those ridiculous allegations supposedly found in the Denning letter."

"Oh."

"It's a pleasure, Mrs. Michaels." Gil emphasized the introduction with a slight nod. He was amused at the woman's not so subtle withdrawal.

"I'm afraid that through no fault of your own, Lieutenant, my wife views you as standing posed to discredit her hero."

Gil sipped his soda and surreptitiously glanced at Sloan's wife to see if she was going to raise an objection to being spoken for. She merely kept her eyes on her drink as Sloan continued to chat away.

"Of course, given the venue tonight, I don't think she'll necessarily be the only one."

"For instance, there's you, of course." Gil raised a brow, and added a smile.

"Of course." Sloan's expression sobered. "Paul's friendship and integrity are unshakable givens I believe in entirely. I hold both very dear."

"Meaning?" Gil favored Sloan with an equally sober expression.

"This fund-raiser is for him. There's no room for dissension here."

"We all know where we are, Paul," Maggie inserted mildly.

Gil chalked one up for Maggie, then he stared at Sloan, content to let the moment stretch until it became noticeably tense.

Sloan cleared his throat. "Well, there I go again." He attempted to resume his former lighthearted expression. "I've repeatedly asked Monica to kick me when I go off on a political tangent. Maggie, Lieutenant, I apologize. I get on that subject, and I have an unfortunate tendency to get intense."

Monica finally spoke up. "Yes you do, and we've

sufficiently monopolized these two already." She claimed her husband's arm. "We're going to circulate. We'll talk to you later."

Sloan spread his hands with an abashed shrug and let his wife lead him way.

Maggie moved on to another group.

Gil was more thoughtful as he mingled. Some, like Congressman White, recognized Gil from his televised conference appearance. Others knew him from farther back, from the time when he'd been an integral part of Paul Thomas's life. Gil didn't find those reacquaintances awkward as much as interesting.

Some of his old acquaintances, politician and nonpolitician alike, expressed genuine regret about the rift that had separated Gil from his former life. Others, he sensed very clearly, were withholding judgment to see whether he had returned as Thomas's friend or foe. Gil thought the latter view was intriguing, because he himself honestly didn't know on which side of the fence he stood.

He knew where duty put him, squarely in the middle. But the party was bringing back a lot of old memories, and he knew that somewhere down the line, no matter what he found out about Thomas, he would have to choose.

Through a sudden part in the crush, Gil caught sight of Maggie. She was just moving out onto the terrace, and she wasn't alone. A tall, sandy-haired man who looked roughly to be thirty-something and highly enamored of her was close at her side. Gil started excusing himself politely as he slowly weaved his way in their direction.

When he finally arrived at the terrace doors, he slowed, approaching cautiously. He didn't want to be seen, but he felt a need to know what the tête-à-tête was about. During their recent encounters, he and

Maggie had never mentioned their personal lives. He felt no compunction about taking a surreptitious opportunity to discover something of hers.

Gil glanced around the door into the lantern-lit darkness. Maggie and her companion were standing not quite a foot away next to an artificial palm. Unabashed, Gil raised an hors d'oeuvre to his mouth, leaned against the door with his back against the crowded room, and listened.

"Cal, I thought you wanted to talk about the interview," Maggie said.

"In a minute, Maggie. Didn't you know, this is a party."

"No, this is old. What do I have to do to get through to you?"

"Stop teasing, for starters. I guess now that the surrogate son's around, the junior protégé doesn't cut it anymore."

Gil's attention quickened.

"You're drunk," Maggie said with disgust. "There's no point in continuing this."

"Not so fast, princess. I wonder what you'll do when your old man dies and makes your cut from his good graces official?"

"You don't know what you're talking about."

"Baby, everybody in this town with eyes and ears knows what I'm talking about. The golden girl lost her crown, and isn't it interesting it seemed to slip right about the time that bastard Stewart split. Isn't it even more interesting how you've gone sniffing around him again now that he's back."

"You're disgusting."

"I'm accurate." Cal sounded amused. "I don't know what you did, but it sure must have pissed Daddy off royally—come back here, I'm not through!"

"Let go of my arm—" Maggie's voice was stony.

Gil knew the time to intervene was probably now, but he stayed where he was, in spite of himself. The scene was riveting.

"Or what, Maggie? You'll scream? Nothing so melodramatic for Paul Thomas's little girl. What would Daddy's supporters think? Or more importantly, if his heir apparent created an unfavorable reflection, what might the paternal fallout cause her to do?"

Gil expected fire. What he heard was Maggie's pain

"I'd cut my heart out again," she said.

As involuntarily as he'd stood arrested before, he now tentatively stepped out onto the threshold of the veranda. He knew by her startled expression that he'd surprised her.

"Maggie, here you are," he said smoothly. "I was beginning to think you'd cut out early."

Maggie recovered and calmly pulled her arm away from Cal. "No, I was just having a discussion."

Belatedly, she made the formal introduction. Considering what had just been exchanged, Gil thoroughly admired her poise. "Gil, Cal Bradly, an old—" she hesitated.

"Flame?" Bradly supplied.

"Acquaintance." Maggie met Cal's eyes squarely.

"She's being modest, Stewart." Bradly held her gaze, then narrowed it with his thin smile. "She's quite the girl, our Maggie, never one to . . . offend."

Maggie offered no comeback, and Gil watched as her sad expression turned bitter. Bradly chuckled again, then sauntered away.

"Why didn't you tell him to go to hell?" Gil asked curiously.

"Because maybe he was right," Maggie murmured after a slight hesitation. Then, as if she guessed he wasn't going to let that slide, she added hurriedly, "Come on, let's dance."

Gil let her take his hand, let himself be led to an adjoing gallery where a live ensemble was launching into a melodic easy-listening selection.

He was a bit surprised when Maggie burrowed into his arms. Her move was sudden enough to let him know just how upset she still was, so he let her have her silence and moved closer, wrapping his arms around her.

The songs changed, but the mellow tempo didn't. All sorts of memories flooded through Gil, all of them having to do with Maggie and gradations of comfort and softness he'd found once upon a time in her arms. And as he continued to hold her through the next song and then the next, he gradually became aware of something else. A fine tremor was shaking her, but when he placed his fingers beneath her chin, she only shook her head and refused to look at him.

He suddenly wanted to track down that grinning son of a bitch and pummel him. But public appearances and personal equilibrium were everything tonight, and so he gazed into the air over her head and they continued to dance.

By the third song, Gil noticed they were attracting comments. He tensed a little, and Maggie brought up her head. But whatever she was about to say was interrupted by a sudden halt of the music that quieted the rest of the dancers and milling guests.

Congressman White seemed to materialize out of the throng, and Gil looked down at Maggie with a question in his eyes. She shrugged, telling him she didn't know what this was about, either.

They didn't have to wait long to find out.

A uniformed waiter threaded his way through the crowd into the gallery. He pushed before him a silk cloth-draped cart, decorated with crystal favors and roses. At its center was an enormous birthday cake. As the many spectators realized there was a cake, they erupted into delighted applause.

Maggie joined them, but after a moment, it occurred to her how still Gil was beside her. She turned to look at him. His profile was a frozen study in desolation, and it made Maggie's hands slow and then stop. Probably no more than a second or two passed before he seemed to catch himself and look down at her, his expression again bland.

She smiled a little more brightly than necessary and smoothly turned away as if she hadn't seen anything. The unexpected glimpse reassured her that whatever his reaction might be, her plan was right.

Chapter 9

After Congressman White's birthday cake had been distributed to all the guests, the party settled into an even groove.

Maggie and Gil resumed their mingling. Sometimes the crush separated them, and at those times Gil found moving around on his own more expedient.

When Maggie found herself alone, she caught occasional glimpses of Gil. He smiled and seemed to be making all the right small talk, but Maggie could sense a melancholy beneath it all.

It seemed as if the birthday surprise had changed the evening for Gil. Maybe that was just as well, she thought, because she was tiring of the party, too. She made what she hoped was a final circuit around the room.

Gil must have had the same idea, because ten minutes into her reconnoiter, she felt his hand on her arm.

"You look tired, Maggie."

"Let's say it would be fine if you wanted to go."

Gil smiled. "Come on, then. You need to say your good-byes to the congressman?"

Maggie made a casual survey of the room. "Since I don't see him around, I won't worry about it. I'll send him a note tomorrow."

The night was still fine when they emerged outside and headed for Gil's car. He opened her door, but Maggie avoided the hand he offered to help her inside.

"What?" Gil said.

"Let me drive."

"Why?"

Maggie pursed her lips in an impish smile.

Gil recognized the look, thought of how many years it had been since they'd played together because of it. "Girl, what are you up to?"

"Give me the keys and you'll see."

Despite his fatigue, Gil felt his curiosity—and, he reluctantly admitted, his anticipation—rise. He tossed up his keys lightly, caught them. What the hell. He hefted them Maggie's way.

She made a clean openhanded catch and walked around to the driver's side, her smile still a tease.

The night was warm but Maggie kept the windows up and the air-conditioning down to a comfortable low. It wasn't long before they cruised into the pricey Buckhead district.

Gil looked over at Maggie thinking now she'd tell him where she intended to go.

She felt his look and kept her eyes on the road. Her smile, however, reappeared. "Just sit back and enjoy, Stewart. Why don't you turn on the radio?"

"Thanks," Gil said a little ironically, amused that she'd issued the invitation inside his own car. He surfed channels and settled on a local country station. The selection that was playing was soft, sweetly melodic, and low.

Definitely surprised, Maggie shot Gil a glance to let him know it.

Gil just smiled, leaned his head against the backrest, and closed his eyes.

Maggie concentrated on the drive, and it seemed as if in no time their destination was just around the corner.

By the time the car stopped, Gil was prepared to expect anything. He was surprised anyway. They were entering the parking lot of an ice-cream shop. Maggie stopped the car and grabbed the door handle again.

"Sit there," she told him when he started to get out with her.

Gil scanned the lot, his cop's eyes alert and watchful.

"Lighten up, Stewart, we're in the high-rent district and yeah, yeah "—she forestalled what Gil was about to say—"I already know the lecture."

"Maggie—"

"Look at it this way, God protects little children."

Gil looked at the clock on the dash. It wasn't quite midnight yet, and there were a few patrons about. "You're no fool, Maggie," he said, completing her thought.

She was right, he needed to relax. Anyway, the sparse number of customers all looked like pretty harmless well-dressed Yuppies out for a late-night stroll.

"Thank you," Maggie said quietly. On the surface, she knew they'd stretched a minor point, but beneath that she appreciated Gil's trust. She opened her door.

Gil watched her as she went inside. He could see her through the glass of the shop, and he saw that she got a number of male looks and feminine smiles. Considering the way she was dressed and the lateness of the hour, many were no doubt speculating that romance was in the air.

Gil sighed restlessly. The depression he'd been

shaking off for the past hour started to creep back. The stars were out, the night was warm, and the sky was clear. Definitely, a night when romance should have been in the air. Yet it wasn't for him, and that made him feel inexplicably lonely.

He kept a thoughtful eye on Maggie, waiting for her to return. When she eventually did, she was carrying a small parcel.

Gil turned in the seat as she set the box in the back and climbed behind the wheel.

"What is it?" Gil tried to see if he could detect anything from the box.

Maggie started the engine. "Can't tell you yet. You'll know, soon."

Thoroughly intrigued now, Gil resettled himself and waited on what obviously was going to be her pleasure. They'd driven about a block down the road when Maggie pulled into the vacant lot of a small municipal park and cut the engine.

Gil raised a skeptical brow. "This is it? We're here?"

"Yeah. Get out."

Since Maggie was already following her own directive, Gil had little choice. He trailed her as she clutched her evening bag in one hand and the box in the other. She made for a picnic table just within sight. As they approached, it seemed to Gil to take on a theatrical effect, situated just under a halogen light as it was and surrounded by a pool of darkness on each side.

Maggie seated herself, delicately arranging her long skirts around her. "You can't stand there all night, Stewart, come on."

Gil sat down facing her and folded his hands on the table.

"Now, close your eyes," she told him.

Gil played along. He heard the rustle of the box and

then the snap of her purse. He frowned, certain the next sound he heard was the flare of a match.

"Okay, you can open up," Maggie said.

Gil did, and went very still.

It was a cake, an ice-cream birthday cake. His name beneath the ubiquitous Happy Birthday was scripted with a flourish. He looked into Maggie's smiling eyes.

"You planned this?" he asked carefully.

Her reply was soft. "Some things, a woman doesn't forget, Stewart."

Gil said nothing, he only stared at the cake.

He was quiet for so long that Maggie's smile faltered. "Gil?"

He still said nothing.

Maggie started to fear she'd offended him after all. She gave it a last try. "That's your candle, you know. It's customary to blow it out . . . if the heat doesn't get the ice cream the candle will."

Gil ran a hand along the back of his neck and looked away from both her and the cake, out into the empty park.

Disheartened, Maggie leaned forward to blow out the candle herself. The quicker they left, the faster they could forget this mistake. She placed her hands on the table to brace herself and was just about to blow when Gil said, "No."

Maggie raised her eyes to his. Gil met her gaze, started to say something, but reached out his hand instead. He slid it along the table until it rested beside hers.

When he moved it a fraction more, she took a quick little breath and felt her fingers enveloped by his. Palm to palm, they sat. The candle burned.

Finally, in an emotion-roughened voice, Gil said, "Thank you."

Maggie's fingers tightened involuntarily. Her voice, too, was thick. "You're welcome."

Gil gave her hand a little squeeze and leaned toward the cake. He exerted a gentle little puff, and the candle went out.

Maggie let go of his hand and reached back inside the cake's box. She pulled out a plastic knife and two plastic forks. After she'd cut two slices, she gestured with the knife that they should eat it out of the box.

They ate without conversation, and for the first time since he'd come back, Gil felt as if he was truly communicating with Maggie.

"I went home today, to see Mama," he told her.

Maggie finished a bite, licked some ice cream from her fork, and reached inside the box for more. "How was she?"

Gil didn't answer right away.

Maggie lifted her eyes, waiting.

"She married. Did you know?"

"No." It was odd, she thought, how thoroughly she had lost touch with his life when he'd left. "What's he like?"

"Decent, I guess. She seems happy enough with him."

Maggie reached for another bite. She let it dissolve against her tongue as she laid down her fork. "How's he feel about having acquired a new son?"

"I talked to him on the phone once. I don't think the conversation qualified him to answer."

Maggie folded her hands on the table. Gil started to pick around inside the box then laid down his fork, too.

"Anyway," Gil continued, "he wasn't home today."

"Well, then, I guess that just gave your mother more

opportunity to spend some quality time with her birthday boy."

"She didn't remember."

Gil had spoken so softly, Maggie almost had to strain to hear. But she had heard. And understood. His unexpected melancholy at White's party suddenly took on a little more clarity. "Well, bully for me."

"What?"

"I said bully for me. Her lapse in memory was my gain because we would have had a hell of a mess if you'd been too full to help me demolish this cake."

Gil stared into her eyes and saw them slowly crinkle at the corners. Her gentle smile took another weight from him. "What about White's cake?" he teased. "It could have put a monkey wrench in your plans if I had filled up on it, instead."

Maggie shrugged dismissively. "That dry old thing? I couldn't choke down more than two bites, and I didn't notice you exactly chowing down."

Gil got up.

Maggie wondered what he was about. He stepped backward over his bench and moved purposefully around the table. Maggie studied her hands wondering why the temperate summer air had suddenly become very still.

Gil walked toward her, saw her head move ever so slightly to track his progress, then she seemed to lose her nerve when he moved out of sight. A couple more steps, and he was right behind her. "Stand up, Maggie."

His voice was as soft as the breeze that caressed her bare skin and, in that moment, twice as dark as the night. Her stomach fluttered, and for a split second, she was tempted to say something flip. But then his strong, cool hands closed over her shoulders, and she was powerless to do anything other than what she'd been asked. She stood.

Gil's hands fell to her wrists and he guided her, with her back still to him, from between the bench and the table until she was positioned directly in front of him. "Now, turn around."

Maggie had to take a steadying breath before she could do so. When she did, her heart stuttered again at the intense look in Gil's eyes. He said nothing, only lifted his hands to her face to frame it.

She watched his gaze drift to her hair, slide caressingly over her face, linger on every feature. Her lips parted when his hands shifted so that the pads of his thumbs could stroke her brows. At the exquisite gentleness of his touch, she closed her eyes and waited for his kiss . . . but he gave her something better.

"Come here," he murmured and folded her completely in his arms, allowed her to move past the barrier around his heart.

Maggie savored the feel of his palm against her nape, the way he applied the slightest pressure to pull her closer. She tucked her head against his shoulder, beneath his jaw, and let her own hands wander along his silk-encased back until they were linked behind his neck.

She breathed in the clean, freshly scented smell of him. She tightened her arms as he shifted to drop a kiss, just one, on the crown of her head. And then the hand at her neck dropped to join its mate at the base of her spine. She thought they swayed but realized that maybe it was just a tender shaking from the beat of their hearts.

"I'm so sorry, Gil," she found herself whispering. "For everything, I'm sorry."

Gil held her closer, absorbed her apology, considered the tears he sensed had begun to fall. There was no easy rejoinder, nothing their brief time together had yet made graceful to say. Still, he was comforted by the way she held him. The strength in her touch told him she could accept his reticence, and perhaps, he thought, the steps they were making together tonight would bring them deeper understanding another day.

At length, he lifted her chin. "We should go." He searched her face. "Are you okay?"

"Yeah." She stepped away from his embrace and raised a finger to her eye. "Yeah."

Gil turned back to the table, where he gathered their trash in one hand and her purse in the other. He tossed the box in a dumpster. "This time, I drive," he murmured when he stood beside her again.

"I'm all right, Gil."

He raised a brow. "I relaxed on the way here, sweetheart. You're exhausted, and I want to make sure you get home safely."

As if his words had sparked a cue, Maggie felt the urge to yawn. She tried to hide it, but saw by Gil's smile how unsuccessful she was. She gave in with good grace and let him guide her to his car.

A short time later, Gil pulled into her drive. "Good night," he said, letting the engine idle. "I had a really . . . terrific time."

"Good, I'm glad. So did I."

He smiled.

She smiled.

He leaned forward and kissed her quickly on the cheek, then he retreated until his back was against his door.

Maggie was relieved. If she had invited him in, he would have accepted. But she hadn't and was reassured by his comfortable restraint, by the obvious fact that he, too, was willing to wait until the timing was better. He was willing to wait, as was she, for something more.

Chapter 10

From his sunroom chair, Sam Peters sat and contemplated the predawn sky while he waited for darkness to fade. Birdsong had just begun to break the preternatural stillness, a sound he loved to listen to this deep into the night.

The eternal transition created a slice of peace before the hectic pace of his life began, gave him time to reflect, to remember, to savor the inherent promise of each dawn.

After more than thirty years, he still found it distressingly easy to recall another space of dawns. They had not heralded the exciting anticipation integral to the palate he'd made of his life. They had simply marked an endless series of days that guaranteed no promises and little change.

The only thing Sam had glimpsed during those long-ago days that held the promise of change was power, and that power squarely lay in the hands of the white postwar landowners and merchants and businessmen who dominated his world. They called the shots by collecting real and imagined debts they were owed from families like his that were poor, black, and disenfranchised.

It seemed as if everyone danced to their tunes, and

many considered their lives bearable only because they were allowed to keep dancing. Even as a child, Sam had grown tired of the tune.

His grades in school had opened a realm of possibilities to him, a world beyond the poor rural South. This world was one where he could fashion his own dance, and the one he'd chosen had carried the jingle of money with it.

High finance—the understanding of it, the manipulation of it, the benefits to be reaped from it—was the direction in which he'd focused his energies. The more adept he'd become at moving through the country's monied corridors, the more quickly the power he had once envied had arrived at his door.

The discipline he chose to specialize in was stocks, bonds, and the brokering of the two. The thrill of the gamble and the incredible rewards for winning he found to be a special delight. Even better, brokering was a trade he could ply anywhere in the country, anywhere in the world.

He'd created his own personal slice of heaven right in the heart of Beverly Hills, a paradise where money bought respect.

His thoughts turned to Jeff, who had been like a brother to him for so many years. He thought of the heights to which Jeff, too, had climbed and, more bitterly, of the ignominious end to which he'd come. Reverie made Sam sad, and the pastel awakening before him dimmed.

But even as it did, he thought of how Jeff would have wanted those who loved him and believed in him to go on. Despite the senseless ugliness in the world, Sam would go on.

He got up and loosened his bathrobe. In the distance, the faint squealing of a braking vehicle sounded outside the grounds of his estate. The world was waking up beyond his patio doors. It was, he reflected, time to greet it. He would start as he had for so many years of his life, with this simple beginning of the day.

The clear blue water in Sam's pool shimmered before him invitingly, though he knew from experience how cool it would be. He anticipated that chilly invigoration as he shed his robe, hitched up his trunks a little, and climbed in from a set of stone stairs at the pool's side.

Two laps into his swim, he started to warm up. After three laps, his muscles started to burn. He flipped onto his back, enjoying the heat of the rising sun that beamed down on his skin. He felt weightless, and his eyes nearly shut with pleasure when a glimpse of something to his side caused him to open them again.

Sam shifted until he was treading water. He saw a tall man wearing a T-shirt with a cleaning service emblem and said, "I didn't order any pool service today. You've made a mistake."

The man tipped his cap politely. "No, sir, I didn't. I'm afraid this is the right address."

"By whose order?" Sam started stroking to the pool's edge. A stupid mistake and confrontation was *not* the way he wanted to start his day.

"You wouldn't want to know." The man reached inside the logo-emblazoned knapsack slung casually against his hip. The silencer-tipped pistol he raised Sam's way gave one deadly spit before it was quickly put away again.

Sam Peters's world narrowed to a pinpoint of light while his life's blood seeped from the tiny wound in his forehead. Slowly, the water claimed his body even as death claimed his spirit and all that he had been. His last thought was of the sun, of the beauty of the dawn. Somehow he was immeasurably comforted to be surrounded by its everlasting light.

Sam Peters's world went black.

Maggie was sorting her laundry when she heard the news. The wire-service report on the radio was brief and brutally to the point. Internationally renowned stockbroker Samuel Peters had been found dead late this morning by a neighbor. He'd died of a gunshot wound while swimming in his pool. Details were to come as the case developed.

Maggie turned off the radio and sat down on her bed. She was chilled. First her father, then Jeff Marrs. Now Sam Peters. An ugly pattern was surfacing. She picked up the phone, needing to talk to Gil.

"Stewart here."

"Gil, good morning."

"Hi."

Maggie smiled a little at the easy intimacy that lowered Gil's tone. Beyond that, she couldn't take much pleasure because of the reason why she'd made this call. "Someone else is dead."

Gil was instantly alert. "Who?"

"Another friend of my father's. We need to talk."

Gil caught Adam's eye from the adjoining desk. His partner watched him with unconcealed interest. "Adam and I can meet you in thirty minutes. Are you at your office?"

"No, I'm home. I'm taking care of some of Daddy's construction business, it's paperwork mostly—" She was rambling. "I'll be at home."

"Fine." Gil hung up.

"What's up?" Adam wanted to know.

"There's been another killing that could have something to do with Thomas."

"And who just gave you that little tip?"

"Maggie Thomas, and cut the crap, Adam. I'm not in the mood." Gil adjusted his shoulder holster and grabbed his suit jacket off the back of his chair. He stood and eyed Adam while he put it on.

Adam's mouth was tight as he donned his own jacket.

While they drove to Maggie's house, Gil filled Adam in on the victim. Before they left, with Myer's permission Gil had quickly contacted the Beverly Hills authorities to see if police were holding back anything significant, from the news crews. They hadn't been, they'd assured him, but upon being told by Gil that the Peters killing could have some connection with his own active investigation, they assured him they would let him know about any further developments.

Gil and Adam reached Maggie's house a little over twenty minutes later. When they got out of the car, she was already standing in the door.

"Gil," she said as he stopped at the threshold, but her eyes were already resting on the man at his side.

"Maggie, I don't think you two were formally introduced at the hospital. This is Detective Adam Carter. Adam, Maggie Thomas."

Maggie held out her hand and Adam gripped it, though he was slow to do so. "It's good to meet you, Detective. Please, come in."

She led them to her living room, where she'd set out a silver coffee service on the sideboard. "I thought we'd need something," she said by way of explanation.

Gil appreciated the thought and was quietly impressed that she seemed to remember the way he took his brew. He reached out to accept the cup she offered and caught the look Adam threw him.

"Detective?" Maggie turned to Adam.

"Black is fine." Maggie concentrated on pouring his

coffee as if it were a difficult task. The hostility she sensed from him made her nervous.

They all seated themselves. Gil and Adam took adjacent armchairs, Maggie the sofa. She tucked her bare feet beneath her, raised her cup, and sipped.

"So, why the panic at this stockbroker's death?" Adam demanded.

His harshness startled Maggie. "This morning, I recalled how Sam Peters used to be one of Daddy's friends. Lately, he hadn't been a visible one, but despite the distance the friendship was still there."

"In what way?" Gil set his cup on a coaster on the coffee table and crossed his legs.

"I was very small," Maggie said, remembering. "Younger than when I met you, Gil. One summer, Daddy and some men he referred to as my uncles took me to a park. I didn't really know Daddy's friends, but I was so young the fun of the day was all that was important to me.

"I haven't thought of that incident in years, but I guess with Sam's death and all . . . well, I guess I've never really forgotten it."

Adam said, "So these uncles were Jeff Marrs and Sam Peters?"

"I believe so," Maggie answered slowly. "And someone else. I can't see his face or remember who he was, but I'm sure of it, yes. There was a third person."

Gil leaned forward. "What about Denning, Maggie? Does Charlie Denning figure into your memories of the past?"

Maggie thought about it, struggled to grasp anything she might have been forgetting. She came up empty. "No."

Gil heard her frustration, knew that her discouragement was real. He looked at Adam. Adam was looking back at him with an unreadable expression.

Gil asked Maggie, "Does your father keep any journals, diaries, personal papers? If he does, maybe they could lend some insight, make it easier for us to attach some structure to these impressions you're feeling." He frowned, puzzled, when Maggie's gaze became bleak.

"I wouldn't know," she murmured, "but I'll certainly look and tell you what I find."

Gil wanted to pursue the distress that accompanied her promise. Instinct was telling him there was something in what Maggie might have to say that could, in terms of the case, produce a little professional rope.

"What about you?" Adam suddenly asked Maggie. "No more notes? Phone calls?"

Maggie overcame her momentary surprise. Of course, Gil would have told his investigative partner about those things. "No, nothing," she answered quietly. "You think that means I'm out of danger?"

"I think we'd all be foolish to let our guard down," Adam replied, then shifted direction. "Anything you can turn up that your father has written will be appreciated." He got up. "Just let Gil or me know."

"I'll do that," Maggie said.

"In the meantime, Gil and I have a few things to check out. By the way, I understand Gil's been keeping an eye on you, but he can't be everywhere at once."

Both Maggie and Gil waited for Adam to elaborate.

"Don't be alarmed if you see me hanging around to spell him every once in a while."

Maggie studied the two men, sensed the tension between them. "I won't. And thanks."

Adam shoved his hands inside his pants pockets.

Gil pulled his eyes from his inscrutable partner and said to Maggie, "I'll be in touch."

Maggie nodded and walked them both to her door.

After they left, she chewed her lip thoughtfully and wandered back over to her sideboard to pour herself another cup of coffee.

"What the hell was the interrogation about, Adam?"

"What the hell is your defensiveness toward that woman about, man?"

"Declining to treat her like a criminal does not equate with defensiveness, partner."

"Yeah, well maybe you should get a clearer bead on who it is you choose to champion."

Gil waited for a red light to change, then smoothly turned the wheel. "Meaning?"

"Meaning she's been checking up on you."

"What?"

Adam let it sink in. "Checking up, as in digging into your past, as in snooping around with the Chicago authorities to get some information about your work there."

Gil tried to concentrate on the road, but he kept thinking of the night they had just spent together. He couldn't believe she was sneaking behind his back. "Explain," he told Adam, tersely.

Adam did. Gil's former captain had recently gotten wind of discreet inquiries being made about one of his former officers. Upon some discreet probing of his own, he'd found the inquiring source had hailed from a very pricey investigation firm based in Atlanta. Nothing as obvious as money had been offered by the Atlanta investigator to the former colleagues of the officer in question, but his questions had, nevertheless, carried a tone of intensity that went just beyond the pale of informality.

The officer's captain had pushed the Atlanta investigator to reveal the identity of his employer. Eventually, with a little pressure, the investigator had given up Maggie's name and quietly faded away. Gil's former captain made a call to Atlanta. Gil hadn't been in, but Carter, his partner had. On a blind hunch, Carter, upon hearing the bare bones of the captain's inquiry, had fielded Maggie's name for a reaction.

"Your old captain," he concluded, "merely confirmed that she was part of the equation."

They pulled into the precinct lot. Gil cut the engine. His expression was neutral when he turned to his partner. "I'll deal with it," he said, then added smoothly, "Would these other leads that we have to 'check out' include taking another look at Denning's place?"

"Gil, I understand how you must feel—"

"Answer the question, man." Gil's voice was still neutral, as were his eyes.

Adam pondered both and backed off for the time being. "Yeah, it would."

"Good. Let's grab some lunch now, and we can be there by two."

"Fine." Adam trailed behind Gil after they got out of the car. He caught a glimpse of his friend's profile and sighed. He hadn't seen that particular set to his jaw since the night at the hospital when Gil had gone to see Paul Thomas and ended up confronting Paul Thomas's daughter to tell her that he was back in town.

Chapter 11

The filth of Charlie Denning's shack caught Gil by surprise again. He preceded Adam past the police seal inside the cramped interior.

"Our people already went over this," Adam commented. "What could we be looking for?"

"Maybe something that's been seen but whose impact was not really understood. As you've suggested, I think we can safely say we've ruled out the obvious."

Adam eyed the kitchen area. "I'll start in there. The drawers and cabinets might have something."

"I'll begin in here." Gil's gaze swept the living room area where they were standing.

They went to work. Gil started with a scarred old bureau that listed beneath the room's only window, along the north wall. One drawer, wider than it was deep, held several scraps of paper, most of which seemed to be notes hastily scrawled as mental reminders for this and that.

The other drawer contained phone numbers, sometimes with names, more often without. The numbers would have to be checked, and Gil put all the scraps he could find inside his coat pocket. Rubber bands, a half-empty tube of Super Glue, a couple of pencils, and a rusted miniature pocketknife rounded out the balance of the drawer's contents. Gil mused that a person's junk drawer could be as revealing as a conversation, or even a handprint on the wall. What was Charlie Denning telling him?

Adam came out of the kitchen. "Nothing. Any luck?"

"Not yet. I'm trying the work area over here. There under that spread? Looks like a trunk. I haven't checked it, yet."

"I got it," Adam said.

Gil moved over to Denning's writing desk. It was a mess. Two dog-eared telephone books hung half on, half off the writing surface. The surface itself was grimed with soiled paper towels and tissues.

Deep inside one of the cubbyholes things got more interesting.

Gil pulled out what at first appeared to be scraps of old newspaper. The scraps were actually a neatly stapled collection of news clips.

Gil thumbed through them, increasingly interested by the theme that emerged. All of the items were reports having to do with race riots or race-based confrontations occurring in the South more than thirty years ago.

The most eye-catching item was of the story that had hit the papers that morning after civil rights leader Medgar Evans's murder. Gil read the sprawling "NIGGER" Denning had apparently put beneath the headline with a heavy black marker. Just the vehemence of that overprint conveyed Charlie Denning's hatred and that of others like him that still reached out across the boundaries of time and death. Gil thumbed on.

A small clip at the very end of the bundle, more

concise than the others, caught his attention. He pulled it out, separating it from the rest.

The article's accompanying photo featured a man with blunt, pale features. A hat was pushed back from his forehead, as if maybe he'd angled it that way to combat the heat. He was wearing overalls and a short-sleeved T-shirt, and he was standing beside a muddy Ford pickup truck. His beefy arms were crossed. The face was ordinary, but for some reason fascinating to Gil. He started reading.

The man was Owen Parsons, and he had been murdered. His body had been found on the morning of August 3, 1959, in a truck—the one he was standing beside?—in a Blundon, Georgia cotton field. He'd been shot once in the chest. His murderer, the story stated, was still at large.

"What?"

Gil started a little. He'd been focused and hadn't heard Adam come up behind him. "Maybe nothing. I don't know." He handed the article to Adam and walked across the room to the window to think.

"Looks like some white trash farm boy to me. Why should he warrant any special thought?"

Gil stared out the window and rubbed his jaw. "Maybe because of the company he's keeping in these clips. He doesn't fit, Adam. Look at the others." Gil stayed where he was, thinking, while Adam flipped through the stack of papers.

A moment passed and Adam said, "All these others talk about race wars and violent crimes. You're wondering what Owen Parsons's relevance could be since his is the only white face in here."

"Yeah," Gil said at length, "that's what I'm thinking. His name didn't surface in any of the interviews we conducted with Denning's guards."

"No. But then again, thirty-plus years is a lot of history for somebody to recall, especially when the party in question may be connected to a character you'd just as soon forget."

Gil turned around and leaned his hips against the window's sagging sill. He studied the floor. When he suddenly raised his head and pinned Adam across the room, the gesture was so sudden he saw his partner start. "Who wrote it, Adam? The article."

Adam scanned the article back up to the top. "Willis Houser, it says."

"I wonder if Houser is still alive? He might be worth talking to if he is."

Adam considered. "He might at that. And for that matter, it might be helpful to track down some more prison personnel who weren't readily handed to us by the warden."

Gil nodded. "It would. We should split up. You check out the prison, I'll check out Blundon. Let's give it"—he shrugged—"two days?"

"Yeah, that should work."

"Good. I've got some more stuff I have to clear off my desk before I can call it a day. I'll probably be hanging around late, so why don't you just drop me off back at the precinct and then go home."

"What about Myer?"

Gil's mouth quirked. "There's nothing we know that he needs to know yet. When we have more, we'll inform him."

Adam opened his mouth to object, but at Gil's look reconsidered. "I just want to be sure we don't keep him out of the loop."

"We won't. In fact, he'll be the first one to know once we have something useful to say."

"Come on, then, let's get out of here."

All the way back to the precinct, Gil was thoughtful. At the entrance, Adam handed him the Parsons clip.

Gil folded it and tucked it in his wallet. He opened his door to get out, and Adam stalled him.

"Gil, about earlier—"

Gil slammed his door and watched his partner through the lowered window.

Adam met the look, knew he couldn't begin to get around the obstinacy behind it. "Just be careful."

Gil answered with a mock salute. "I'm a big boy."

"Big boys can still get hurt."

Gil stepped back and turned away. "See you," he said over his shoulder.

Adam watched him until he got to the doors, then he drove away.

Gil checked his watch. It was going on eight. The closer he got to her door, the more his steps lagged.

He was feeling angry and betrayed, and when he rang her bell and she opened the door, he felt something else. Saddened. He couldn't return her impulsive smile. He watched that smile falter and stepped around her.

Maggie shut the door with foreboding. "What's going on, Gil? I didn't expect you back tonight."

Gil shucked his suit jacket as he walked into her living room. He tossed it on a chair and turned around to face her. His question was very quiet. "Have you been spying on me, Maggie?"

Maggie felt a cool little jolt go through her, but she held his hard gaze. "It's not what you think," she began.

Gil crossed his arms. "Suppose you tell me how it is? Start with giving me a straight answer to my question."

"You obviously have the answer or you wouldn't have come here like this. However, if you want to discuss my reasons, perhaps we can talk."

Gil didn't move. "I'm listening."

Maggie ran a hand through her hair. "Could you listen sitting down? Please?"

Gil held out for a long count, assessing her nerves, then he turned to the chair behind him and sat.

Maggie used the interval to settle herself on the sofa. "What do you know?" she asked.

"You mean how did I find out?"

"I mean what I said, what do you know? It would help me to hear exactly what it is I'm about to be damned for."

"The answers to both questions are probably close enough to being one and the same. The cops your investigator was snooping around gave it away. My old captain got suspicious about the inquiry and called the precinct here to ask questions. It got back to me."

Maggie dipped her head. He was furious, and given their history who could blame him. She sighed, knowing that all she could do was to try her damnedest to make him understand that her motives hadn't been malicious. The last thing she wanted was for them to slip back to where they'd been before.

"I just wanted to understand your life now." She looked closely at him and forced herself to keep talking despite the icy mask that hardened his face. "After you came back, there were things about you that were still indicative of the Gil I used to know. But in other ways, you seemed so different. I just wanted to understand why."

"Easy solution, Maggie. Why didn't you just ask me?"

"Would you have answered anything so personal?" For the first time since he'd walked through her door, his eyes shifted. Maggie took heart because she knew she had him.

"I would never have believed you really would have wanted to know. I'm not sure I believe it now."

She gave him a chiding look. "Come on, Gil. How can you say that now. How can you say that after last night?"

"I say it especially because of last night. When I left you at your door, I believed we had gotten beyond our deceptions, Maggie. Now I'm wondering if you ever intended to confront me directly, or if you were just going to let your hired lackey do your dirty work so that you could hoard the goods to yourself forever?"

"Goods?" Maggie frowned. "You talk as if you think I was trying to deliberately uncover something negative against you."

Gil's expression flattened for the briefest moment, and he avoided her gaze. "Aren't you?" he said quietly.

"No," she looked straight into his eyes, willing him to believe it. They were approaching a watershed here, and for her part, she was determined not to screw things up this time.

Gil wondered what she was thinking when she hesitated. Was she conscientiously organizing her thoughts—or, he thought cynically, marshaling her lies? God knew why it was so important to her after all these years to try to tie him up in knots again. Then again, he mused, perhaps her motives had to do with what had always driven them, her father's approval.

"Let me cut to the chase, Gil." Maggie was finding it very hard to read him. "Your old friends on the Chicago force—"

"Couldn't have given you any juicy gossip because they didn't really know anything to tell," he interrupted. "But since you've proven yourself to be so persistent in going after the information you want no

matter what the consequences might be, let me save
you some suspense."

Every bit of bitterness behind Gil's words abraded
Maggie's composure. She suddenly considered that
perhaps she had been foolish. Whatever was eating at
Gil might be something she had no right to pry into.
She was getting the uneasy feeling she'd stirred
sleeping dogs she would have done better to let lie.

Gil saw her reconsidering and took perverse pleasure in what he was about to reveal, even if much of it
turned out to be at his own expense. "What your
investigator couldn't tell you, Maggie, was something
he couldn't have gotten from Chicago because nobody
there knew."

"Gil, you don't have to tell me this."

"On the contrary. You've shown me that I do, no
matter how much I'd prefer to let it die. What your
investigator didn't tell you, Maggie, was that for two
years after I ran away from this town, I drank."

Stunned, Maggie whispered, "You were an
alcoholic?"

"My sober acquaintances called me a drunk."

Maggie uncurled herself from the sofa, needing to
move, needing to get some space.

"Disgusted?" Gil said, watching her cynically.

"No," she said, trying to analyze what it was she
did feel. "I'm not disgusted, but"—realization
dawned—"I think you are. Still."

"Damned right. Any drunk who lives to survive
learns to view self-disgust as a healthy emotion, if he
has any sense at all. Post-preservation, it's called."

"Gil . . ." Maggie groped for words, for understanding. "Why?"

"Lots of reasons," he said more calmly, thinking
back to the addictions counseling he'd eventually
forced himself to seek out.

Maggie felt worse than appalled. "We did that to you?"

Gil's head reared up, his anger quick and fierce. "No one did it to me, Maggie, you give yourself and your assumed sense of power too much credit. I did it to myself."

Hurt and embarrassed at what she knew had been a naive assessment, she looked away.

Gil sighed. "Back in those days, I was dealing with a lot of stuff. It all seemed to culminate with Brooker, but even if that case hadn't come along, I think something would have blown things anyway."

"I'm sorry."

"I don't want your pity."

Maggie didn't know what to say, and she didn't like this feeling that with every word she was stumbling even more. "I'm just trying to understand," she said defensively.

Gil watched her. "Then back down," he said evenly, "and let me try to help you."

Maggie sat forward and rested her forearms on her knees. "Go on."

"As I said, I was grappling with a lot of stuff." He stared off sightlessly into the distance, introspective. "You have to have at least guessed that much. As I recall, even before we split we were having our share of fights."

"Disagreements."

"Disagreements," Gil murmured, as if he was discounting that triviality. "But about what, Maggie?

Indeed, she thought, about what? Their lives together had been a long time ago. There was, she supposed, a possibility that with time her memory had smoothed over some of the rougher patches of their union. Now that Gil had directly challenged her to think about it, she searched her memory, trying to remember honestly.

There had been intimacy. After they'd left childhood behind, their fast friendship had evolved into something deeper. Gil had not only become her lover, he'd become her confidant, and she his. But in the end, she'd still sided with her father . . . Why?

If the bond with Gil had been that strong, why had she run from him when he'd needed her most? Trying to figure it out, she kneaded her brow while she sat in the soft peripheral light shining from the single lamp Gil turned on.

"Why did we fall apart, Maggie? That's the question that kept plaguing me after I had gone. If we had been as strong as we thought, Brooker wouldn't have torn us apart."

Maggie looked at him, startled that his comment and her thoughts were so closely aligned. And she wondered again about his recent revelation.

"Yeah," he said, guessing her thoughts. "Maybe the Brooker thing was partly the reason for the booze. But like I said, the rest of the reasons went deeper.

"In the aftermath of everything here, I started questioning a lot of things about myself. My beliefs, my motives certainly, but even beyond that I started reevaluating my goals to see how much they were truly mine."

"What do you mean?" Maggie found herself hanging on his answer. So many of the things he was expressing were parallel to assessments of herself she had been compelled to eventually make.

Gil dropped his head against the back of his chair. He half closed his eyes. "I was so ripe for a Paul Thomas when I met your father. At the risk of sounding pitifully clichéd, I had a house, but I didn't have a home. I was full of need for understanding, affection, for somebody who cared about not only the me that was, but the boy who could be . . . something."

"Yes," Maggie murmured more to herself than to Gil. She remembered. As Paul Thomas's child, she hadn't lacked for any of the things Gil was so candidly expressing. But, as an adolescent and later an adult, she'd been forced to closely examine and question the abundance of those very things that had presented the emotional paradox in which she'd found her problems.

"Even after I started loving you," Gil continued, "after I let myself become assimilated into your life and your father's, I couldn't stop making comparisons between what I saw on my streets every day of my life when I wasn't with you. It got to a point, I guess, where I started feeling guilty."

"For what?"

Gil shrugged. His eyes stayed closed. "For selling out. It was almost as if the existence, the goals, everything I had with you two was part of some privileged fantasy while the cruder existence of everyone else and everything else I knew was what was real."

Maggie sat in silence, admitting to herself that she wasn't entirely surprised. Hadn't she sensed his conflict? Hadn't it contributed to the simmering emotional distance she'd felt in their relationship, but hadn't wanted to admit? They'd both avoided that reality, but their hearts had been aware of it, and in the end it had driven them devastatingly apart.

"Is all of this news to you, Maggie?" Gil finally turned his head against the chair and opened his eyes. "Somehow, deep down, if you really think about it, I don't think it can be."

Maggie owed it to not only him but to herself to be forthright. "I think I always sensed that these things you're saying were there, but I didn't have the

courage when it counted to admit it, even to myself."
She smiled bitterly. "You weren't the only one living
with demons, Gil."

At one time Gil's first inclination, given Maggie's
gilded life, would have been to scoff. Life and the
maturity he'd gained from living it urged him to
reserve his judgment now, especially when she
seemed so sad.

"What happened, honey?" He frowned a little at the
endearment that had come so naturally to him.

"If you were struggling with trying to live up to
Daddy's expectations, I was probably struggling at
least half as hard to live them down."

Gil smiled a little, though it was bittersweet.
"Golden child syndrome?" he probed softly.

Maggie's lips curved briefly. "It can be hell being
the only child of a 'great' man. Sometimes, it can
smother the life right out of you until you get to the
point where you start wondering where he leaves off
and you begin."

"And he wasn't helping you find the answers
easily?"

"No. After you had gone, I started wondering why.
The conclusion I reached didn't comfort me."

"What was the conclusion?"

"That letting me fly was something Daddy just
didn't consider to be to his advantage."

Why hadn't they ever discussed any of these things,
Gil wondered. There was melancholy, yes. But there
was also a real liberation that obviously was too long
overdue.

"You have flown, Maggie," Gil said. "You've only
to look at your life now."

"You don't know at what price I've acquired it, Gil."

He waited for her to elaborate while she got up
from the sofa and turned on two more lamps.

"Do you want some coffee, water, or anything?" Maggie headed for the kitchen even as she fielded his unspoken question. "I need something."

"Coffee, maybe. I'll come with you."

Maggie left him to follow and headed for the refrigerator. She ended up pulling out a couple of eggs, some cheese, and a green pepper, then she took some spices down from the cabinet.

When Gil joined her, she simply scooted over to make room at the counter. He rolled up his shirtsleeves, fished a knife out of a drawer, and started to slice the pepper. Maggie smiled a little inside because the moment was redolent with the easy intimacy they used to share. Minutes later their omelettes were done, and she poured coffee to go with them at the small glass-topped breakfast table.

Somehow, the shared chore of preparing the simple dinner made it easier for her to speak now.

"The extent to which Daddy showed his displeasure at my independence, or I should say, my move toward independence from his plans for the course of my life, astounded me." Maggie sipped her coffee, speaking in the same contemplative tone she'd used in the living room.

Gil heard her, but he couldn't fully imagine what she was suggesting. "Tell me."

Maggie carefully put down her cup and leaned back in her chair. She watched Gil with eyes she knew were expressionless because she was deliberately trying to blot out the pain. "I'll sum it all up in the last words he said to me, face-to-face.

" 'Maggie,' he said, 'you're my only child and I really want to love you. But at this moment, I only wish . . .' "

"What, babe?" The endearment this time was deliberate. He could tell by her fragile composure, she needed something with which to brace herself.

Maggie swallowed the thickness in her throat. "He said, 'At this moment, I only wish you were out of my life for good.' "

Chapter 12

Gil paused in the midst of raising his cup to his mouth. "He couldn't have meant it, Maggie."

Again, Maggie's lips curved. Again, the smile was without humor. "You think not? So did I, until he started demonstrating that what he had declared was true."

That dark statement brought all sorts of ominous and, Gil was sure, outrageous imaginings to mind. "You care to explain?"

"Foremost, he wanted me to go into politics. If not as an actual politician, he at least wanted me to pour all of my energies into helping him advance his social agendas, his civil causes. I refused, choosing to enter the public arena through another door."

"Your magazine," Gil said.

"Yes, my magazine, the 'country's leading forum for black political expression.' What you and a lot of other people don't know is that my professional pride and joy is a product that nearly didn't come to pass. When I set out to found it, Daddy tried to sabotage me at every turn."

Gil was finding this incredible. If it was true and she had prevailed anyway with the degree of grace and success that was apparent—well, she was a very formidable woman. It would have taken such an adversary to best Paul Thomas.

"He drastically cut back the allowance money he had been providing me for starters," Maggie told him. "Then he made it clear to me that I was no longer welcome to have access to his money. He knew that would force me to seek backers for my project, so next he manipulated that Good Ole' Boy system we all know can work so well by quietly venturing the suggestion that my project wasn't sound."

"And there are," Gil said, continuing the thought, "an awful lot of people who, over the years, probably owe him some substantial favors."

"Precisely. Actually, in hindsight, opposition was very good for me, I guess. It caused me to value the merit of work as more than just holding down a job. Every dollar I earned was a future mark that counted toward something I became determined to make for myself.

"Getting the initial backing I needed was frustratingly slow, but when I got to the point where I was finally strong enough to step outside the family network to solicit the rest of my backers, I was able to do it with personal assurance that for the first time my solo efforts were real. The support I won was pure victory."

Maggie hesitated, then said, "In the early days, I used to wish desperately that you were here to see it."

"Why?"

Maggie murmured softly. "I wasn't so naive, so spoiled that I was unaware of your disdain, Gil. You loved me, yes, but on a much more real level I always sensed that you didn't completely respect me."

"Maggie," Gil searched for the words to deny it, but denying it was so difficult when she was, he reflected, largely right.

The old Maggie had been sweet when it suited her, a challenge to him, smart. But she'd also personified a sheltered lack of awareness that had grated against his deepest insecurities, or more specifically, against what he'd told her earlier. She'd conflicted with what he used to consider his "double life." Apparently, he hadn't concealed the hurtful brunt of his dissatisfaction at all.

"I thought I made you happy," he said quietly. "And now with what you're telling me—hell, you make me feel small. Ashamed."

Maggie shook her head and reached across the table to touch his hand. "No, Gil. I see things more clearly, now, too. We're older, maybe that's why it's easier to do so. Yes, at the time, it hurt me deeply, but I never said anything because the greater pain would have come from losing you."

Gil looked at their joined hands, still grappling for the right thing to say. "I'm sorry" was the best he could offer.

Maggie's smile this time was poignantly genuine. "I guess that's my cue to say, oh shucks, that's all right, it made me a better person." Her smile faded. "The truth is, I'm not bitter about it anymore, but at the time, especially when it coincided with Daddy's arrogance and increasingly patronizing attitude, it hurt like hell."

Gil studied her slender fingers, then he tightened his hand around them. For a long while, they sat with their own thoughts, saying nothing to one another. Gil's foremost realization was that until this moment he'd been patronizing her still. This woman before him was the quintessential essence of the Maggie he had loved. But she was also so much more, all of it special and seductive and mature in a way that was much more potent to him now than even in the days when he'd—arrogantly—assumed the habit of thinking of her as "mine."

Gil cleared his throat. He needed to create some distance in order to rethink many things. Unfortunately, the device to do it was merely a tangential side to the other topic in his life with which he had struggled so hard to reconcile.

He released her hand, but rested his beside hers on the table in order to keep her warmth near.

"Maggie, we've known from the beginning that my job, my professional obligation might wind up making me your father's worst enemy." He watched her closely for her reaction.

Maggie slowly shook her head. "Not an enemy, Gil. No matter what's happened in your life, no matter how many things in it and about it have changed, I can't believe you've become so cold-blooded."

"Focused," he countered.

"No. In light of what you felt for Daddy . . . what I believe you probably still feel—it would be cold-blooded. You can't push all of your old emotions so ruthlessly under the carpet, like dirt you're trying to hide. Even if you can fool others, you'll never be able to fool me."

Despite what had passed between them, the closeness he sensed they had started to reclaim, a part of Gil still couldn't help being wary. What, a little voice cautioned, if she was just laying retaliatory groundwork to use in her father's defense, if circumstances came to that?

"My feelings about your father one way or the other have no bearing on this case, Maggie. Maybe that's what scares you."

Maggie frowned. "I don't understand."

"I asked you once how far you were willing to see this thing with your father, if you thought you could deal fairly with the consequences if the situation turned into one you'd find hard to live with."

"I remember."

"You couldn't answer me then, Maggie, and I didn't expect you to. What I want to know is this, can you answer me now?"

Maggie glanced away, looking inward.

Gil watched her retreat. Somehow he hadn't expected her withdrawal, and it disheartened him. "Well," he murmured, "that's that."

"You don't know what you're talking about, Gil."

"Are you trying to tell me you don't love him anymore, that you feel no loyalty because of the way he's treated you?"

"I told you, you've got it backward. He doesn't love me."

The conviction with which she obviously felt that to be so still rocked Gil a little, but her eyes were too steady, too hurt to be the deliberate reflections of a lie. He'd known the spell of Paul Thomas, observed the man and his daughter together for years. In spite of the rift with her father Maggie spoke of, how could she really believe she was telling the truth?

"I've only told you about the external things, Gil," Maggie murmured after a while. "There are lots of others you might empathize with but never truly understand. They're things that are irrevocably . . . momentous to me."

Gil was intrigued. "Such as?"

"He deliberately discarded his child. After Brooker and after you—well, Daddy and I could never go back to the way we were. Those blinders you referred to not so very long ago were well and truly lifted from me, and I began to see."

"What did you see?"

"That Daddy's intention for years had been to hold

onto his little girl, *his* little girl. His heir and champion." She added more quietly, "His sycophant."

Gil remembered her pain at White's party, his surprise at her taking her old lover's crap so docilely. "Go on."

"There's something else that I never told you. Of course"—she shrugged—"I wouldn't have. But I'm a little surprised you never guessed."

"It's a night for revelations, it seems." Gil shrugged, encouraging her.

"I realized about a year or so after Daddy pushed me away that some of the seeds of our rift had actually been planted long ago. They directly involved you."

"How?"

"Put simply, I was jealous of you."

"Me? But you had everything, Maggie, that's ridiculous."

"I didn't have your ability to convey with the same seriousness who I was and what I was capable of to Daddy. He seemed to accept that from you much more easily, almost from the start."

Gil didn't know what to say. He'd never seen—or perhaps he'd been too self-absorbed to see—this girl Maggie spoke of who was so insecure.

"Don't worry, Gil, I got over it. Another benefit of hindsight, courtesy of maturity." Maggie watched Gil wrestle with what genuinely seemed to be a revelation to him. In a way, his obvious surprise and lack of awareness made her feel better, reassured her that that particular struggle of hers had been more her problem than his.

Gil gazed down at their hands, uncomfortable with this turn in the conversation, maybe because now that she'd pointed it out, he sensed the depth of its truth. Trying to shift the conversation a little, he said, "You never answered my first question, you know, about

Chicago." He lifted a finger when she started to speak. "Whatever you found out couldn't have been as comprehensive as what I can tell you."

Maggie simply nodded, knowing he was right.

He absently ran his hand over the glass-topped table. "I don't want to tell you now, Maggie. I—I think we've both done enough soul-searching tonight." He raised his eyes, hoping he'd get her agreement.

Maggie nodded slowly, understanding. She wanted to hear it all, but she understood that in light of what had passed tonight, perhaps it was more important to wait.

"Let's back way up, then, Gil. Why else did you come, here tonight?"

Gil smiled. That she could still get to the heart of the matter and anticipate him warmed him. "Does the name Owen Parsons mean anything to you?"

She shook her head. "Why should it?"

"Maybe it shouldn't. I just have this feeling." He explained about his visit to Charlie Denning's shack.

"No," Maggie repeated. "There's absolutely nothing that name tags in my memory. But you think he may provide some link to Denning's death?"

Gil pushed himself away from the table. "Like I said, I don't know. But I did call to check on the reporter who put together the story, Houser is his name, to see if he was still living, if he was anywhere close around here."

"What do you think he can tell you?"

"More than his printed story did. Maybe something that can hook it up to Denning in my mind." He walked over to the sink and rinsed off his plate. "Then again, maybe he'll tell me nothing. I'm going to pay him a visit."

Maggie got up and joined him. She handed over her plate and reached under the sink for the bottle of dishwashing detergent. "We'll see," she said, nudging him over. She picked up his plate, squirted a bit of the liquid on it, and started to wash.

Gil took the cleaned plates she handed him and set them on the draining board while he watched her, waiting for some elaboration. She glanced up at him once, the look in her eye telling him plainly that elaboration wasn't forthcoming.

"Maggie, the footwork of all this is police business," he told her flatly. "You can't go."

"This is my father and a case that may be jeopardizing my life. I have a right to go, and I will." She finished with the dishes and dried her hands. That done, she leaned her derriere against the counter and crossed her arms, waiting.

"You can't force this issue." Gil crossed his own arms and shifted his weight, using the counter as a prop, too.

"I was hoping my appeal to your reason and sense of fair play would be enough."

He really hated it when she assumed that smooth reasonable tone. It necessitated discussion marked with some modicum of reason, and that usually clashed with what he wanted more—his own way. "What good do you think you would do?"

"I could filter what Houser has to say through my memories of Daddy's past. I may hear something Houser tells us in a very different way from how you hear it." She could see that she'd gotten Gil's attention.

"Even if you have a valid point, I would still be unwise to allow a civilian to ride shotgun on this. You'd be in the way."

"If you really believed that, Stewart, you wouldn't be talking it out with me now in what sounds suspiciously to me like a rationalization."

Gil almost smiled. "If I were to consider this, you'd

have to convince me of your utmost discretion before I allowed you to come along."

"My word." Maggie assumed a straight face. "I wouldn't want you to fall out of grace with your partner."

Gil thought of Adam, of how his friend was trying to look out for him. "He's all right."

"Yeah, he hates my guts."

Gil's face tightened, and he walked away. He picked up his suit jacket on the way to the door.

"Did I say something wrong?" Maggie was only half joking as she joined him.

"Don't take this lightly, Maggie. Letting your guard down is a very good way to get yourself hurt."

Maggie instantly sobered, because she sensed Gil's figurative meaning as well as the literal. She'd only meant to extend the surprising goodwill that had come out of this unexpected evening instead of offending him. But offend him she had, somehow. "I am taking everything seriously, Gil." She raised her hand to his face, and stroked his jaw.

"Everything."

Gil held her eyes with his, then he turned his lips briefly into her palm. "Good night. I'll let you know something more specific about Blundon tomorrow."

Maggie shut the door behind him, clicked off her porch light, and stood staring at the wood for a moment. She lifted her palm to her own cheek, transferring the imprint of the lasting impression that mattered most to her as Gil drove away.

"He stayed inside there a pretty long while, and the look in her eye wasn't exactly adversarial when he walked out." The assassin shifted his cellular phone against his ear and waited more with curiosity than interest for what the congressman was going to say.

"Be ready to move, but remember, there's still no need for haste. Making this particular move could be nasty."

"Besides, the original mission comes first, right?"

"Maybe not, if this situation is evolving in the way you seem to suggest. Stand by."

The assassin sat in his car thinking after the congressman hung up. He had some evaluating to do, too. If he was clever, he would still come out of this with an advantage. He put the receiver back in its cradle and smiled. It was like his employer said.

He still had time.

Chapter 13

As it turned out, Gil wasn't able to get back to Maggie until two days later. A stubborn point on one of his other cases necessitated tracking down and reinterviewing witnesses, two of whom were irritatingly recalcitrant about giving him what he wanted.

He was tired, irritated, and decidedly in a bad mood when Maggie's phone rang five times before she picked up. Her breathlessness exacerbated his annoyance.

"It's Gil."

"Oh"—she took two restorative breaths—"I was outside weeding with my earphones on. If I hadn't taken them off to talk to my neighbor, I never would have heard your call. Is the trip on?"

"Yeah. Can you be ready to leave tonight?"

"Why tonight? Why not get a fresh start in the morning?"

"Why not leave the itinerary to me. You're the one horning your way in on this thing, if I recall."

Maggie did a slow ten count. Apparently, he was having a bad day. "What time?"

Gil expelled a short breath. "I suppose I should apologize for my pissy mood."

Maggie smiled faintly. "You just did. What time?"

"I still need to clean up some stuff here at the office, but I want to be on the road by nine. Can you be ready by eight-thirty or a little after?"

"Of course I can. This sounds like an overnighter. Should I be prepared?"

"Yeah, probably just in case. Everything should be straightforward, and we should be ready to head back tomorrow sometime during the day, but—"

"I'll be ready to go when you get here." Maggie hung up. She hadn't anticipated staying overnight. For a second, the thought gave her pause. The next moment she chided herself for being silly. This excursion and everything connected was purely business. She shouldn't need any reassurance that Gil would do everything in his power to keep it that way.

Gil's common sense wasn't the only piece of sanity that was intact, Maggie reminded herself. No one needed to counsel her to adhere to his dispassion, to follow his lead.

It was eight-forty by the time Gil knocked on her door.

"Hey." Maggie stepped back, inviting him in.

Gil glanced at his watch and raised a brow.

"I'm ready," Maggie protested. "I can see your day didn't get any better."

Gil sauntered inside and closed the door behind him. He was feeling impatient and restless, but the last thing she needed to know was that his discomfort had nothing to do with his day and everything to do with the night he was about to spend, albeit professionally, with her. She came walking toward him now from a room at the back of her house with a small overnight bag in hand, obviously, as she'd said, ready to go.

Gil took the bag from her.

"Oh, wait!" She hurried back to the kitchen, and Gil

saw her open the refrigerator door. When she slammed it and trotted back to him, he looked askance at the package in her hand.

"This isn't a camping trip, Thomas."

"It isn't a penance, either, or is it against some cop law to go prepared when you hit the road?"

Gil didn't need to hear anymore to realize he was being ridiculous. "Come on," he said tersely, leaving her to follow.

Maggie sighed and trailed him to the door. She knew what was bothering him. It was the same thing she was trying very hard to submerge beneath her joking and wisecracks.

Gil tossed her bag in the trunk and unlocked her door. Shortly thereafter, they were on their way.

They headed south once they were out of the city. Darkness precluded admiring the passing scenery, so Maggie reached over and turned on the radio. Gil spoke to her once to tell her that they had, roughly, a seven-hour trip in front of them. After that, he didn't seem much inclined to talk.

In fact, Maggie had expected the awkwardness that had begun at her house to continue. She was relieved that as the miles wore on, the more comfortable she felt. Maybe the benign intrusiveness of the soft pop music she selected helped. Maybe they both just needed time to remind themselves that this time together didn't have to be a big deal or anything else they didn't want it to be.

Maggie was surprised to find herself waking up a while later. She hadn't felt tired and didn't remember falling asleep. But when she looked at the dash, she realized a little over two hours had passed.

"Where are those Twinkies?" Gil murmured.

Maggie stretched and chuckled. "Oh, ho, the mono-lith speaks."

"Hunger has a way of cracking even the best of us stone faces."

"They're in the back. Hold on." Maggie turned on the seat and scrambled to her knees so that she could reach the box behind her.

Gil looked over once to see what she was about. The sight of her neat, tightly jeaned little tush brought a rush of his earlier tension back, but this time it was gentler, tinged with nostalgia. He remembered the first time they'd traveled somewhere significant together.

He had been eighteen and combined the earnings from the part-time job he'd been working the past two summers at Thomas Construction with another after-school job he'd scrounged up during the regular school year. He had socked away enough money to proudly purchase his first car, a Chevy. Though it had looked good, it had been a wreck.

Of course, he hadn't thought so, probably because it was the first major item he'd ever had the means to acquire on his own, free of parental prescreening or scrutiny. He'd loved that old car, and had known even then that because it had been so special to him Maggie had loved it, too.

The summer he'd bought it, he'd convinced her to take a drive with him to a friend's lakeside picnic one Saturday afternoon. A bunch of kids from his high school were gathering at a local lake to celebrate the end of summer, and he was adding his own imminent enrollment in college to the festivities.

As he'd anticipated, the party had been slightly raucous. But things had stayed under control, considering the amount of skinny dipping, pounding music, and endless quantities of hot dogs and beer. He could tell that Maggie had been a little intimidated at first by the older kids, until she'd relaxed enough to realize she hadn't been the only sixteen-year-old, or even the youngest one there.

As the day wore on, she'd had a great time, loosening up enough to join the fun with a crop of kids who, for the most part, came from economic and social circumstances much humbler than her own. She'd even drank a little beer, not enough to get tipsy, but certainly enough, Gil had carefully assessed as the evening wore on, to pleasantly float.

Her mellowness and his had worn on with the afternoon so that by the time evening approached, their moods were just right for the miraculous and unplanned lovemaking that had ensued. It had only been Gil's second time with a girl, and it had been infinitely precious to him because he had been Maggie's first.

"Here you go," Maggie peeled the cellophane from one of the pastries she'd extracted and held it out to Gil.

"Thanks." Gil took it and bit off a substantial bite.

"What a smile you had there, Stewart," Maggie had been studying him, wondering what was going through his mind. "I know these things can hit the spot, but the anticipation for them can't ever be that good. What gives?"

"Just stuff," he said. "Did you have dinner?"

"If that's a full-service offer, I'll forget the grilled cheese six hours ago and say no."

"Fine. We'll stop somewhere."

They settled on a Shoney's two exits later. It was late enough that the service was quick, and once they'd loaded up on hot buffet selections, they agreed the old-fashioned country-kitchen fare tasted fine.

"How would you feel about finding a hotel or motel somewhere?" Gil asked her when he started pulling money out of his wallet for the bill.

"Sounds good." Especially now, Maggie thought, after their meal. She caught Gil stifling a yawn and felt more comfortable with his suggestion. Obviously, she wasn't the only one who was suddenly bone tired.

They settled on a chain operation not too far down the road. It was going on one a.m. when Gil pulled into the lot. He collected both his own bag and Maggie's from his trunk.

Inside, Gil dispatched the registration quickly and painlessly, to Maggie's relief. They'd been given adjoining rooms, and Gil didn't balk when she pulled out plastic to pay for her own.

At her door, he took the room key from her hand and inserted it inside the computerized lock. He pushed her door open and picked her bag up from the floor, then preceded her inside. Maggie followed him into the narrow entry and threw her purse on the bed while she watched him make a visual inspection of the tiny space the room allowed.

"All safe?" She kicked off her shoes and sat on the single bed.

"Yeah. Put the chain on after I leave. Let's be ready to roll by eight, okay?"

"Sure. Good night."

Gil saluted her at the door, looked her over with a slow, enigmatic smile, and left.

Maggie didn't waste time sitting when she could be sleeping. She showered, donned a T-shirt, and crawled under the thin covers.

Her last thoughts before she drifted off were of Gil and that smile he'd given her. Was he sleeping already? If he wasn't, what was he doing? Her eyes closed, oblivion slowly beckoned, and she didn't think about it anymore.

* * *

Gil was still contentedly lost in a deep sleep when the wake-up call he'd requested penetrated and jarred. He dragged himself to the edge of the bed. A glance at the curtains showed him it was going to be another clear, hot beautiful day.

Thirty minutes later, he met Maggie in the hallway. She was just walking out of her room as he was walking out of his.

"Good morning," she said, sauntering his way. "You look rested."

"I'm feeling better. You?"

"I slept just fine. Do we stop for breakfast first, or are we off?"

Gil had to smile. "For such a little thing, you always could eat. Sorry, we'll have to forgo food. We have a brunch date with Mr. Houser, and we'll just be making it as it is."

"No problem." Maggie hefted her bag over her shoulder along with her purse.

No problem, Gil thought falling behind her a little to take advantage of the thoroughly pleasant view from the rear. She had said she wouldn't be a problem and dammit, she wouldn't be. Still smiling, Gil took in the jeans, the sleeveless black cotton shirt, the comfortable worn Dockers, and thought there were problems, and then there were problems.

Back on the road, Maggie twisted the cap on the bottle of orange juice she'd snagged before they'd left. After she'd taken a long, cool drink she set it in the cup holder next to the styrofoam cup of coffee Gil had wangled from the kitchen. Deftly, she peeled the plastic lid off his cup and then sat back with the atlas Gil had pulled out. She spread it on her lap.

"Thanks," Gil murmured, picking up his drink.

Maggie nodded absently and studied the map. "We're not actually going to Blundon, right?"

Gil took a long restorative sip. "That's right, not unless we have to." He didn't plan on having to, not with her along. The town had to be backwoods at best, and in some parts of the region, progress for blacks still evolved very slowly. Of course, reminding her of that would just make her insist, and they'd have to fight about it, and that was a fight she definitely wouldn't win.

"Houser should be able to give me everything I need," Gil continued. "Augusta is where his paper was based and where he was headquartered before he retired in '85."

"So do you need me to navigate?"

"Not really, I mapped our route out pretty well in my head last night."

Maggie folded the map and tucked it in the pocket at the bottom of her car door. So that's how he'd spent his night. "What did Houser sound like on the phone? Vague? Interested? Annoyed—what?"

"Hesitant at first, as if he genuinely didn't remember what I was talking about. Open after that, but still a little cautious."

"How much did you tell him about Denning or anything else?"

"Not much. It's always a good idea not to give your subject time to prepare. Takes away the spontaneity of the interview."

"I guess so."

Neither said much more for the rest of the ride. Just along the outskirts of Augusta, Gil got off the highway and soon was cruising along a set of cross streets until he found the one he wanted. He then located the mom-and-pop diner they were headed for. He parked, noticing that there was only one other car in the lot.

"Popular place," Maggie commented as she closed her car door and stretched.

"I'm just looking for one patron, so it doesn't matter." Gil met her around the car and touched her arm to urge her inside.

The interior was noticeably darker than outside. The shades had been lowered to half-mast, but rather than dampening the atmosphere inside, they made the wooden paneling, checkered-cloth-covered planked tables, and buff-colored walls all seem rather cozy. The half dozen or so diners were all geriatric. Gil recognized the one he sought from the description he'd gotten over the phone. He was sitting alone in a corner booth by a window.

"Come on." He took Maggie's hand.

"Mr. Houser?" Gil asked, standing beside the old man's table.

The white-haired man tilted his head up, gave the once over to Gil and Maggie, and nodded. "That's me. Sit down."

Maggie scooted in and Gil squeezed in beside her. "Thanks for agreeing to meet with me. Just water," Gil told the hovering waitress who had followed him to the table. "Maggie?"

"The same."

The waitress smiled and left.

Houser reached around to a hip pocket and pulled out a pipe. "Mind?" His hesitation was merely polite before he lit up.

Maggie did mind and wasn't looking forward to eating smoke for lunch, but she was here to be unobtrusive and to observe. In fact, feeling as if she were being watched, she looked up from her menu to catch Houser observing her.

"You a cop, too?" Houser's thick white brows rose in inquiry?

"No, I'm not."

"Maggie is my assistant," Gil smoothly diverted.

"You said over the phone that the Owen Parsons killing was one that particularly stuck in your memory, Mr. Houser. I'd like to talk about why that is, if we may."

Houser squinted over his pipe. "First thing you have to do is start calling me Will. Everybody does. I'm eighty-two, but that Mr. on the front of my name coming from boys like you never fails to make me feel like I'm a hundred-and-two."

Maggie smiled at the sentiment, though she was uncertain about whether Willis Houser had used the term "boys" in a generic sense, or in a way that was racially significant.

Their waitress returned, and after they put in their orders, Gil got back to the conversation. "You said over the phone there was a lot of bad feeling in Blundon after Owen Parsons was killed."

"Yes," Houser nodded. "But what you have to get straight right off the bat is this. It wasn't because a lot of people were sad to see him gone, they weren't. Parsons was a pig. It was a bad feeling that lingered with most people because they were speculating about the way he had died."

Their sandwiches arrived. Will Houser dug into his with overt single-mindedness. Maggie and Gil exchanged wry glances and started on their own meals, knowing Houser was taking pleasure in setting the pace and dramatic tone.

Houser chewed and swallowed his third mouthful before he chased it with his root beer and took up his story where he'd left off. "Popular opinion said Parsons wasn't murdered by one of his many old enemies he'd managed to keep pissed off. Opinion said he got what was coming to him after he tangled with some drifters."

"Did the police follow up on that?" Maggie took a sip of cola.

"Didn't have any real leads to go on, so speculation just sort of died, just like 'ole Owen."

"But the talk didn't," Gil pointed out. "What started it?"

"A fight, an exchange of words, whatever you want to call it that some folks saw between Parsons and some city boys passing through the morning of the day he was shot. Parsons was having a drink, as usual, at a little no-account diner in Blundon. They've torn it down since then. Anyway, some fellahs came through and stopped for gas. Owen came out to see what the strangers wanted. They weren't talkative, so just for the hell of it, Parsons started giving the colored pump jockey a bad time."

"Define bad time," Gil said.

"Parsons was a proud and active Klansman. Need me to clarify?"

"No," Gil murmured. He could imagine only too well. "Go on."

"There were some words between Owen and the strangers. Afterward, they drove off. Owen left the diner about an hour later and wasn't seen again until a farmer found him that night slumped in his truck with his brains blown out."

Gil watched Houser intently. "And the drifters?"

"They were long gone, Parsons was dead, and even though the talk continued to make the bar rounds for a while, that was that." Houser pushed his plate aside and folded his napkin. He set it down. "Until about a year ago."

"What happened?" Maggie was thoroughly caught up in the story and its telling.

"Somebody else started asking questions about Parsons, not unlike you two. He wanted to know if there was still anybody around who saw what had happened that day, who might have some details that could give some substance to the talk. He even put out the word that he was willing to pay." Houser lit his pipe again.

"Who was it?" Gil pushed.

"A stone cracker, if you'll pardon the crudity, miss."

Maggie waved his concern aside. "Don't worry about it."

"His name," Willis Houser told them, "was Charles Denning. I believe, Lieutenant, that's the man you're investigating who was killed?"

Gil held Houser's canny gaze and leaned back. "You know it is, Will."

Houser smiled. "There's one other thing you might be interested to know, since you haven't asked."

Gil inclined his head.

"Those boys, those drifters who were passing through?"

"Yeah?"

Houser took two precise puffs of his pipe and leaned back himself. "They weren't just ordinary trash drifters. They seemed unusually well-educated for these parts during that time." He set down his pipe.

Maggie said, "What do you mean?"

"They were black."

Chapter 14

That was it. Gil saw in his mind's eye the collection of Denning's clips. With the inclusion of the Parsons clip, the connecting theme of racial violence and confrontation hadn't been abandoned after all.

Owen Parsons had been murdered, and common speculation in his hometown was that his murderers had probably been black.

If those obvious bells and whistles going off in his head had merit, they needed to be validated by a clear connection between Parsons and Denning.

"I can see you thinking, Lieutenant," Houser said mildly. "Have I provided some answers?"

"At the least, some missing facts. What else?"

Houser lifted his thin shoulders, then let them drop. "That's all I've got."

Maggie was subdued. "Were you the one who talked to Denning?"

"I was. He was an ignorant old coot. But I'll give him this, for someone who only had an article to work from, he did a damned good job at backtracking."

Gil reached his hand across the table. "Thanks, Will. You've been a help. Don't worry about lunch, it's on me."

Will smiled and smoked. "My pleasure, and all that. What will you do now?"

Gil slid out of the booth. Maggie was right behind him. "Digest everything. We'll see what happens after that."

"Good luck, then." Houser turned his head, his interest seeming already to have shifted to whatever was going on beyond the window on a lazy summer day.

Maggie seemed equally fascinated with her window view after she and Gil hit the road again. She sat with her hands folded, not saying anything. Gil left her in solitude with her thoughts. If they were anywhere in line with his, he knew she needed some time to herself.

The miles ticked off, and Gil glanced over Maggie's way once to gauge how she was doing. She was dozing, but a worry line marred the smooth perfection of her brow even in sleep. He pulled his attention back to the road. As more miles slid past, he could hardly believe it when the dash clock told him nearly four hours had passed.

Maggie's soft "damn," distracted him.

"Those men . . . Daddy just can't be involved in any of that, Gil. You know it, you know him. He just can't be."

Gil couldn't allay Maggie's plea because he was having trouble dealing with the same concern. "You said yourself he, Marrs, and Peters were like brothers. They would have been in college just about that time."

"Yes. But I knew Jeff and Sam, and they were no more capable of killing someone than myself." She rubbed her arms, suddenly feeling chilled. "God, I can't believe I just said that. I can't believe we're even giving the possibility serious consideration. In the first place, who's to say those men who drove through

Blundon that day killed Parsons? And in the second, even if those men did commit a crime, how do we know they were Daddy, Jeff, and Sam?"

Who was to say they weren't, Gil's cop logic silently replied. But in his heart, he was having as hard a time as she swallowing the possibility of Paul Thomas being a murderer.

He wanted to tell her not to worry until he had something concrete that would either confirm or deny today's revelations. But when he turned his head to say it, he saw a tear tracking down her cheek.

"Oh, honey, don't cry."

Maggie licked away the tear that darted to the corner of her mouth. "I'm sorry," she whispered. "I'm just . . . Gil, I'm scared."

It was going on seven. Maggie needed some dinner, Gil decided, and even more than that, a chance to gather herself. About a mile back, he'd spotted a road sign for a country inn that sounded, right now, a whole lot more appealing than a noisy chain diner or restaurant. Five minutes later, he made the necessary turnoff and soon after that spotted the oak and timbered building to his right. He pulled in.

"Gil, I'm not up to people," Maggie protested.

Gil opened his door. "That's why I chose this place. I don't think typical tourists are something we'll have to worry about."

She put her hand on the door handle, still hesitant.

"Come on, honey, we need to talk," he coaxed.

Maggie got out and once they were inside, she was relieved to see that despite the dinner hour Gil had been right. The decor surprised her a bit. Its design and the dress of the other patrons indicated the establishment was a little more upscale than it had appeared on the outside.

Gil quietly requested an out-of-the-way booth. After

they had been seated and served their coffees, Maggie ventured, "Let's say for argument's sake the suggestion of Daddy and the others having been involved with this Parsons killing is possible. Murder is extreme, Gil. What conceivable motive could have driven these particular men to that particular crime? For me, the answer to that question is far from clear."

It was for Gil, too. "Let's concentrate, then, on a point we can more easily speculate about. You said after the Brooker episode, after he 'turned' on you, a change in your father's personality seemed evident. I can't believe any change that compelling happened overnight. When you think back, can you remember any sort of gradual indication of what was to come?"

Maggie thought about it. "Daddy was always exacting, you know that. But the rules he set and his strictest wishes were always issued with a gentle hand. That was the most shocking thing about his change toward me, his loss of gentleness."

Their server arrived with their meals. Maggie waited until their soups were served, and after they were alone again, she pinched off a portion of the hot buttered corn bread that had also been placed on the table.

"In fact, in the days before our final break, I used to attribute his gruffness to everything that had happened with you. Then after you left and his impatience with me got worse, I attributed that to his being disgruntled because he set down his demands for me and I rebelled." She paused abruptly.

Gil had been eating, occasionally looking at her as she talked. "And now you're wondering if maybe something else hadn't been working beneath the exterior you'd known all your life."

At that moment, Maggie resented him. "How easily you niche everything, Gil, every word, every emotion.

When did you become the expert on other people's lives?"

He stopped eating. "Especially after I so royally screwed up my own?"

As quickly as her ire flared up, it died. "I'm sorry . . . I'm sorry. It's not you, I didn't mean to attack."

Gil made a decision. "Perhaps it's time for me to fulfill a promise I made to you the other night." He pushed his empty bowl away, surprisingly at peace with his sudden decision to talk, to share everything with her. "I want to tell you about the real dose of medicine that cured my drinking. I want to tell you about Chicago."

So much had happened today, was still happening that for a moment Maggie didn't honestly know if she wanted to take on another burden, even if it was Gil's. But then she looked into his eyes and saw clearly that he was sharing not to dump on her, but to give to her: something of himself, another part of his trust.

"I'm listening," she urged, and leaned back to listen.

For an uncomfortable moment, Gil felt on the spot with her simple acquiescence. He wondered where to begin and fiddled with his napkin. "My decision to leave Atlanta was very sudden, so I hadn't really planned on where I would go. I didn't have any family that I knew of living anywhere else, and my mother wasn't in the habit of worrying about me long-term, so my options were wide open.

"The last thing I wanted to do for a living was police work, so I decided to make a clean break with everything no matter where I ended up. North seemed as good a place as any, and it had the added bonus of being far enough away. Quite randomly, I chose Michigan as my new home.

"As for making a living, my construction background was as solid an anyone's could be, thanks to your father. So I took a job as a crewman with a firm that specialized in low-scale building, mostly commercial ventures, homes. As for the crew, well, it was typical for the guys to hit the bars after work, just for something to do.

"Barhopping doesn't lead to instant alcoholism," she commented gently.

"No. But when you take to that hopping with a monkey on your back, the odds increase dramatically.

"After about six months, I started feeling guilty for running away. I couldn't escape the feeling that every day I showed up for the anonymity of that construction work I was letting myself down, letting down all the high aspirations and ideals your father, despite everything, had instilled in me.

"But at the same time, I'd look at myself in the mirror every day and rebut those feelings with, 'what's the use?' I told myself it was like a lot of guys I knew on the streets always said—stick your neck out for someone or something else other than yourself and you're only begging to get hurt. So I continued to work and drink and hide until the work got harder, the drinking got easier, and every time I did both I was dying inside."

Maggie sat listening to him, hurting for him. No small part of what she felt stemmed from the awareness that her own narrow-mindedness and insecurity had partially contributed to Gil's old and deep-seated pain. Impulsively, she leaned forward and reached out her hand. Gil was baring his soul, but she found it was she who sorely needed the contact.

Gil didn't look at her, but he took the hand she offered all the same. Her touch, her lack of judgment that had clearly inspired it made it much easier for him to find the words for what he wanted to say.

"After a year with the company, people started

noticing I was getting sloppy on the job. A month or two after that, I started receiving official reprimands. My supervisor wouldn't fire me outright because he knew I was one of the best workers he had." Gil's mouth twisted. "When I was sober.

"One year and six months into my new profession, my new life, my employer called me into his office and calmly informed me that if I didn't seek help for my addiction, he would fire me. I remember just sitting there frozen, feeling so angry at myself and embarrassed. Everything I had vowed years before to not let my life become was hurtling toward me like a stone.

"My employer told me the company would pay for a counseling program, that regular reports would be forwarded. Then he dismissed me, told me to go home."

Maggie honestly didn't know what she had anticipated when Gil had hinted at this tale so casually at her home. Whatever she had expected hadn't been anything like this.

"So"—she cleared her throat a little—"so you obviously took your employer up on his offer."

"Yeah, seeing as how it was one that I couldn't refuse. Six months and three weeks after the next day, I received a clean bill of health from the clinic. More importantly, I walked out with a renewed perspective on my life. With police work, I'd chosen the profession where I really belonged. So I quit the firm and moved again. In Chicago, I reinstated myself on the police force."

"You prospered there," Maggie voiced. "You were well respected, well liked—" She broke off at his rueful look. "Yes, I got at least that much information for my money. But why did you leave all that success behind?"

Gil pulled his hand away and signaled their server for two more coffees. "Because of some home truths I learned through Life Lesson number two."

Maggie found herself simultaneously spellbound and disturbed by the tale Gil told.

He'd been working homicide when he'd caught the case. It involved a sixteen-year-old hooker.

"When I got to the dump she was renting, it was apparent she'd been brutalized before she'd been killed. Routine tests were conducted to make it all official, but it was clear to me she'd been sodomized and beaten before her throat had been cut.

"The elements of the case that made it so unusual, so volatile were two facts. The first was, she was black. The second was, two days into the investigation when I still hadn't turned up any prime suspects, an eyewitness who lived in the victim's building swore she saw a white cop leaving the victim's room minutes after the victim had screamed.

"The witness was even able to produce a startlingly accurate description of the man which, sure enough, brought in a composite match to a veteran patrolman named Evan James. Unofficially, James was a problem inside the force long before this happened. He had a history of brutality, and the charges leveled against him came from a number of alleged victims who were black.

"Naturally, it wasn't long before the local press got wind of it and had a field day sensationalizing it. I'd already lived through Brooker, and I couldn't believe I was swirling in a similar racial cauldron again.

"What about James?"

"He insisted on his innocence. But both conclusive and circumstantial evidence went heavily against him. Serology tests came back with a positive match of his semen to that found on the victim. James admitted he'd been in the habit of visiting her infrequently. In fact, he further admitted he had been with her the day she was murdered. But, he insisted, he'd been long gone at the time when the witness swore she saw him leave.

"Beyond that, bruises James had on his hands and scratches he had on his face—wounds he said were sustained in an altercation with a street punk we could never find—were consistent with the sorts of injuries a medical expert said the victim could have inflicted prior to her death.

"Most damning of all, prints on the knife that was found in a dumpster two blocks away were a match. In short, James's loud protests weren't nearly enough to keep him out of jail while the investigation went on."

"And how did you ride it out, Gil? What did you believe?"

"I wanted to believe what most every other black cop on that force wanted to believe," Gil told her honestly. "A bad apple, a known racist had finally gone too far and set himself up for some comeuppance in a major way."

Maggie tilted her head, reading Gil. She could sense what was to follow by his tone more than by what he was saying. "What did you do?"

"On the eve of James's indictment, I went to his cell to talk to him at length. Understand, there had never been any love lost between us, but the vehemence of his continued protests in the face of so much evidence bothered me. That vehemence was inconsistent.

"Men like James, men who are basically cowards aren't great thinkers or great intellects. When the tide of whatever it is that moves against them starts to look insurmountable, resignation sets in and bravado usually becomes their common resort.

"After a while, James's protests stopped sounding

so defensive and brash to my ears. Instead, they started sounding desperate, the way a desperate man sounds when he's sincere. I left his cell that night actually starting to doubt his guilt. Given what a sorry human being he was, the fact that I could side with him surprised me. I hated it."

Maggie thought of the Brooker case with all its parallels, all its obvious ironies. "How did it end?"

"I went back to the victim's building while the city's most high-profile suspect was being indicted. I started canvassing tenants again, hoping like hell that I wouldn't really turn anything up. I kept knocking on doors, hoping every single tenant would deny any scenario contrary to the one that had been branded into the city's conscience by the media. I even remember thinking my conscience was going to let me off the hook because nobody was contradicting the story and I was almost home free.

"Then I came to Carmen Arrondez's apartment. She was last on my list."

Maggie looked out into the room of patrons, blocking out the desultory din to concentrate fully on the ugliness and tragedy that underscored what Gil told her.

On the night of the murder, Carmen had heard noises coming from inside the victim's apartment. She, like everyone else, had known what the girl did for a living. Most of the time, it was just easier for her to block out the sounds than to wonder. But it was the desperation of the girl's scream on that particular night that had hung onto Carmen's conscience and wouldn't let go.

She'd cracked open her door just as a man in uniform was quietly closing the victim's door. But this man hadn't matched James's description. He hadn't even been white. Carmen had become frightened when she'd seen the black cop return less than an hour later, going from door to door in the hallway, flashing a photo around, and gesturing occasionally toward the victim's door.

When the eyewitness had actually ventured to the victim's apartment a short while after the black cop had left, she'd found the door unlocked and walked in, and the rest had been history.

But armed with new information Gil had taken Carmen to the station to help produce a second composite of the other cop. It matched one of James's most vocal detractors.

After that, events moved quickly. The eyewitness, upon threat of perjury, caved in and confessed that while she had noticed James go into the victim's apartment on the day the victim was killed, and other days before that, she hadn't actually seen him come out. She'd heard the victim's door slam, and used to unusual comings and goings at that apartment, had assumed his leaving had been what she'd heard.

Most damaging, however, was the eyewitness's confession that Carmen's cop had asked her prior to discovery of the girl's body if she would be willing to testify under oath that she had seen James leave the victim's apartment shortly after the time she should have been killed. Disgusted with the way this particular cop—James was no stranger on the streets— had repeatedly used the girl, the witness had agreed. A subsequent search of the rogue cop's apartment turned up minuscule amounts of the victim's dried blood in his carpet fibers. His confession—in return for consideration of leniency—to having coerced a manipulation of evidence samples against James pointed the finger to others within the force. In the end, leniency was denied and he was hit with a murder rap instead.

"James was released and reinstated," Gil concluded. "The cop who had set him up went down, I was made a lieutenant for my work on the case, and shortly thereafter, everybody's life went on."

"But justice was served, Gil." Maggie attempted to counter Gil's bitterness.

"Yeah, justice was served all right. I learned in a very hard way that racial boundaries aren't what determine good guys or bad guys at all. And, most neatly of all, the tarnished force I worked for reinstated itself in the public eye chiefly because it cleaned up its very public mess on its own. Hurrah."

"I'm sorry," Maggie finally said, unable to respond to his despair. Perhaps given the insurmountable issue of race in a country whose prevailing mood was paranoid at best, there really was no easy solution or simple panacea to stories like Gil's. Even so, the story had made Gil's point clear.

"Do you ever wonder why things that should be the most straightforward in life are sometimes the most confusing?" At length, Maggie looked back around at Gil.

"Not anymore. I think sometimes it's hard enough just to try to keep up with the whys and wherefores of things you can plainly see."

"Like Daddy."

"Maybe like your father," Gil corrected. "Like I've been saying, Maggie, sometimes the things that seem the most obvious to us have to be reassessed, because all of the factors at play aren't always evident to the naked eye."

"Especially, if murder is involved."

"Yes, especially then."

Chapter 15

"It's getting late," Gil said. "You ready to go?"

"Just two more hours on the road, right?"

"About that, yeah." He pulled out his wallet. Maggie watched him extract some money. He was counting it when she registered the fact that a band was playing somewhere nearby. Their waitress came up to the table with a tired smile, and Gil started settling up the bill.

"Where's the music coming from?" Maggie asked, curious.

"Next room," the waitress said. "Every night, local musicians come in here to play. It gives them a chance to be heard, and the patrons really like it." She took Gil's cash and smiled at them both. "Enjoy your evening, folks."

Gil stood up after the waitress left.

Maggie stayed where she was and said impulsively, "Before we go, can we dance?"

Gil hadn't anticipated such a request. In fact, he'd only now just really paid serious attention to the music. It was an easy blend of young country and pop. He started to voice a gentle refusal, but then he saw the look in Maggie's eyes.

It was restless, but even more than that she still

looked a little lost, as if she needed some sort of anchor to hold onto.

He reconsidered. It was only one dance, and he told himself he wouldn't be tempting folly if it was only for that short while that he held her in his arms. He held out his hand. "Come on."

Maggie got up and walked beside him to the next room, not understanding what had prompted her to do this. She was glad, nevertheless, that she had once they stood on the threshold of the darkened ballroom. They waited for the song that was playing to end, standing where they were out of sight of the three other couples who moved languidly inside. When the music stopped and soft applause followed the dying notes, Maggie felt a twinge of hesitation.

And then Gil took her hand and urged her along. She was being ridiculous, she told herself, going with him. It was only one dance, and they'd shared a million dances in the past.

This time, the ballad was pure country, and Gil pulled her close. To her surprise, Maggie felt stiff as they began to move. Gil obviously sensed it because she felt his arms tighten around her. "It's okay, baby, I've got you," he murmured, and she tried to relax again, letting her senses re-accustom themselves to being held securely in his arms.

Gil knew the instant her nervousness started to fade away. He felt it in the almost imperceptible sigh she emitted against his throat, he felt it in her fingers when they rose hesitantly to his shoulders and hovered before gaining the courage to twine around his neck. He wouldn't have been a man if he hadn't succumbed to the urge to pull her closer. When she moved into him easily this time, it was he who almost sighed.

Maggie lost herself in the mournful tones of the steel guitar, in the poignant pulse of the acoustic instrument it accompanied. She could almost imagine the notes sliding and swirling around them, binding them together until the longing of it moved within her heart, the pulse of it inside her blood.

"Maggie, Maggie," Gil chanted, failing to move them apart when one melody slid softly into the next, taking encouragement that Maggie's lack of protest meant she was feeling this long-lost magic, too.

Maggie tightened her arms around Gil's neck and let herself be moved. Everything outside this inn, outside this room at this moment seemed unreal. The one thing she held close in her arms right now felt like the only reality, or at least, the reality she was indulgently willing to be true.

The selection that held them enthralled slowly ended, and Gil gathered himself to encourage Maggie to come away. In stark contrast to when they'd begun moving together, she seemed almost boneless now, as if it would take very little for her to fall asleep.

"Come on, honey, let's go," Gil urged softly.

Maggie turned her head slightly. "No, I want to stay."

Gil looked down at her, studying her face. Her words surely referred to the dance, so why did he have the feeling she was making a request for something more.

Maggie felt Gil's probing gaze, and after she recovered from her own surprise at what she'd said to him, she gathered the courage to meet it. They stood there clasped together, unmoving, while a scattering of couples smiled at them and maneuvered around. A fine tension surrounded the moment and Maggie tried to look away, but an internal wanting greater than her will kept her gaze locked on his.

Arrested by her determination, Gil let the moment between them stretch until the unspoken question between them became charged. What would happen, he wondered faintly, if they did throw caution, common sense, and all the other responsible emotions to the wind to let their hearts take charge.

And then Maggie smiled.

I dare you, her gesture seemed to say, and if that wasn't plain enough, Gil could see the challenge in her eyes.

As if that had been the cue he'd been subconsciously seeking, Gil answered his own question. He stopped thinking and took her hand tightly in his own. They were almost to the lobby door, and he could feel her disappointment with every step.

Just as he could feel her nervous elation when he leaned down and said against her ear, "I'll go get the bags."

Maggie watched him walk to the car, and she knew she had very little time to decide whether or not she was about to make an insurmountable mistake. They'd both studiously avoided even thinking about today or the next in any personal context. The concept of tomorrow was a possibility she wasn't really ready to seriously consider. And she knew that despite the many ways in which Gil had changed, on this matter he was in full accord.

She was frowning at the ground when she felt his touch on her shoulder. Too late, the warning voice inside her said.

Then she looked up at his face, and the moonlight touched his eyes. There was worry there, she saw. But there was also anticipation and softness. And maybe, her heart read, even a little fear. That last realization settled her nerves and quieted that little voice more effectively than anything else could have. She touched the hand at her shoulder with her own.

"Let's go inside," she told him.

Gil released the breath he hadn't known he'd been

holding and wrapped an arm around her waist, suddenly eager to comply.

Maggie only felt the slightest qualm when he registered them into a room together, but not for propriety's sake. It was because a step had been taken, and the chance for either of them to turn back had faded and was gone.

The room they were given was on the second floor. They slowed their steps then waited by the elevator, arm in arm.

When moments later they stood at their door, Gil released Maggie only long enough to insert the key, and then the door was closing, she was standing flush against him, and their bags were hitting the floor.

Maggie expected Gil to kiss her first, but when he moved from her slightly, she realized he was searching for the light.

"No," she begged, "don't turn it on." Everything about this decision seemed so ephemeral, so magical, so out of time that she wanted only the glow of the moon to illuminate their bodies. She wanted to preserve this moment in her memory as something sharp and crystalline clear.

Gil clasped her wrists and took her with him as he backed into the room. A few steps in, he turned her until the backs of her knees were touching the bed. She complied with his unspoken command and sat down while the pressure on her wrists tightened. He leaned over her, whispering her name, then he kissed her, a fleeting touch of his lips to hers, before he backed away.

Maggie heard the rustle of his clothes but could only see his shadow as he moved across the floor. At the window, he parted the heavy drapes, letting the snowy liner linger. Their privacy was insured while nature's night-light spilled inside bathing the bed and floor with its glow.

Maggie closed her eyes when next she felt his touch . . . a hand at her throat, a drifting caress, his mouth at her shoulder, more tenderly at her breasts. "Move over," he breathed.

When Maggie complied, her back was against the coverlet, and he was kissing her mouth with insistence. As she parted her lips, he deepened the contact until the exchange became erotic, wet and slow. Her hands lifted to his hair, and the cool, wavy strands were no barrier to her massaging fingers, to his warm skin below.

"Let me move a little, honey," he whispered softly, then he drifted from her arms and was gone.

Maggie sensed his impatience as they shed their clothes. Gil's movements were laden with steadiness but his arms were tense when they encircled her again.

Shifting skin welcomed shifting skin, beating heart welcomed beating heart. Maggie relished the sensations, but savored Gil's responses even more.

"I want to kiss you here," he said, "and there . . . and there." And Maggie kissed and caressed him and smiled to discover she could make him shiver, too. Then that minute bit of consciousness left her when he shifted her, and parted her and prepared her for more.

He whispered something against her ear, but she couldn't hear because she was gasping at his touch, which had turned intimate, sizzling, and deep. She arched against his hand and softly called his name, and when his fingers left her she was ready and knew Gil felt the same.

His palms trailed a path along her stomach and then up, causing Maggie to arch even more. For incredible moments she felt suspended, as if the crests of her breasts and the center of her body were joined in a world ruled by his encompassing touch. "Don't make me wait," she pleaded, but it was as if he'd never heard her, or did and didn't care.

Gil dragged a hand between them until it was nestled against her heat and slowly aided his flesh in a tantalizing press. It was a taking without penetration, and it brought Maggie to the brink . . . and then she tumbled over into a tide that pulsed around her, rhythmic and strong.

The pleasured sound she emitted wrung a breathy reciprocation from Gil. He kissed her mouth, stroked her tongue with his, turned up the heat until she was aching once more. . . . And then she was falling . . . falling . . . and Gil was there to catch her. He whispered words meant to calm but he was acutely tense, and Maggie was very aware.

Gil shivered at the sensation of her small hands upon his back. As they glided up and back down, he wanted to tell her this felt so good, like coming home. But she wasn't ready, and truthfully, neither was he, so he focused on the experience of having this woman, his Maggie, in his arms.

His thrust was strong, and Maggie took him deeply, completely inside. He wanted to pause to savor the moment, but the pleasure she inspired was so right, so intense, he was powerless.

Her legs clasped him to her tightly, and he shuddered. Her hands dropped to his flexing buttocks, and he groaned.

"Come on," she chanted against her ear, and he was lost, only able to surge against her again and again. The sensation low in his body deepened and clawed, and Gil suddenly lifted his head from beside Maggie's neck. He wanted her to watch him when it happened.

He wanted her to see how much he could feel with her even after all this time.

She whispered his name, and then he was so close to peaking he couldn't think at all. He thrust hard and quick until the tension inside him broke. His back arched, and for a breathless beat his body went still. Maggie's hips moved silkenly against his, heightening it for him, milking the release that shook him and spasmed on . . . and then he was shuddering in the enervating aftermath.

Maggie's arms came around him, and she relaxed her legs to claim more comfort for herself. She wondered what he was thinking. Was he searching for something to say?

In the past, she had always needed the words, yet tonight she found comfort in the quiet that surrounded them. It still startled her to think of how in so many ways she'd been so naive for so long.

"Maggie," Gil began, rousing himself against the drowsiness that beckoned.

Maggie placed a slender finger against his lips. "Don't, Gil. It's okay."

Gil studied her, trying to see if she was placating him or if, in this, too, she really had changed. She gave him his answer when she closed her eyes and tucked her head beneath his chin.

He wanted to thank her, but he was more comfortable holding her instead. So he did, content to let the newness of what they had just shared simply be.

Chapter 16

The sun was completely up and shining strongly through the blinds when Maggie awakened. Gil sat relaxed and quiet against a pillow he'd propped along the headboard.

"Good morning." She lifted her head from the hand that had been pillowing it and turned, pulling the covers to her chest. When she scooted up Gil raised an arm, inviting her to snuggle in beside him.

"How are you doing?" His fingers absently played with her hair.

"I'm good." She smiled with a hint of tease. "More than good."

Gil smiled back and continued to play with her hair. "I need to check in at the precinct this afternoon, and to touch base with Myer and Carter."

Maggie swung her legs over the side of the bed. Abruptly, she felt a little cool.

"Maggie?"

"Hm." She sat with her back to him, hoping her awkwardness would miraculously go away.

"I don't have any regrets."

Maggie looked back at him over her shoulder, feeling, with that simple statement, a little reassured and, thankfully, more at ease. "Neither do I, but we need to think about this, Gil. There's so much to deal with, so much to erase—"

Gil reached over to cup the back of her head. He exerted enough pressure to make her lean in close against him.

Maggie broke their kiss slowly, understanding that Gil was trying to give her some encouragement, trying to tell her that he had believed her last night when they'd lain together and she'd told him everything was okay. The look in his eye was deliberate now as he reached out and twisted a corner of the sheet in his fist while she tried to hold it snugly against her.

Maggie resisted but Gil was determined to make a point, and so she took a deep breath and let go. He lowered the sheet and smiled at her, and again she felt another bit of her tension ease.

Gil swung his own legs over the bed, then he held out a hand. "Let's go get showered."

"Let's," she agreed.

An hour later, they were back on the road. As Maggie had said back at the inn, there was still much they had to discuss, but Gil didn't feel too inclined to do so just now. He wanted to let the drive sustain the lull over his senses. Business that had to be faced back home would bring them back to reality soon enough.

Maggie suggested they stop for lunch less than one hundred miles from home, and Gil teased her for it since they'd both eaten substantial breakfasts in the inn's dining room before they'd left. But they did stop, and Maggie reflected on how good it felt to be teased by him. How incredible it was that they'd managed to move beyond the wariness and mistrust they'd both felt when they met again.

The outskirts of Atlanta were less than thirty minutes away when Maggie said, "Gil, don't drive me straight home. I want to stop at Dad's."

"Why?" Gil kept his eyes on the road.

"He keeps personal papers there, journals, private things. If there's something within all of it that could help explain anything, I've got to know."

"You don't have to investigate it today, Maggie."

"I want to know."

She was determined; he heard it plainly and knew that if he didn't drive her she'd just come back later in the day without him.

"Since you're determined, I'll stay there with you. That way if something turns up, we'll both see it."

Had she not known better, Maggie would have interpreted his last comment to mean that he didn't trust her to turn anything that could be incriminating over to him. Briefly, habit tempted her to call him on it, but she desperately wanted to believe in their newly found trust, so she kept silent.

She gathered her purse off the floor when Gil swung the car into the driveway of her father's home. Though she was determined to do this now, she was anxious, and when Gil reached over to pat her hand, she knew she hadn't been able to hide her apprehension from him.

"We may not find anything," he reminded her.

"I know that." Still, she felt tense.

"Then, just remember this. Everything usually has a reasonable explanation no matter how ambiguous it may look from the outside."

Maggie couldn't help but recall Gil's revelations, his stark experience with that particular truth. When he cut the motor, Maggie nodded inwardly. "Let's go." She opened her door and stepped outside.

Gil closed his door and remembered his impression of the Thomas estate the first time Paul Thomas had brought him here for a visit. He'd been such a young boy, so easily impressed, so malleable about many things if it meant Paul Thomas too would be impressed.

The house was still beautiful, its grounds still extensive, fertile, green. But what for so long he had remembered as being vast seemed surprisingly diminished. He viewed it not through the eyes of a boy, but through those of an experienced man.

Maggie was turning the key in the side door's lock by the time Gil reached her. She walked inside the kitchen and tossed her purse on the counter. Again, Gil smiled because her very casualness went another notch toward demystifying the sanctity with which he had once viewed everything and everyone inside this house.

Maggie started toward the hall, eager to get to work. "Let's start in the study. It seems the most logical place to stash something you might want to hide."

"Whatever it is we may find may not necessarily be something your father feels he has to hide, Maggie. Don't condemn him yet."

That brought her up. She stopped where she was and turned around to look at him. "You're right, I know that, of course. I guess I was just thinking this would be easier if I walked into it expecting the worst."

Gil touched her arm. "Don't."

Don't what? Maggie wanted to ask, think this excursion could be easier, or expect the worst? As if he could sense that question hovering at the corner of her mind, he sidestepped her and kept walking until he was standing at the closed study door.

"When did he start locking it?" Gil wanted to know.

"He didn't. I did, after the accident. It just felt right somehow, as if I was shutting off a private sanctum he was powerless to defend."

Gil wondered at that, turned it around in his mind

because coming from anyone else it would have sounded as if they'd had something to hide. But in the next moment he realized habit had prompted his instant doubt.

As of last night, even before they'd had sex, he and Maggie had shifted to newer ground. That was significant enough to convince him that as long as they were moving forward, he was going to make a stronger effort to trust.

The study wasn't heavily furnished, and aside from a series of ceiling-to-floor bookcases, a bureau, and Thomas's desk drawer, there weren't many places Gil could see that they would need to search.

"I'll look in the bureau here." Maggie singled out a key and gave her ring to Gil. You look through the bureau over there."

"Fine."

Gil found an assortment of files, many that had to do with Thomas's construction firm, others that had to do with colleagues and employees he'd associated with through past elections. He found the rough-draft manuscript of a couple of campaign speeches as well as a more recent draft, whose cover letter had been drafted by Sloan Michaels. Curious, Gil took a closer look at the notes Michaels had made.

Part of his advisory expertise was evident at a glance. His incisive eye had effectively cut through a lot of grandiose banter Paul had penned, and Michaels had reshaped the thoughts into a package that was tighter, at times funnier or pithier, but always clear in an effectively sound-bitten way.

Sloan Michaels obviously understood that elections were won or lost, for the most part, electronically. He possessed the art of steering a man who had been raised in an era of glad-handing to the realities of a society where the fastest tongue won.

"What do you have there?"

"Hm?" Gil kept reading.

Maggie kneeled beside him. "You look so engrossed."

"It's a draft of one of your father's recent campaign speeches, or rather, I should say, Sloan Michaels's handiwork."

"Oh."

Gil looked up. "You don't like him, much, do you? I noticed that once before."

"Yeah, at White's party. You're right, I don't."

"Why not? Seems to be an eminently amiable kind of guy."

Maggie slanted him a sardonic eye. "You noticed."

"Hard not to, babe. What's the story?"

"A short one. He's an ambitious politician who strikes me as bitter because he knows he can't go the distance on his own. He held a local office back in California, didn't make it, and shifted gears to enter the advisory field."

Gil went back to the speech for a minute, then inserted it back in the stack inside the bureau from where he'd taken it. "He seems to have made a wise choice. Your father hasn't benefited too shabbily from the association, and Michaels seems content."

"Men like him are never content." Maggie wandered across the room to a table that was a companion to the bureau Gil was exploring. Her search turned up more of the same sort of material Gil had already found. The drawer yielded little more than a business account ledger for his firm and miscellaneous form letters to constituents who had contributed monetary support to one campaign or another.

Gil joined her in the middle of the room. "Is there anywhere else here where he lives, so to speak? Any safes, lock boxes, anything else that he keeps secured away or out of casual sight?"

Maggie shook her head. "You know Daddy, he's the original man with nothing to hide."

Gil heard the bitterness again, or maybe it was just a precursory emotion to disillusionment. That was a defense mechanism he knew all too well. "Maggie—" A sudden crash made Maggie jump. Gil whirled around. The noise had come from upstairs.

Gil's first inclination was to tell Maggie to stay here, but his second had him pulling her along so that he could be sure she was safe and sound with him.

They hit the stairs, and Maggie tugged on his hand when they arrived in a rush at the landing. "It sounded like it came from down there." She motioned in the direction of what Gil remembered to be the portion of the hallway that housed her and Paul Thomas's bedrooms.

"Stay with me, Maggie, and do what I say."

She didn't argue.

A second crash sounded from behind the door to their right. The commotion seemed to entail an abundance of breaking glass. The shocking loudness of it made Maggie cringe against Gil's side. Gil leaned down and drew a small caliber pistol from beneath his pant leg. Maggie wondered how he'd managed to conceal it this morning while they'd dressed. The sight of the gun, no matter how small, unnerved her, and when Gil took her hand she held on tight.

He leaned against the door, listening. "Whoever you are in there, I'd advise you to give it up now. I'm a cop. I'm armed, and I'm coming in." He looked down at Maggie.

She swallowed and kept her eyes trained on him because she'd never seen his face this hard.

"Stand over there out of sight range and don't move until or unless I tell you," he whispered. "Do you understand?"

She nodded and lowered tense eyes to the doorknob he held. "I'm going in on the count of three," he whispered, and started counting. On the final count, he hit the door, wrenched it open, and dropped to a defensive roll. Maggie couldn't hold back a gasp, certain, as she was, that he was on the verge of shooting or getting shot.

Silence. And then Gil said, "It's okay, Maggie, you can relax. Come in."

Maggie stepped around the corner into her old bedroom. At first she was confused because everything seemed to be completely intact. Then she saw the window by the farthermost wall in the corner. It was shattered, and at its foot lay two bricks. What looked to be scraps of paper had been tied with twine to each one.

Gil walked over to the shattered window and looked out. He relaxed his hand holding the gun and turned to kneel down. The note from the first brick he looked at and discarded. The note from the second he read a bit more thoughtfully, then passed on to Maggie.

Maggie's heart was still jumping when she turned the paper right-side-up to read.

Niggers, unlike black cats,
don't have nine lives.

"Son of bitch," Maggie muttered, furious. "How *dare* someone do this to us." She crumpled the note. "What did the other one say?"

"Nothing that makes sense."

"Those letters Sloan received. God, Gil, it's the same thing, isn't it?"

"Maggie, calm down."

"How can I calm down when someone is trying to kill my father?"

"I'm staying at your place tonight." He could see Maggie think about it for all of two seconds before she opened her mouth to protest. "I don't want any arguments on this, Maggie, I mean it. We've discussed it before, I'm not sure you're safe, and this incident may have just confirmed that."

Maggie stared at him and relented. He was just trying to protect her, and she'd been prepared to lash out because she was angry about needing that protection. And she was scared.

Gil saw the conflict in her face and pulled her close. "You are not going to get hurt, I promise you that. I'll take you home, then I'll touch base at the precinct, but not before I call and arrange for someone to watch you while I'm there."

"There's no need," Maggie protested. "I have to get some work done at the office, too, some of Daddy's business as well as my own. Pick me up there when you're finished."

She'd be surrounded by hundreds of people, Gil thought. In his mind, he saw the words scrawled across the paper he'd discarded.—*Don't think your nigger bitch daughter won't die, too.* If someone was really trying to hurt her, that someone would most likely take their best shot when they thought she was alone.

"Come on, then, let's go." Gil ushered Maggie out of the room ahead of him. While she walked, he backtracked into the room. He retrieved the discarded note and tucked it inside his shirt pocket, then he followed her. They left through the kitchen door they had entered and got quickly into Gil's car.

The man by the shrubs not ten feet away watched Gil's car drive off. He'd seen by their set faces that his messages had been received as he'd wanted. The stage

he was setting was just about right. Only one final act
was needed before finishing off the plan.

Adam swiveled around from his terminal so that he
could look at Gil. "Through her window? Is she hurt?"

"No. We were downstairs when it happened."

"You were there, too?"

"Yeah, I called her this morning to ask her if she'd
had any luck finding anything that looked interesting
among her father's things, and she told me she hadn't
looked yet, but that she'd do it then if I wanted to
come with her." Gil didn't feel too bad about the slant
he put on the truth. He knew Adam, and he knew eva-
sion was easier than trying to explain what had really
transpired.

Adam said, "How early did you call? She wasn't
home when I cruised by late last night."

"She's a grown woman, Adam. I doubt if she fol-
lows a curfew, and house arrest, the last time we
spoke to her, wasn't exactly a condition of the call."

"No need to get sarcastic, okay? I was just asking."
Adam scratched his head and leaned back in his chair.

Gil thought his partner was going to ask what he
really wanted to know, and suddenly he didn't care;
in fact, he was ready for it. He'd spent eight years
uncomplicating his life. Today, he was just ready to let
the chips fall where they might.

But Adam didn't ask. Instead, he requested the low-
down on Houser. Gil gave it to him lean and spare.

"So what we have is a possible connection between
Paul Thomas and these other two men who have been
murdered." He shook his head, "Aside from the town-
rumor angle, Gil, I don't have to tell you it seems
pretty thin."

"No, you don't. Then again, we both know cases

have been made on circumstances that seem even thinner."

"Then, what we need to find is a connection between Parsons and Denning, and Denning and Thomas."

"Yes. What did you find out at the prison?"

"We've got an interview in three days. The warden did some checking, said there was at least one, maybe two more inmates we might want to talk to. They go back to the beginning of Denning's time in there."

"Why the holdup? Why can't we see them now?"

"One's sick with bronchitis, and he can barely breathe let alone talk. But his condition is chronic, and the prison doc figures it'll be no longer than another three days before it runs the worst of its course."

Gil dropped into a chair next to Adam's. "What about the other one?"

"He's in solitary. It'll be three days before he gets out."

"Ducky."

"So what do you want to do next, I mean right now?"

Gil told Adam of his immediate intention to guard Maggie at her house.

"I suppose she explained all nice and neatly why she was prying, without your knowledge, into your life?"

"Yes."

Adam sighed deeply and picked up his empty coffee mug. He stared into its interior. "Hell, man, maybe I am all wrong about her. It's just that . . . when a chick screws you over that bad, it just doesn't seem like you should be able to trust her again. That's all."

"And you've got to know how much I agreed with you at one time."

Adam's eyes stayed on his cup. "You love her?"

"I don't know."

Adam looked at Gil from under his lashes and sighed again. "Oh, man."

Gil rubbed his jaw. "Yeah."

Chapter 17

"Sloan, Henry, thanks for coming." Maggie gestured them over to the small conference table that occupied one end of her office. A deli lunch, procured by Jerry, had been arranged there for them.

Henry took in Maggie's jeans and shirt before he pulled out a chair for her, then selected his own. "Slumming today?"

Maggie waved his remark away. "I hadn't planned to be here at all, but since I am, I thought it would be a good opportunity to talk to the two of you alone."

"About what?" Sloan chose a turkey sandwich on rye, a cola, and a small container of potato salad.

"Daddy. His past. His future."

Both men paused in spreading their selected sandwich condiments on their bread. "Sounds awfully serious, honey," Henry said, "What's going on?"

Maggie pulled over a can of soda and popped the top. "Have either of you ever heard of a man named Owen Parsons."

Neither man showed any sign of recognizing the name. Henry took a bite of his sandwich and chewed. Sloan did the same, but he responded first. "Should we have? In my case, the answer's no."

"Same here." Henry said. "Who is he?"

"Someone who lived a long time ago. If his name draws a blank, then it doesn't matter. What about Charlie Denning? We've never talked about his so-called accusations and what this mysterious document he claimed to have written could have said."

Henry pushed away his food and crossed his hands. "I didn't think we needed to, seeing as how whatever that lunatic claimed couldn't have been anything but lies."

"Sloan?" Maggie asked.

"I'm the new kid here. All I know about your father is what I've learned over the last three years. But I will say this, during all that time, I've never seen a hint of anything or anyone as vindictive as this Denning person appeared to be."

"What about the letters?" Maggie asked.

Henry frowned. "What letters?"

Briefly, Sloan told him.

"Damn. He studied Maggie. "I thought when you and Gil were doing that smoke and mirrors for the media, the show was a farce. Now I suspect I've been wrong. There's reason to believe Paul's life really is in danger, isn't there?"

"Perhaps, yes," Maggie said.

"And you've actually called us in here because you know something that suggests Charlie Denning may have been holding more to his chest than a bunch of lies?"

"No," Maggie said with frustration, "that's what I don't know, and it's making me crazy. You've known him longer than any of us, Henry. And you, Sloan, well, we all know that things come out during the course of a campaign that don't necessarily get leaked to the ears of children or wives."

"Suppose you tell us what you suspect," Sloan suggested.

Maggie thought about it and finally shook her head. Gil would be furious if he knew she'd scheduled this impromptu lunch. He'd be livid, and probably rightfully so if he found out she'd been telling tales out of school about the case, so she said, "I can't tell you anything with any assurance, and I don't want to burden either of you with unfounded suggestions that turn out to be half-cocked."

Sloan laughed cynically. "Try again, Maggie. You can't tease us like this and leave it."

"I'm afraid I can, Sloan. I am." His patronizing attitude raised her hackles.

Henry intervened. "At least tell us if any of these—allegations—you're entertaining have to do with anything that's illegal?"

"No." She wasn't lying precisely, she told herself, because even though the matter was criminal, her father's involvement, because it was still questionable, wasn't. "I guess what I really want to know is if there's anything that's struck you as particular lately concerning Daddy's frame of mine, his habits, anything like that."

"You already know my opinion of your father, Maggie," Sloan said. "If there's a finer man in the political arena today, I don't know about him." He pushed aside his sandwich wrapper and sipped his drink.

"Henry?"

"You know what he's lived through. Even though you were a child you have to remember some of that turmoil yourself. Answer your own question, Maggie. Has the Paul Thomas who's been your father for thirty-two years demonstrated any possibility of being related to this—shadow character—you've created in your mind?"

That was, of course, the question that had been

plaguing Maggie ever since she'd listened to the story of Willis Houser. No matter what she told Gil, it bothered her still.

Sloan looked at his watch. "If that's all, I've got to go. There's a lot I still have to do back at the office today, not the least of which is compiling a list of rowdies who may be excessively angry at Paul for your Lieutenant Stewart."

"What do you mean by *my* Lieutenant Stewart, Sloan?"

He smiled slightly. "What could I mean? Don't take offense." He pushed his chair up to the table. "Good-bye."

Maggie waited until he was gone. "What does Daddy *see* in that man?" she exploded.

"A very competent campaign manager, I imagine. Managers don't have to be lovable. You've lived as the daughter of a politician long enough to know that by now."

He was right. But the father she'd once known would never have abided that man's attitude, never tolerated him as someone he chose to have around.

"One thing that Sloan said, though," Henry said. "What about Gil?"

"What about him?"

"Maggie," Henry said chidingly. "It's no use being coy with me. Are you involved with him again?"

Maggie felt warm. She'd never been able to lie well, and it was twice as hard to do it while she was looking her old friend in the eye. "No. I'm not."

Henry didn't say anything for a long time.

Neither did Maggie, and by the time Henry finally did respond, she felt confident she had reclaimed a little more of her composure.

"You two were awfully—intense—before your breakup. I wouldn't approve, but I'd understand if you found that attraction to be something you can't quite leave alone now."

Maggie didn't feel in the least like laughing, but she had to smile. "I never could pull anything over on you. I don't know why I tried."

"So, how deep is it?"

"Not very. We've simply discovered that we don't hate each other like we thought we did."

"Well, that's a start."

"For what?"

"A future? A beginning?"

Maggie tilted her head. "Why do you care, Henry? You never approved of us even when Gil was the fair-haired boy."

"I know you've always thought that. I used to assume your response was the result of Gil's influence."

"I'll admit I was a little young, Henry, but I wasn't quite that innocent. You're contempt was plain."

Henry didn't deny it. "It wasn't because of what you felt for him, or, I'll admit it, what I knew he honestly felt for you. I resented Gil for different reasons."

"Such as?"

"The rough character he was, the way his edges were so unrefined. After your mother died, your father did everything he could to give you polish, to see that you grew up to be a reflection of the lady your mother had been. When he then practically adopted a mongrel like Stewart, insinuated him into his life, into his home . . . well, I was a bit dismayed."

"I never knew you were such a snob, Henry."

Henry didn't take offense, instead he thought seriously about what she'd said. "It wasn't snobbishness, Maggie. You've had a pretty easy life, but your father and I and a whole generation of blacks like us didn't.

"Many of our lives were filled with poverty, and,

too often, dead-end choices. Our visions of the future were of oppression and despair. So when we saw opportunities to crawl out from under the weight of our problems, those of us who could seized them. We refused to look back."

"So how does all that relate to Gil?"

"Gil was the embodiment of a dangerous, ultimately self-defeating attitude I saw, and still see, afflicting so many black young men. At his birth, life dealt him an unfortunate hand. His response was to turn his anger and suspicion on things he couldn't have, instead of finding constructive ways to claim a little piece of the prosperity he saw for his own. The white man was his enemy, the foot on his neck, the easy excuse. I'd lived twice his lifetime and never seen men who victimized themselves by that backward rationale ever amount to much of anything."

"Gil was a boy, he wasn't a thug," Maggie pointed out.

"No. But he was something worse. He was a prisoner of his own mind. The chip on his shoulder was huge."

Maggie answered slowly. "Maybe in the beginning what you say was true. But there was also something in Gil, right from the start that was very fine. Daddy saw it. It took me a while, but eventually I saw it, too."

"Perhaps you were right, in fact, I think I'll shock you by admitting this, as well. I think Gil Stewart has become a fine young man. Nevertheless, I'm still not convinced he's the right man for you."

"Why?"

"Because he has the capacity, like no one I've ever seen, to get thoroughly close to you, close enough to break your heart."

What could she say when he was so right? For a moment Henry's observation frightened her.

Henry reached out and took Maggie's hands. "I meant what I said to you not so long ago. Don't let Gil Stewart take advantage of you. Whatever this thing is he's planted in your head about your father, examine it carefully. Gil Stewart has every reason in the world to hate the man.

"Oh, I'll admit he had feelings for Paul Thomas once. But even then, he was the outsider in your lives."

Maggie studied their joined hands.

"He still is, Maggie."

Maybe he was, she mused. Then she looked into her friend's concerned eyes and thought, ah, but Henry, you don't know him deep down where it really counts. You never did, not the way I do.

Maggie turned their hands over until hers were on top and she could give Henry's a reassuring pat. "Don't worry about me. I'm going to be just fine."

"So is your father, little girl. Believe that."

"I do. And I've kept you away from—?" She looked at him quizzically.

"Golf," he laughed. "I'm a respected senior politician, what else?"

Maggie smiled and pushed back her chair. "Thanks for coming."

Henry met her at the office door. "Thanks for asking me, for trusting me to be frank with you. I only wish I could put your mind more at ease."

"Somehow, you have." Maggie realized that was perfectly true.

"Good." Henry kissed her cheek and left.

Twenty minutes later, the assassin dropped into his easy chair and picked up his phone. The run he'd enjoyed had been the first he'd had time for in nearly a

week, and it had been particularly invigorating.
"Yes?"

"We've got to accelerate things. The final hit has to
be moved up."

"Final?"

"I'm still delaying the ultimate measures we've discussed because of . . . other things."

"When do you want it done?"

"Within the next week. I'll leave the particulars to
your expertise."

"Wise. I haven't let you down yet."

"No." The congressman's voice held no joy.

"I'll be in touch." The assassin hung up. It appeared,
he mused as he got up and headed for the shower, the
schedule was going to have to be speeded up.

It was after seven when Gil picked up Maggie. He'd
called about two hours before that, so she'd known to
expect him late.

"Hi," she said softly as she climbed inside his car.
He'd parked at the curb in front of her building.

"Hi." He took one hand off the steering wheel long
enough to smooth a welcoming rub across her back.
After they'd merged into the heavy traffic he asked,
"How was your day?"

Maggie glanced at him, trying to discern a double
meaning. Gil just continued to drive, so she relaxed.
"It was productive. Yours?"

"Same. Listen, you probably don't feel like cooking,
I know I don't, and I don't want to go out. Would you
mind if we ordered something in?"

"Like a pizza?"

"Yeah, like that."

"Of course I don't mind. In fact, why don't we do it
up right. There's a little video place not too far from

me. We'll rent a movie, pick up some sodas. Have a real date."

"What a deal."

She did, and by the time they'd collected the rest of everything they'd agreed they needed to make the evening complete, they were hauling an enormous pizza, a case of colas, a bag of popcorn, and a pack of peanut butter cups into Maggie's house.

"Why don't you shower first," Maggie invited when Gil used his foot to push her door shut. "You look beat."

"I'm not going to argue." He set the food down on the kitchen counter. "See you in a few minutes."

Gil headed for the bathroom. It seemed such a disgustingly domestic moment, Maggie had to smile.

While he was gone, Maggie poured their popcorn into a bowl. She took down glasses from the cabinet and snagged an ice bucket from a nearby beverage cart. The candy was left in its cellophane wrappings. As for the main course, well, pizza just wasn't pizza if it wasn't eaten from the box.

Gil emerged in short order wearing a fresh pair of loose, low-slung khakis. Droplets of water still glittered in his hair, and an anticipatory smile was on his face. "Smells good. Hurry with your shower, woman. I'm only willing to wait so long."

Me, too, Maggie thought hopefully to herself. When Gil's mood was teasing and loose like this, he was irresistible.

She did hurry, for despite her playful mood she had only nibbled at lunch.

When she walked back into the living room a little later, she had the distinct pleasure of seeing Gil drop the remote control. She knew the smooth brown skin of her legs teased Gil's eyes in a silky extension that ended only where the hem of her ivory tap pants concealed what his mind's eye could visualize. The top she wore was just as pale and not a bit of skin was exposed beneath it—until she moved and her midriff became a visible peekaboo.

Gil stooped down to pick up the remote. "Must have slipped," he mumbled.

"I've had that problem myself," Maggie said solemnly.

Gil tried not to smile. "Let's eat," he said to her instead.

They did, every last crumb of pizza and two thirds of the popcorn. They decided to take the sodas into the living room so that they could pop the movie they'd selected into Maggie's VCR.

She didn't feel like sitting in a chair and neither, apparently, did Gil because he joined her with alacrity against the sofa, where she'd settled herself comfortably.

"So, what is this movie you talked me into?" he muttered.

"Not the love story I wanted, so stop complaining. It's categorized as—"she turned the box over—"a romantic adventure. I believe that means we reached a compromise."

"Um, hm," Gil was noncommittal.

Maggie scooted over to the console and slid the movie inside. She was about to scoot back when she felt Gil's hand circle her ankle. Her head came up, and a question was in her eye.

"Lint," Gil said succinctly. "You had a piece of it on your foot."

"That isn't my foot."

"You're going to be prickly when I'm trying to rid you of lint?"

Maggie's mouth quirked. She came back to him on hands and knees, keeping him in sight. A moment later, she decided she needn't have bothered because the movie was starting and Gil's attention shifted solidly to the opening scenes. They were predictably, Maggie thought cynically, of the heroine's plight.

Actually, Maggie thought later, the film was pretty entertaining. She found herself genuinely caught up in the action. So did Gil evidently, because after that first flirtatious foray, he hadn't moved.

The climax was moments away, the villain in hot pursuit of the gorgeous hero. The heroine was suitably distressed. Maggie was literally holding her breath and nearly screamed when Gil's arm shot out and she found herself flat on her back beneath his grinning face.

"You fraud," she gasped, pushing at his shoulders. "I thought all you cared about was this damn movie and the food."

"Yeah, well, hurrah for me." He dropped a kiss to her nose and smiled. "Gotcha."

Maggie laughed, and Gil did, too, before he took his kiss from her nose to her cheek, to her chin, and finally, when she wasn't laughing anymore, to her mouth.

She twined her arms around his neck and kissed him back, tangling her tongue with his, hearing the music of the movie credits soar triumphantly.

With languid ease, Gil lifted his head. "So, did you pull out this little"—he gestured at her outfit—"nothing, just for me?"

"Uh, uh, mister. I pulled it out"—she raised her head and pressed a quick kiss to his chin—"exclusively for me."

Gil easily read the look in her eye. He matched it with a roguish twinkle of his own. "Lady," he murmured, "I like your style."

One of them, Maggie could never remember which, felt around and located the remote control. Once the television was shut off, there were no more distractions, no more diversions.

Gil quickly divested Maggie of her top, and pants, then he rid himself of his own clothing. Between kisses, which became increasingly deep, he asked the way to her bedroom.

"Right here," she managed. "Tonight, our bedroom is this floor."

Gil's reply was a whisper. "Good enough."

And it was. At the height of her passion, Maggie moaned and arched. Gil's mouth was deliciously warm as he sucked strongly at her sensitive nipples, then his tongue transformed the sensations with wet, thrusting caressess. The measure of them perfectly matched the rhythmic touch he bestowed between her thighs.

At some point, Maggie thought she cried out.

As the strength of his climax hammered through his body, Gil knew he did.

When it receded for both of them, they couldn't stop panting, couldn't catch their breaths. But then, it didn't really matter.

Much later, Maggie felt Gil's chest rumble.

"What?" She didn't hear what he said.

"I said let's do takeout more often."

Maggie's own stomach shook from his suggestion, and the joyous laughter signaled her pleasure in what they were rediscovering and forging anew between them.

Chapter 18

Maggie's phone rang, and Gil's first impulse was to answer it until he remembered he wasn't sleeping in his own bed. He listened to her fumble, find it, and mumble a sleepy, "Hello." He was almost asleep again when Maggie demanded, "Who is this?" He came fully awake.

"Listen, you didn't have the guts to tell me who you were when you called my office. I don't know how you got this number, but I certainly don't appreciate being harassed at my home—what?"

Gil reached over her shoulder, trying to take the receiver from her. Maggie resisted. "What?" she repeated. More time passed before Maggie quietly hung up the phone. She scooted up against the headboard and brought her knees to her chin.

"Tell me what it is." Gil could see her pallor and was faintly alarmed.

"It was no prankster. That person knows who murdered Jeff and Sam, who tried to murder Daddy, who threatened me."

"How do you know?" Gil asked carefully. He scooted up beside her.

"Because the message was for me to, quote, 'leave it alone,' or else be killed next."

"I'm getting a tap on your phone before the day is out. What else did this person say? Were any names mentioned, how can you be sure it wasn't a joke?"

"I just know, Gil. Don't ask me how, I just know."

"Are you going to your office today?"

"I don't have to. I've got a load of work to do for Daddy and had planned on kicking back and doing it here."

"Do it downtown. It'll be easier for others to help you watch your back there." Gil swung out of bed.

"What are you going to do?"

"Go to the prison. Adam and I have something that just might lead somewhere."

"Will you be able to pick me up this evening, or should I drive in?"

"I'll pick you up. Now, let's get moving; I have a feeling it's going to be a very long day."

So did Maggie. What she didn't tell Gil was that she had the additional feeling the day wasn't going to end in a very pleasant way.

"Well, shit, is he going to die or is he going to recover?" Adam raised a languid hand as Gil walked in. "Fine, then. Tomorrow." Adam slammed the phone down on his desk. "Stalled again. Our interviewees are still incommunicado."

Gil set down a cup of coffee he'd gotten from the hallway vending machine. "That doesn't necessarily mean we can't be productive anyway. It occurs to me that we've been looking at this backward. Instead of questioning why Charlie Denning knew Owen Parsons, maybe we should have been asking ourselves how Owen Parsons knew Charlie Denning."

The angle was so obvious, Adam was arrested by its simplicity. "Because, if they knew each other before prison, which they most probably did since Charlie wasn't making many friends while he spent thirty years locked up behind bars, maybe it was Owen who kept the association going."

"With recorded visits," Gil continued.

Adam smiled. "Yeah."

"Yeah."

Adam was already on his feet.

"Wait a minute, I need to take care of something first." Gil called Maggie's office building manager. A polite request here, a casual dropping of rank there, and he hung up with the promise that added security would be put outside her suite for the day and, if necessary, the rest of the week.

"So, how was Maggie last night?" Adam held the precinct door open for Gil, and then they headed for their car.

Gil pinned Adam with a look.

"Shit, I didn't mean that the way it sounded. What I meant was, is she doing okay? Is she holding up all right?"

"Yeah. I think whoever's got a bead on her might be starting to crack, though." Gil told Adam about the early-morning call.

"What about additional killings, any mention of that?"

"I'm not sure," Gil answered, and that bothered him. When they'd left Maggie's house, he'd walked out with the distinct feeling that she hadn't been telling him the entire truth.

Maggie handed the cabbie the appropriate fare, thanked him, and walked up the drive to her father's house. She hoped that Gil didn't call her before she got back to her office.

The last time they'd been here, she'd started to tell him that her father had a wall safe in his bedroom. She hadn't had the chance to finish when they'd been so violently interrupted.

The temptation of the safe's contents had been bugging her ever since, and after this morning's phone call she couldn't bear to delay looking in it.

An added urgency was there because now she had a name for the person who could be a living connection to all of this. She hadn't wanted to tell Gil anything before she had the chance to check it out herself. She knew there was absolutely no sensible reason for her reluctance, but she'd been acting purely on emotion when she'd clammed up just as she was acting purely on emotion now.

She let herself inside the house and headed for the stairs. At the foot of them, she couldn't help but remember the last time she was here, the terror she'd felt and later the fury. She started to climb but stopped when she reached the landing.

Her father's bedroom was down the hallway and to the left. Her room was to the right. With a morbid curiosity she couldn't resist, she headed for it.

The room was as they had left it, the glass shattered, the bricks lying heavily on the floor. A soft summer breeze fluttered the lightweight curtains in and out of the sash, and the sudden sense of violation Maggie felt was so strong that she quickly backed away and left.

Inside her father's room, she could still smell the tobacco he liked to smoke in the evenings and the clean, woodsy cologne that had been part of her memory ever since she was a child. He'd first shown her the safe as part of a game.

He had been the pirate, and she the lady fair whose treasure he'd come to plunder. Since her kingdom in those early days after her mother's death had been this very room where she could be closest to her father, it was only fitting that their most valuable possessions resided in here.

Maggie walked over to the wall that faced the foot of his huge four-poster bed. The painting of the seashore that she'd always loved was the most whimsical keepsake they owned that had been left by her mother, a woman whose childhood along the coastline of Maine had given her a love for the ocean. What she could no longer be surrounded by in the South, she'd taught herself to paint.

Maggie reached up and tenderly dismounted the special painting. Behind it was a tumbler. In her memory was the combination that had resided there for, it seemed, a lifetime.

Inside the safe, she found a manila packet the size of a legal pad. She opened the flap and reached inside.

The first sheet of paper she pulled out was a letter. Its salutation read, "My love," and it was dated the fall of 1958. It was signed, Mary Larson. Maggie scanned the page, touched that every word her mother had written before she'd become Paul Thomas's bride exuded the affection whose memory still sustained him nearly thirty years after her death.

She reached inside the envelope again and tugged out the other papers that had been stuffed inside. She found love letter after love letter, each resting beneath its mate. For every letter her mother had written, Paul Thomas had responded in kind. Maggie sank down to the bed and read each one.

Nearly an hour passed before she put down the last letter. The writer of these essays was no killer, on that she'd swear her life. A tear splashed the back of her hand, and it startled her because she hadn't even known she'd been crying.

Carefully, she inserted the letters back inside the

envelope and put the envelope back where it belonged, at rest.

Further back in the safe, Maggie's hands touched something else. It felt like a cloth-covered board. She pulled it out. It was a diploma, her father's from the Southern university where he'd earned his political science degree so many years ago.

Maggie opened it and read the academic words. She was about to close it and put it back when the corner of something stuffed between the backing and the diploma caught her eye. She worked it out with her nail until she could see what it was she had discovered.

The photograph appeared in the faint sepia tones so common to images of nearly forty years ago. There were four subjects in the photo, and as she mentally peeled away the layers of time and did the necessary adjustments, her heart started to pound.

Four fraternity brothers. Four college graduates. Four young black men whose futures would later be measured by prestige and accolade. Four bosom friends whose lifelong alliance would be cut short only after one of them was critically injured and two were brutally murdered.

Paul Thomas. Jeff Marrs. Sam Peters. And one other.

As of this morning, she knew the name of that fourth. Blake Manderly. If her caller was telling the truth, Blake Manderly was to be the next victim of the other men's killer.

She'd wondered if Blake Manderly had even been associated with the other two men in her father's life, or if he was just a taunter's unrelated lie. Now she knew. She had to tell Gil.

Maggie shoved the diploma back inside the safe, shut the door, and relocked it. After the picture was rehung, she hurried from her father's house.

* * *

"Maggie, slow down." Gil tucked the phone between his ear and shoulder, and grabbed a pen. "Tell me again."

"The fourth man in the picture is Blake Manderly. He's an aspiring politician running for city county council, and the caller this morning gave me his name."

"As another victim?"

"Yes. Maybe. Gil, I don't *know*."

"Then, take your time, honey, try to tell me."

Adam moved closer to his partner to read the pad over his shoulder and to listen.

"The caller was a woman, Gil. She was still trying to disguise her voice, but she wasn't as successful as the first time when she called at my office."

Gil thought about that and filed it away. "What did she say?"

"She said, 'The others didn't have to die, but since they're dead, I can't let another one die. Stay away from Blake Manderly, or you'll be next.' "

"And that's when she hung up?"

"Yes."

"Now, one last thing. Did the woman at any time during the conversation mention other specifics? Names? Dates? Locations?" Gil paused, thinking. "Could you hear any discernible background noises, cars, a television, other people, a child? Anything?"

"No. I'm sorry, no."

"That's all right, Maggie, you've done fine." Gil looked at his watch. "I'm going to meet you in your office in about thirty minutes. I want to take a look at that picture myself."

"Good."

"All right. I'll see you soon." Gil hung up.

"She has something that moves our victims closer to the Parsons angle?" Adam asked.

"We can't be sure until somebody, maybe Willis Houser, gets a chance to take a look at the photograph."

"Why Houser? By his own account, he got his story secondhand. He wasn't there."

"By his own account, he's damned himself in my eyes. Few octogenarians' recollections would be that clear if they were based on hearsay. And even if they are, I think it would be awfully hard to muster emotion as strong as the outrage I saw banked in that old man's eyes while he talked."

"So you'll get the photo from Maggie—?"

"And overnight it to Houser. Either he'll recognize the men, or he won't. I don't want to take the time to go down there again."

"And leave Maggie alone?"

Gil looked at him. "That's right."

"I'd still like to make it to the prison before the end of this afternoon. Do you think you'll be able to go?"

Gil clicked his tongue. "I don't know. I'll call from Maggie's office by one. If not, go on without me."

"Okay. Gil?"

Gil looked back over his shoulder, his hand propped against the open door.

"What I've been saying about Maggie . . . oh, hell. Maybe love can be forever."

For the first time, Gil allowed himself to think of committing beyond the noncommittal. "I'll count on it, man."

"Mr. Houser—Will—I'd like you to do something for me." Gil pulled Maggie's phone cord closer to him and leaned back in her desk chair. "There's a photograph I want you to ID, if you will . . ." Gil explained to the reporter that he had the picture of four men, who, because of the photograph's age, he couldn't identify. He thought it might be related to the Parsons case and asked Houser to please get right on the identification if Gil overnighted the picture.

"I'll do it," Houser said after a pause. "Send it on."

"Thanks. I appreciate it."

"Hell, boy, I ain't altruistic; I'm just damned curious."

Whatever, Gil thought. "Thanks, again."

Maggie had been watching Gil from across the room. "He'll do it?"

"He will."

"That's good."

Gil knew that she had to have mixed feelings, but there was absolutely nothing he could say to comfort her. Whatever the truth turned out to be was something they couldn't change. They would simply have to deal with it once they knew the full story.

At the conference table where she stood, Maggie took another look at the photograph. Each man had his arms slung around the shoulders of his fraternity brothers. There was so much hope in their faces, so much youth, so much joy. Had it all come to nothing? Might this whole situation turn out favorable yet? She picked up a manila folder and laid the photo inside.

Gil contemplated the folder over her shoulder, then he reached for her and pulled her into his arms. As she raised her hands to his shoulders and clung to him, Gil rested his chin on her forehead. He stared sightlessly out at the panorama beyond her window.

A thousand memories of Paul Thomas, of his daughter, of all the happiness, purpose, and ultimately pain they had brought to his life crossed his mind. Would this final chapter they were going to have to play out be the most painful of all?

He sighed. "I'll be back for you by six, okay?"

Maggie nodded, knowing she'd only get through this by trying harder to be strong. "I'll be waiting."

Chapter 19

The doorbell broke Maggie and Gil's preoccupation. They looked at each other across her dinner table, then in the direction of the door. It was a little after nine. Maggie scooted back her chair.

"Wait," Gil said, getting up with her. "Let me get it."

Maggie followed him to the door.

"Who is it," Gill demanded.

"Me, Adam."

Gil opened the door, and Maggie's heart stopped jumping.

Adam walked inside. "We got lucky on Parsons."

"What did we get?" Gil started walking back to the kitchen, leaving Maggie and Adam to follow.

"For the first five years Charlie Denning was in prison, he had only one regular visitor."

"Owen Parsons," Maggie said.

"Yeah."

Gil said, "Is there anybody around who might remember those visits, anybody who's willing to talk, whose incarceration dates back that far?"

"The warden says there's one guy who could fit the bill. He started serving time just a little over a year after Denning went in."

"So, I guess the suspense is just going to continue."

Maggie carried her plate and Gil's to the sink and started rinsing.

Gil caught Adam's look behind Maggie's back and shrugged. Adam cleared his throat. "Ms. Thomas, I had another reason for coming over here."

Maggie turned, waiting.

"About the way I behaved the last time I was here, and my attitude, I'd like to apologize."

"Why?"

"I just didn't need to be so tough. That's all."

"Well, thanks then, I guess."

Adam fiddled with a saltshaker.

"Look," Maggie said, "since you've made the trip over, the least I can do is offer you some dinner. Have you had any?"

"Not yet. I'd sure appreciate it."

Maggie smiled a little. "Call me Maggie, or I won't give you a bite."

"Thanks, Maggie."

She turned back to the stove and reached inside the overhead cabinet to pull down a fresh plate. "Has anything been done to warn Blake Manderly?"

Gil answered. "We haven't been able to find him."

Maggie turned, the apprehension in her eyes clear.

"No, that's not what I mean," Gil clarified, understanding her consternation. "He's taken off for a vacation somewhere in the wilds of the Smoky Mountains, according to his secretary. I wouldn't worry overmuch. If we can't find him, odds are small that anyone else looking for him will, either."

"Someone's looking, Gil, mark my words."

"At any rate, he's due back in two days." Adam added a thanks as he dug into the plate of stew and biscuits Maggie set in front of him.

Maggie took her seat. "You're welcome." She reached across the table for a napkin, put it down again. "What if . . . what if in spite of everything you try to do, Manderly still dies?"

"And there's nobody left to round out this killer's roster except your father and you?" Gil read into her hesitation. "Maggie, listen to me." He made an effort to keep his voice soothing, his reassurance clear. Still, Maggie was very solemn when she looked up.

Gil waited until he was sure he had her complete attention. "Your father has around-the-clock surveillance. Neither I nor Adam are going to let anyone get to either of you. And nobody," he stressed, "is going to get to you in your own home while I'm here.

"As for Manderly, Willis Houser will have that photo in his hands tomorrow. If those men in the picture are the ones connected to Parsons, we'll know better how to move in order to intervene with Manderly."

"Especially, if the guy we talk to at the prison comes through for us," Adam added.

Maggie knew she'd have to be content with that. Her fingers touched the napkin again. She folded it distractedly while Adam ate his meal and Gil sat quietly, obviously deep in thought.

"Well"—Adam pushed away from the table—"Gil, let's leave around eight o'clock in the morning."

"Sure."

"Maggie, thanks again."

"I'll walk you to the door." Maggie started to get up.

"No need," Adam stopped her with a raised hand. "I know it's hard to not let all of this get to you, but the situation is just like Gil says."

"I'm trying to have faith in that, Adam."

He nodded. "Right."

As it turned out, Gil walked Adam to the door and Maggie sat where she was, watching the men, wondering what Gil quietly said to Adam just before Adam left. Gil locked the door and came back to the table and touched her cheek, then he went over to the sink for some water. Apparently, he wasn't going to tell her.

Later that night as Gil was sleeping and Maggie lay wrapped in his arms envious of the seeming ease with which he slept, she desperately wished for time with her father. Not since she'd been a very young girl had she needed his comfort and reassurance like she needed it now.

The frightening part of that need was the deeper fear that she would never be able to experience those feelings again, not in the same way.

Gil's arms tightened around her, even in sleep. Though Maggie took comfort from the involuntary way he pulled her near, she still found herself pondering the nature of that comfort.

Even in their best days, she and Gil had never fully come together with the equality she felt they were according one another now. They'd loved hard, and they'd been friends. But they'd also been children in so many ways, needing to taste the realities of life, needing to learn how the experience could force them to grow.

She twined her legs with Gil's, wanting more of his warmth on this night in particular when she felt so chilled. Were they loving each other now?

After traveling such hard roads, first the one that had driven them from each other, then the one that had kept them apart, were they really finding a way to make long-lasting repairs?

The question lingered, then grew hazy for Maggie as sleep finally drew near. Her last conscious thought was that with all her heart she hoped they'd survive this crisis to find the answers. She'd lost so much in her life, she desperately wanted the second chance to keep what was becoming for her supremely dear.

The first thing that struck Gil about Ned Clausson as he shuffled into the prison interview room was that Clausson still looked weak. His second was that beyond the debilitating effects of his recent illness, Ned Clausson had been soul weary for years. It was evident in his eyes, which didn't flicker, as he sat down at the table, in the bored expression unchanged by even the merest curiosity about these strangers—these cops—who had come to visit him.

Ned Clausson was living just another changeless day in the thirty-fifth year of an incarceration that was set to go on forever. Perhaps, Gil thought, Clausson had simply discovered that the easiest way to accept that harsh judgment was to school himself not to care.

Gil held out his hand. "Mr. Clausson, thanks for agreeing to meet with us."

Clausson looked at Gil's hand. With little show of interest and slightly less animation, he reached out and took it.

"You want to know about Charlie Denning," Clausson stated.

"Whatever you can tell us," Adam replied.

Clausson looked at his thumbnail. "He was a mean son of a bitch. He was funny, though. Helped make the time go by."

"What made him mean?" Gil casually hooked an arm behind his chair.

"The good Lord, I reckon. What makes any of us turn out mean or good?"

Gil thought about it. "Maybe you have a point. Specifically, though, we want to ask you what you remember about the time during which Charlie was your cell mate. Four years is plenty of time to have discussed special acquaintances, family, visitors, whatever."

"Who are you interested in in particular?"

Adam said, "A man named Owen Parsons."

Clausson rocked his chair onto its back legs. "Parsons," he repeated. "I don't know about no Owen. Only person Charlie used to act like he gave two shits about was his half brother, Dewy. Seems to me Dewy's last name was Parsons."

Gil sat very still while realization dawned. That's why that news photo in Denning's shack had fascinated him. Denning's resemblance to his half brother had been evident. They'd have to confirm, do some record checking, of course, but he already knew the connection Clausson had revealed was true.

"What did Charlie tell you about his brother?" Adam picked up the conversation.

"Not a lot, until after he'd been murdered. When Charlie saw the article in the paper, all he could talk about was how he had to get out of here so that he could get him some justice."

Gil said, "You mean revenge."

"I just said that, didn't I?"

Gil smiled a bit. "What kind of revenge?"

Clausson shrugged. "Whatever it took to settle the score."

"Did he have any ideas about who it could have been?" Adam folded his hands on the table.

"Niggers."

"Why?"

"Because with Charlie it was always niggers." He only glanced at Gil then shrugged. "Nigger this, nigger that, the man was obsessed."

Adam qualified, "A racist."

"Card carrying, until he got religion."

Gil raised a brow. "Religion?"

"Yeah. Some jacklegged preacher got to talkin' at him one day after everybody else had lost the patience to listen. Started telling Charlie how it was time to mend his ways, get rid of his hate, start lovin' his brothers"—for the first time, Clausson laughed—"and how that was supposed to mean his black brethren, too. That really bit old Charlie's ass."

"But then he started to believe? What caused the epiphany?" Gil watched the laughter die out of Clausson, the dull scrim of boredom settle back over his waxy features.

"He got superstitious after his brother died. I could never figure it, but Charlie really started to believe that his time was near, too. I guess that's why he gave that old preachin' fool the time of day. Whatever, Charlie started to readin' and quotin' the bible like he was gonna get taken any minute."

"Sounds like you two were pretty close," Adam observed. "But you lost touch after he got out, isn't that so?"

Again, Clausson shrugged. "Wasn't that close, what've been the point of his keeping in touch? Prison memories are something you want to get rid of when you get out, not hold onto. Besides, there was the other thing."

Gil watched him, waiting.

"Charlie wouldn't want to have nothing more to do with the likes of me or anyone like me once he got on the outside. There wouldn't be any fun in it, any sport." Clausson rocked forward, thumping his chair back on all fours.

"What kind of sport?" Adam said.

"Charlie was queer."

That one surprised Gil. "How do you know?"

Clausson gave Gil a look that told him to get real. "In here, you know. I mean, there's some guys that's just lonely, and a lonely man'll do a whole lot of things he didn't think he would've just to push that feeling away. But then there's others in here who like it.

"There was this young guy, a boy really, who came in not too long before Charlie and me stopped sharing a cell. The boy talked tough, but I could see he was scared. And he was weak. I knew right off it was just a matter of time before he got tagged.

"Charlie just laughed when I talked with him about the kid. Started sayin' how if the boy couldn't defend himself, he deserved what he got, just like all the other faggots who was goin' to hell. Then, one day, I was doin' my laundry detail. I was in the laundry room sortin' clothes, and I heard him, that young boy over in the corner. He screamed a little once, then he just whimpered. I started over but heard some more things that told me he wasn't alone. I went back to what I was doin'."

Adam said, "You knew that boy was being raped, and you just let it happen?"

"I have to live in here."

"So how is Charlie connected to all this?" Gil asked.

"By the time the noises finally stopped, I was haulin' a pile of clothes into a bin. I was turned for just a second over toward that corner, but I was able to see two men walkin' away. I was turnin' back when I saw a third."

"Denning," Gil guessed.

"Yeah." I met his eyes for a second. He smiled, and there was something wild and crazy in that smile. He'd liked it. I could tell that he knew that I could see that he liked it. And I could tell the knowin' turned him on more.

"That night in the cell, he didn't say much and I didn't say much, either. He just laid back on his bed with his legs crossed and that shit-eatin' smile. We quit bein' cell mates not long after that."

Gil knew prison rape was common, but that awareness still didn't lessen his disgust. "So you had no more significant contact with him from basically that point on until after he got out?"

"Yeah, that's right. But I guess his premonition came true after all, didn't it?"

Adam leaned forward. "How's that?"

"Nigger did kill him, I mean accordin' to the papers and all. That Paul Thomas must have slapped ole' Charlie down pretty quick because accordin' to Charlie all he was livin' for was his chance to get Thomas."

Gil stood and Adam did the same. Gil said, "Thanks."

Clausson just nodded and started rocking his chair again. "Hey, Lieutenant," he called softly when Gil was at the door, ready to signal the guard to open up.

Gil turned. "Yeah?"

"It's just come to me. You're the one involved in that trouble with Thomas a few years ago. You gonna really have the balls to go after the old man if your search for Charlie's killer tells you he's the one?"

Gil turned away and wrapped hard on the room's metal door.

For the second time, Ned Clausson laughed.

* * *

On the drive back, Gil could feel Adam's eyes on him, waiting for him to make the next move. Gil said, "It seems that maybe we're looking for some answers that lay in unlikely places. We've been thinking of Denning as the lonely guy, no family, no friends to connect with on the outside. If Clausson's to be believed, and I think he is, maybe we've just been looking for the wrong kinds of friends."

Adam said, "There's an area not too far from where Denning was renting. Could be a joint or two there where somebody might have seen him, remembered something, have some input."

Gil nodded. "We'll check it out. First, I want to see how Houser's possible ID panned out."

When they arrived at the station, they didn't have to wait long.

The secretary handed Gil a pink message slip. "He said to give him a call whenever you got in."

"Thanks," Gil glanced at the slip and turned away to head for his desk. He punched in Houser's home phone and had only to wait for two rings.

"Will, Gil Stewart."

"Lieutenant. A question first. Why did you want to send this photo to me?"

"I figured your recollections were a little vivid for a third-party bystander. Was I wrong?"

Willis Houser took a while to answer. When he did, he said briefly. "No, you weren't."

"Why didn't you tell us while we were there?" Gil ignored Adam's questioning frown at "us."

"For very good reasons, I thought. I still wasn't sure I wanted to get involved. When you called me about that story, it threw me. It was all so long ago, I guess I've spent a lot of years trying to forget it. Now you bring it all back up, and I just . . . well, then you called about this photo and I knew I didn't have a choice about being involved anymore. I am involved."

"So, are the men in that photo men you recognize?"

Houser sighed. "I look at those men, Lieutenant, and I see babies. Unfortunately, the answer to your question is yes. I recognize them. The four men in your photograph are the men who stopped in that diner."

Gil felt no professional elation. In another way, though, he was relieved a critical question had been resolved. Even so, the answer he had just found didn't explain everything. Whether it went further and connected to the bigger Denning question was one that still needed to be answered.

"Thanks, Willis."

"It only proves they were here, Lieutenant. On its face, it doesn't prove one thing more."

"I'll be in touch," Gil said, and hung up.

"We?" Adam wondered. He perched a hip on Gil's desk.

"We," Gil gave Adam a level look. "Don't give me any shit about it now. Houser's answer was yes, which means we have the possibility of a motive. But we still don't necessarily have the proof that would conclusively support Paul Thomas as a suspect."

Adam swung a leg back and forth, looking around idly. "Aren't you stretching just a bit, Gil? You just said it yourself, we have motive."

"No, we have the possibility of a motive. In order to determine if the implications of that motive are probable, we need more. We need to find that concrete link between Denning and Thomas."

"We need that document Denning wrote."

"But since we don't have it, we'll never get what we need by throwing wishes into the air. I want to find

Denning's post-prison hidey-hole. Chances are it's burrowed somewhere around his shack."

Adam got off the desk. "You wanna look now?"

"Yeah, the sooner the better. If my memory of that neighborhood serves, there are a couple of bars nearby I know of."

"Your memory's solid, man. Let's go."

Chapter 20

Maggie hesitated outside her father's room. In the last few days, his condition had been updated from serious to stable. Lai had ordered physical therapy to begin. Maggie was waiting for the therapist to finish today's session.

"How's it going?" she asked him when he walked out.

"Very well, Maggie. His hands have good tone, his leg muscles are responding well. I'm done, so you can go in."

"Thanks."

Inside, Maggie pulled a chair up to the bed and sat down. With one hand she absently fiddled with the strap of her purse. She wrapped her other hand lightly around the bed's protective railing. To her own surprise, she felt tears well in her eyes. She dropped her head to the cool metal under her fingers when they overflowed.

"Oh, Daddy," she whispered, wishing he could hear, wishing he could reassure her she had no reason for the fear she felt.

"I didn't let you down," she told him. "I'm just not like you. I don't thrive in public confrontations and the kind of celebrity you've embraced all your life."

Maggie reached over the rail and grasped his still hand, intertwining her fingers with his. "I'm fighting, Daddy, in my own way. I understand the struggle goes on, but I can't be the public activist you are. I just wish you could understand that I get the job done as well as you in my own quiet way."

"He understands, Maggie."

Maggie jumped a little at the sound of Sloan Michaels's voice behind her. She raised her head, but didn't turn around.

"In the way of men who are old and more than a little set in their ways, he just finds it hard to tell you so," Sloan said.

Now Maggie turned, certain that she had herself sufficiently under control. "I didn't hear you come in."

"Sorry if I frightened you. I always visit Paul about this time during the day."

Maggie let go of her father's hand and folded hers around her purse. "None of the nurses mentioned it to me."

Sloan shrugged. "They probably thought you already knew. How is he today?" He walked closer to the bed.

"Same as yesterday. Same as the day before that. A little better with no indications that the progress is going to reverse."

Sloan gripped the railing and looked down. "Good." He turned a bit so that he could cross his ankles while he leaned back against the bed. "And what about you? How are you holding up?"

Maggie made a dismissive movement, letting him know that the question wasn't important. "I'm holding up fine. How's the campaign going?"

"His support is out there, and it's solid. No more hate mail, I'm happy to say. In fact, the letters and financial pledges we've been getting at headquarters show overwhelming support and hope for his recovery."

"That must make you very happy." Maggie's attention settled back on her father.

Sloan frowned. "I'm not sure I liked the sound of that."

"What?" Maggie asked absently.

"I sensed a less than charitable attitude in your voice."

Maggie looked at him sharply as she realized that her dislike for him had unintentionally sharpened the words she'd let slip out. "I'm just a little stressed, Sloan, don't pay any attention to me."

"No, Maggie, I'd like to get this out in the open." He paused, apparently choosing his words with care. "I've sensed, almost from the beginning when your father hired me, that you don't like me."

Maggie kept her eyes on her father.

"Am I wrong?"

"No, Sloan," Maggie said, deciding to be honest. "But it's not really dislike. I guess I'm just a bit taken aback by your—aggressiveness. Your campaign style always seemed a little abrasive to me."

"And now?"

Maggie watched Sloan, realizing he was perfectly sincere and more than a little curious. "Three years have passed and you've more than proven your professional worthiness. You've justified Daddy's faith in you twice over. I guess that's all that counts in the end."

Sloan said slowly, "But you still don't like me. Personally, I mean, not as your father's campaign manager." He unfolded his ankles and moved a little closer to her. "I've always liked you, Maggie."

Now it was Maggie who didn't like Sloan's tone. She looked up at him, holding his gaze squarely, wanting him to clearly understand. "Yes, I think I've probably always sensed that. It's the nature of the 'like' I've always questioned."

Sloan's eyes skimmed over her, lingering over the neat bodice of the navy suit she wore, over its short skirt that tastefully hugged her slim thighs, over the long, smooth, silk-encased expanse of her legs. He murmured, "Just say the word, Maggie, and I'll be happy to show you."

Maggie was aware of her father's slumbering presence right beside them more keenly than ever. She kept her eyes level with Sloan's, her distaste for him acute. "I don't think your wife would approve."

Sloan's eyes shuttered and with an almost imperceptible stiffness, he backed away. "I've intruded." He made a point of looking at his watch. "I'll leave you with Paul."

"I'd appreciate that."

He inclined his head and gave Thomas a parting glance. His words were directed at Maggie. "I'll see you later."

Maggie watched Sloan leave, reassured that her instinct hadn't been rooted in fanciful overdrive. Sloan Michaels was a hell of a campaign manager, but he was a man who, on a personal level, she wanted to steer clear of.

As Sloan Michaels accelerated out of the hospital parking lot, the one who watched him coolly debated. The time to act, he decided, had arrived.

Gil cut the engine in the tiny lot of The Bar. He gave the sagging establishment a once-over and looked at Adam. Adam was giving the place, the second one they'd visited, the same.

"The ambiance is certainly right," Gil commented as

they made their way to the black, security-screened door. "Let's hope this one pans out."

Adam opened the door, stepped inside the dark interior, and felt Gil walk in behind him. "So is the clientele."

Gil took a look around, noticed the looks were returned, and also noticed that the longest looks lingered on him. He thought he could understand why, taking in the abundance of pale faces and of Johnny Reb memorabilia that decorated the bar and walls.

Gil raised his brow at Adam's rueful look. They spotted some empty stools at the end of the bar, walked over, and perched and waited.

"Help you?" The bartender looked at Adam.

"Maybe. Two," Adam ordered. He pulled out a prison mug shot of Denning while their drinks were being fetched. He held the photo up where the bartender could get a good look at it while he set down their beers. "Ever seen him around here?"

The bartender squinted, then slapped his damp dish towel down on the surface of the bar. Methodically, he started to wipe. "Who wants to know?"

Gil reached inside his suit jacket and pulled out his badge. He flashed it and tasted the minor satisfaction of watching the bartender do a double take.

The man recovered. "It could cost you."

"So that's a yes?" Gil asked.

"I said it'll cost you." The bartender's tone informed Gil the penny he had prepared to throw him was going to have to be upped to a dime or two. Gil pulled out some change.

Adam watched the twenty hit the bar's surface with some surprise. From the corner of his eye, he gauged his partner. While the bartender scooped up the money with a faint smile, Gil's expression didn't change. The hard resignation in his eyes, however, could have sparked flint.

"I might have seen him," the bartender said. "Come in here, a few weeks ago. Hung around a few nights just drinking beer, and then one night after that the routine changed."

"Changed how?" Adam asked.

"He met his buddy. Young guy, well he was younger than Denning, which could have made him a youngster even if he was closer to thirty than twenty."

"Was he?" Gil picked up his beer.

"What?"

"Closer to thirty than twenty?"

"I'd say so, though with that long hair of his and the biker's build, it was hard to tell."

"So he was a biker, then?" Adam waited for the bartender's response, realized the man had deliberately wound down, and pulled out another bill.

The bartender scooped it up. "Don't think so. He never rode in or hung around with the others I knew for sure were bikers who could have been his buddies. Besides, he had the look."

"What's the look?" Gil took a token pull from his beer, then set the bottle back down.

"Hustler. Older college kid maybe, or some rich dude slumming for kicks. Denning zeroed in on him right away. By the third night the guy showed up, Denning was sitting at his table like he was a regular, and I could tell the two of them were getting tight."

"So this guy was deliberately letting Denning pick him up," Gil said.

"Looked that way. Beats the hell out of me as to why. Denning didn't look like he had nothing on him that could do anything for the kid. And if the kid was looking for money, Denning didn't look like he had any of that to spare, either."

"But they hung tight," Adam said.

"Yep. Right up until the night they walked out of here together." The bartender shook his head, flipped over the dingy towel, and continued to wipe.

"Can you describe him?" Gil asked. At the bartender's look, he elaborated, "The kid."

The bartender flipped the rag over his shoulder and shrugged. "I guess. He was either late twenties or early thirties, about six foot. Longish blond hair he had tied back with a thong, and I guess he was good-looking in that soft, sissy kind of way."

"And you never noticed him coming in here before Denning started coming in?"

"No. Around here, he would have stood out."

No doubt, Gil silently concurred. "He still come around?"

"Sometimes."

"He ever leave with anyone else."

"Once. The guy was a regular and younger than Denning. Never talked much and he ain't been back since."

"What's the kid's favorite time?" Adam finished his beer.

"Late. After eight or nine or so."

"If we were to ask you, could you definitively point him out?"

The bartender looked calculating.

"Yeah, for a fee," Adam said.

The bartender nodded. "Probably. You thinking the kid did him?" His smile was snide, as if he'd just realized the irony in his choice of words. "*Killed* him, I mean."

Gil ignored the question. "Any night we might get luckier on than the next?"

"Thursdays or Fridays," the bartender said, thinking about it. "If he pops up, it usually seems to be then."

Gil got down from his stool. Adam followed. Gil said, "See you around."

The bartender went back to wiping down his bar.

Inside the car, Adam cut Gil an eyelash flutter and a smile. "So, Thursday's tomorrow, partner. Is it a date?"

"Eat shit, man," Gil replied. His own smile was faint. "Yeah, it's a date."

Gil could tell as soon as Maggie opened his car door that she'd had a bad day. He took her hand and tucked it beneath his on the seat between them.

"Tell me about it?" he invited.

Maggie shrugged.

Gil let it ride. They'd be home soon enough.

Maggie kicked her shoes off as soon as they were inside the door. "I'm going for the shower. There are some leftovers in the fridge."

Gil took in the stiff way she rubbed her back before she disappeared out of sight. He shrugged out of his jacket and hung it in the front closet, then he went to the kitchen and put some coffee on. There was some pot roast in the refrigerator. He sliced it cold and arranged it on a plate. He also added tomatoes, celery, the remains of some potato salad, and a few rolls that he warmed in the oven.

Maggie took in the impromptu meal arranged on the kitchen table and was touched. In the short time she'd had to get to know Gil again, she'd found that while he was fully self-sufficient around a house, he hadn't quite reached the stage of domesticity. This simple meal would have taken some effort.

"Go ahead and eat." Gil stood behind her and closed his hands on her shoulders. "I'll be out in a minute."

Maggie closed her hands on his and squeezed them lightly, then he was gone.

She was still thinking about her visit with her father, the reconciliation she'd initiated in the face of his silence, when she became aware of the fact that Gil had seated himself across from her.

"What's wrong, Maggie?" Gil folded his hands on the table and delayed his own meal, waiting for her to speak.

"I went to see Daddy. I couldn't get the photo, Blundon, Denning, everything out of my mind. That's all."

And now he had to tell her something, unsubstantiated though it was, that was going to make all of that even worse. He served himself some food, deciding that two or ten minutes from now wasn't going to make much difference given her already down state of mind.

Maggie sat with Gil while he finished his meal. Even though they didn't talk, she took a measure of comfort from just being close to him. When he pushed his plate aside and got up, holding out a hand to her, she took it.

On the sofa, Gil drew her into his arms. Maggie tucked her feet beneath her and leaned back into his embrace, feeling warmed, comforted.

"Willis Houser called back today, Maggie."

She couldn't help stiffening. "And?"

"The photo is a match with the men he said passed through that diner."

"God."

Her voice was a whisper, and Gil felt helpless when her warm cheek touched his wrist.

"All it proves is that your father and the others were in Blundon the day of Parsons's murder. It doesn't prove they were involved."

Maggie twisted around until she could see Gil over her shoulder. "Can you honestly still believe they're innocent?"

No, he couldn't. But neither, he could have reminded her, did he have any evidence that conclusively linked them to Parsons, and therefor to Denning and his murder. "Adam and I are checking into another lead on Denning. It looks promising, and if it works out, we could very well have another angle on the motive."

"To take the heat off the one that's just presented itself in terms of my father."

Gil pulled her close again. "Yes."

For the longest time, Maggie was quiet, then she said, "Blake Manderly is due back in town tomorrow, right?"

"That's our understanding."

"Will you talk to him immediately?"

"We'll talk to him soon. I want to follow up the Denning thing first."

Again, Maggie lapsed into silence.

Gil wondered what she was thinking, and when she suddenly turned around in his arms, he wondered what she was about. As she pressed her soft lips to his stubbled jaw, he started to guess. And when the insistence of that caress transferred itself to his lips, he understood what was driving her.

Sex wouldn't erase the sadness she was grappling with tonight or tomorrow, he could have told her. But as she twined her arms around his neck, and whispered, "Please," he understood that she already knew that. She wasn't asking for oblivion, she was asking for surcease.

And because he loved her, probably had never stopped loving her, he didn't spoil the moment by talking. He concentrated on giving her what she needed, the comfort and intimacy for which she asked.

Gil turned her again, until she was lying soft and pliant beneath him. He turned the kiss she had initiated into his own, deepening it until her breath was his, until his breath was hers, until the heat and wetness of it made them both tremble.

Her hands moved to the waist of his pajama trousers and beyond until the softness of them became a caress over his naked skin. She shifted her legs to allow him better access, and Gill took advantage. He drew his hand along the silkiness of her chemise-covered breasts and rib cage until it touched the hem where a flash of smooth skin showed through. He edged his hand down farther until he removed her tap pants, and they, like his pajama bottoms, were discarded in the hushed room.

"Oh, Gil, oh, God," Maggie moaned as her flesh started to heat at his touch. His fingers stroked and slowly invaded. Maggie gasped as the intensity of it became too much.

"Gil!" She shuddered, and arched as the world fell away in a warm tide of soothing release.

"I've got you, sweetheart," Gil said against her lips, against her throat, and then he slid deep, deep inside her while she still rode the undulating wave of her pleasure.

When her legs clasped him to her, Gil started to thrust. When she meshed her trembling mouth with his, he deliberately slowed to delay the act. When she whimpered and begged him to move, he slowed even more until each penetration and withdrawal for both became achingly prolonged.

Maggie's body was arching again, seeking desperately the mercy of release when Gil suddenly groaned and grew even harder inside her.

His body started to shudder, and Maggie urged his orgasm by holding him tighter, stroking the backs of his thighs, tangling her warm tongue with his.

At the peak of his desire, Gil tore his mouth away and gasped. For an endless moment, the movements of his body against hers were rough, driven, in a blind search for deliverance. He groaned as his pleasure gripped him at last, leaving him utterly lost in Maggie.

As the fierce throbbing that held Gil captive started to lessen, then relent, Maggie's world grew still again. Gil was murmuring love words to her, stroking her lips with his, lowering the gentling caress to her sensitized breasts. She sank her fingers into his hair and cradled his head against her, sighed as he sighed and felt the dawning peace of the aftermath she'd craved all along.

"I love you," he thought she said, right before she touched his brow and slept. "And I love you," his heart echoed as he followed mere paces behind, at peace in this merging they could at last experience so thoroughly together, body, soul, and mind.

Chapter 21

They knew he was the man they were looking for as soon as he walked inside the bar. Gil settled sideways in the booth to observe the newcomer while Adam took another drink of his beer.

"He's young, all right," Adam noted, watching their target choose a table by the opposite wall.

Gil watched the "kid" pass under a dim bar of light, suspended from the ceiling. "He ain't no kid. Thirty, if he's a day."

"Got a pretty face, too. No wonder Denning went for him."

"Hm," Gil said. In fact, Gil was thinking their man had a decidedly cunning face. He assessed the patrons who were already there, studied two and then a third as they walked in. A fourth, he subtly tilted his beer bottle at, and in no time the man who had been summoned joined him.

Not a kid, Gil thought. In fact, as he watched the two men lean cozily into each other across their table, he decided the bartender's assessment of hustler was probably apt.

"Think they'll go home together?" Adam idly wondered.

"I'll find out. I'm going to follow him while you go

back to the city to stay close to Maggie and home base. I may need you as a fast link."

"Sure you don't want that the other way around?"

"Yeah, I'm sure. If there's anything to find out, I want to discover it myself."

Adam eyed Gil, then turned back to his beer.

Gil felt the censure behind the look. "Listen, man, I'm not pulling rank. It's just . . . you know the stake I've got in this. I want to be on the scene if anything serious goes down fast."

"Just like Maggie wanted to be on the scene in case Willis Houser had something relevant to offer?"

Gil's gaze didn't shift from their quarry. "Yes, just like that."

"Jesus, Gil, I hope you can stay as objective about this thing as you need to."

That brought Gil's head around.

Adam finished his beer. "I just feel like something very bad is going to happen, and when it does, I don't want to see you take it in the rear."

That made Gil smile. "Colorful choice of words, considering where we are."

Adam chuckled in spite of himself and signaled for another beer. "I'm serious, man. So"—he gestured at the table across the room when the bartender brought his drink over—"that him?"

"That's him."

Adam slipped the man a bill, then huddled over his drink, dismissing him.

"Good thing we got lucky in one night," Gil commented. "That character could make this annoyingly expensive."

Adam shrugged.

Gil sensed Adam's impatience with his diversion. "Look, man, everything's under control. Stop worrying about it."

Ten minutes later when their quarry made a move, Gil noted with interest that he wasn't alone. The table-mate followed his young companion, who paid their bill. They headed for the door together.

"If I'm going to follow, it's now or never," Gil observed.

Adam pushed himself up. "Let's go."

They lingered at the doorway, and Gil surreptitiously peered through the door's dirty mesh window. The hustler climbed inside a sporty little car and his companion got behind the conservative wheel of another. Gil touched Adam's arm. They were out of the door and at their own cars by the time the sports car and its tail pulled onto the road.

Gil allowed the two men time to open up a respectable distance. While the distance was still controllable, Gil pulled out behind them. Adam, he saw through his rearview, turned the other way.

Gil followed the lead car for about five miles before it turned down a heavily shaded road. Gil could just make out a street sign in the dark. He recognized the area as a pricey one that was close to a lake. He was unfamiliar with the specific blacktopped street they traveled on, however.

He and the cars ahead of him were so isolated that Gil had to cut his lights and hope he didn't drive into a swamp before they reached their destination. Fortunately, the ride wasn't long. They ended up at the lushly treed property of a country cabin.

Gil let the two cars pull onto the property's circular driveway and cut their engines before he cut his own several yards away. He had the cover of a low-branched pine, and pulled a pair of powerful binoculars from under his seat.

Definitely, a hustler, Gil saw, training his glasses on the cars. The young man met his companion by the front walkway and pulled him into a very heated embrace. When the men moved apart, they were still holding hands. The grip didn't break even as the hustler reached inside his shirt pocket for a key to unlock the door.

Gil lowered his binoculars after they were inside. He checked the illuminated dial on his watch. Eleven o'clock. He got as comfortable as he could by bracing his back against his door and putting his feet up on the seat. His guess was that he was in for an all-nighter. It wouldn't be the first time, and when the sun came up, he'd be curious to discover the next stage of the game.

Gil slept fitfully. Three times, he found himself jerking awake. Each time, the prey's car sat right where he'd parked it. The fourth time Gil roused, he saw the dullness of the vigil changing. The sun was coming up, and some action was happening at the door. He grabbed his binoculars.

The mark was walking out of the door, and he was alone. He got inside his car and drove away from the end of the drive opposite from where Gil was parked. Gil trained his binoculars back on the door and saw nothing more.

He raised them to a second-story window he'd not been able to make out last night. A curtain moved. Gil got a glimpse of the hustler, clad in a low-slung pair of jeans. He was watching the car Gil had just observed drive off to into the sunrise. Moments after it was gone, the hustler stayed at the window, a study in contemplation who thought himself completely alone. The curtain dropped.

Short minutes later, the front door opened and the hustler walked out clad in running shorts, T-shirt, and tennis shoes. He raised his face to the sun briefly, then he set off down the drive away from Gil, his legs setting a strong, measured pace.

Sucker sure could run.

I'll be damned, Gil thought, reconsidering his dismissal of Buster.

The sports car was parked. The cabin was sitting in the middle of nowhere. The hustler would be back, Gil knew. He relaxed and picked up his cellular phone.

"Carter," Adam answered sleepily.

"Rise and shine. I need a favor."

"What?"

"Run a check on this address." Gil recited the cabin's location.

"Got it." Adam hung up. Gil shifted, trying to get more comfortable than he'd been last night.

An hour later, the runner jogged back into sight. Gil watched him unlock the front door, barely looking winded, and push his way inside. The next time he came out, he was wearing jeans, canvas shoes, and a white polo shirt. Over his arm, he'd draped a white jacket.

After the man climbed inside his car, Gil unfolded himself and prepared to follow. The hustler drove off in the same direction he'd taken for his run. Gil took his time, knowing he wouldn't lose him on this secluded outgoing road.

When Gil got to the end of the blacktop drive, he spotted the sports car about a half mile down the cross street that bisected the road he was on. Gil turned to follow. His cellular beeped.

"Meet me, man," Adam said without preliminaries.

"I'm a little busy just now."

"Do it anyway."

Gil watched the car ahead of him. He knew where the hustler lived. "I'm a few blocks from that coffee shop we discovered last week. Can you get here in ten minutes?"

"I'll be there."

He was there when Gil pulled into the shop's lot.

Adam said nothing, but his look promised much as he led Gil inside. They were seated and handed menus before Gil said, "Tell me, man."

"That property you called about? It's leased to a Joseph O'Connor, ex-con, convicted drug dealer, and all-purpose unsavory guy."

"How unsavory?" Gil accepted his coffee from their waitress and listened to Adam speak once he took a long, hot sip of his own.

"While he was a juvie, he was busted four times for criminal assault, twice for prostitution. He did some rocky time in two halfway houses and a foster home before the system gave up on him and sent him on his way.

"On his own, he started in with the drugs, selling and using. His sometimes clientele is what warrants special attention."

Gil drank some more of his coffee. "You're killing me."

"Doctors, lawyers. Politicians." Adam held Gil's eyes. "Political aides." Calmly, he took another sip from his cup then set it down.

"Son of a bitch."

Adam held up a hand. "While I was doing my checking, I got a line on an old cop buddy of mine who's originally from the West Coast. He told me a story. Seems there was one personage in particular who helped Joe O'Connor earn his fifteen minutes of fame in their California hometown."

"Go on," Gil urged.

"He was a bright young man who ran for congress sixteen years ago. He won his House seat and served a successful term. He was closing in on a reelection when a case of very bad judgment fouled him up."

Gil was impatient for the point, but the course of Adam's tale held him intrigued.

"On the eve of the reelection, the congressman and his wife were attending what was already being regarded by political insiders as a victory celebration. About an hour before the polls closed and the official victory count everyone anticipated came in, the wife went looking for her absent husband. Sometime before, she later said, he'd quietly disappeared from the heart of the party action.

"The congressman's wife was on her way to a lounge that had been assigned to her husband that night for his personal use. The story goes that before she reached the lounge, she was drawn to a nearby restroom by curious noises. When she peeked inside, she got the surprise of her life.

"Her hubby was locked in what my buddy tastefully phrased as an amorous huddle with their trusted chauffeur—"

"Whose name was Joseph O'Connor," Gil guessed.

Adam nodded. "As you can expect, the congressman's wife caused some commotion, enough to bring other spectators rushing to the scene. The situation got worse.

"The congressman claimed he was a victim, that he had been drugged and tricked into the compromising position. The chauffeur argued that the congressman's participation hadn't been coerced.

"When the election results rolled in a short while later, the victory everyone had gathered to celebrate was announced. But after proffering an official explanation of not wanting any media fallout to besmirch the honor of the office he respected, or his effectiveness in serving it, Sloan Michaels resigned twelve hours later."

"What happened to O'Connor?"

"Michaels refused to press charges, claiming that he just wanted the whole unfortunate episode over for everyone, especially his wife. Soon after, Joseph O'Connor disappeared."

"And Michaels?"

Adam smiled cynically. "We're living in the era of *A Current Affair*, where more people are interested in watching the show than in taking the time to get the facts behind a legitimate current affair. Michaels and his wife went underground until the tittering of the local media died down. And as usually happens, a juicier story superseded a local congressman's disgrace. People lost interest.

"When Michaels resurfaced on the East Coast six years later, it was as a very effective behind-the-scenes aide to a high-profile senator who still holds office today. He moved on to other political powerhouses after that. Those alliances did the trick in winning back the professional respectability Michaels enjoys today."

"And his personal life?"

"He and his wife seemed inseparable. Any nasty little whispers from the few who still recalled the O'Connor affair simply lost spark in the face of the apparent heterosexual monogamy that Michaels enjoyed. General consensus became that Michaels, an obvious rising star in the political arena, indeed must have been the victim he claimed to have been.

Gil's smile held little humor. "I'll be damned."

"That's not the best."

"Do tell." Gil was thinking back to the comment Maggie had recently made about Michaels not being able to live with the memory of a failed political career. He should have pressed that comment, should have asked her for what she knew of Michaels's checkered past. But they'd been concentrating on Thomas and what clues his papers could reveal, not on the enigma of Sloan.

"The registered owner of that cabin you followed lover boy to last night?" Adam began.

"Is Sloan Michaels," Gil finished.

"Yes."

Gil dug inside his pants pocket for appropriate change and threw it down on the table. "When your friend was giving all of this juicy information up, did you ask whether or not he could produce some sort of identification of O'Connor? A photo, perhaps?"

Adam checked his watch. "Of course. If we get lucky, his answer should be coming in over the fax at the precinct in less than thirty minutes."

"Where's Michaels this morning?"

"Out of town, according to his secretary. He apparently had some personal time coming and decided at the first of the week to use it today."

"We need to get to the precinct, then."

"Adam, this is just in for you."

The office secretary lowered the phone receiver from her ear and held up a fax. Gil was at Adam's side when his partner snatched it, read, and smiled.

"Well," Gill murmured over Adam's shoulder. "The hair of the photo's subject was much shorter, but it was lover boy."

Adam flipped to a second sheet that had been stapled to the xeroxed news photo. "There's more. He's been mobile, a jack of all trades and apparently master of none. Waiter, cook, retail clerk, med student—"

"Really." Gil got a sudden bad feeling. "Anything more to that last one?"

"Didn't go for the brass ring because he's no doctor. But it does say here that he's been licensed as a general health care provider."

"Shit." Gil's bad feeling suddenly got worse. "Let's go."

Joe O'Connor waved a greeting at two of the nurses who had just come on duty on his floor. They nodded back. One of them smiled at him shyly. The other turned away, not quite able to conceal a giggle.

Silly women, O'Connor thought. Why didn't they just come straight out with what they wanted instead of posturing behind silly flirtations.

Joe had never had problems expressing what he wanted. In fact, it was his need that guided his actions now. It had always been clear to him that despite what Sloan said, Paul Thomas was going to have to die.

Sloan was way too committed to the man. Over the last year, that commitment had become intolerable. Anything that wedged a barrier between himself and Sloan was not to be permitted, but Sloan couldn't see that because he had been mesmerized by the brightness of Paul Thomas's political star.

When Sloan had explained to him why Marrs and Peters had to die, Joe had taken care of it. There were worse things than murder, and Joe had either seen or done them all. Killing for love this time was a novel experience for him.

Before the killings of Marrs and Peters had been plotted, Sloan had explained to Joe that Paul Thomas would have to be hurt as a distraction. Joe had accepted that, but he'd almost considered killing Thomas at that point. He'd only hesitated because he hadn't yet seen the absolute necessity, hadn't yet observed Sloan's commitment to the man.

Joe had intended only to maim Thomas, just enough to create a convincingly tragic accident for the public, as Sloan had wanted. Sloan had carried out the next step, inflaming the public's ire by creating the racial slant through manufactured hate mail. Hate crimes currently topped the list of politically incorrect deplorables. When they were directed at civil rights icons like Thomas, sympathy and support were nothing less than guarantees. Indeed, a multitude of those responses in the wake of the accident, to Sloan's delight, had come pouring in.

Though the hit and run was more severe than Sloan had wanted, Sloan had come to welcome the political advantage it gave the campaign, and in turn, himself. Of course, his own advantage, Joe thought, had been the burst of affection Sloan had expressed to him.

That's why Sloan's most recent threat of throwing him back into obscurity had prompted Joe's final actions. Paul was irrevocably in. Joe was out. To Joe, that meant Paul had to die.

After all the years they'd been together, after all they'd shared—things no friend, no political mentor, and certainly no wife of Sloan's could ever truly understand—Sloan was still determined to push Joe away. He was determined to deny that his deepest feelings bound him to Joe as surely he'd ever believed his affections had bound him to his wife.

Sloan's rejection of his nature had become more driven as he'd transferred his need for Joe into a need for the power and adulation Paul Thomas's success could bring to him. His delusions of grandeur had prompted him to start laying the groundwork to cut Joe and the embarrassment he represented out of his life.

But with Thomas gone, Joe knew all of that would change. Sloan could tell himself he didn't want Joe, could even tell himself he despised Joe. But Sloan had always taken Joe back whenever Joe had come running, and Joe knew he always would. Joe was in Sloan's blood, and despite everything, Sloan was in his.

Joe nodded to another nurse. She smiled and greeted him by name. He was a popular guy, he mused, but then, his likability had helped him to stay one step ahead almost all his life.

As the corridor leading to Thomas's room came into sight, Joe thought about the surveillances he'd run at Sloan's request on Maggie and her boyfriend, the cop. As far as he could tell, neither of them were getting close to him or Sloan. That meant dealing with them still wasn't absolutely necessary.

Thomas would join his dead friends, and afterward his daughter would be left with her grief, and the cop, with no leads to follow, would be diffused. In fact, there would be no one alive who was directly tied to Denning's little mystery. Finally, Joe knew that because nothing existed to tie him to Denning, his seduction of the man would never come to light.

Joe's surveillance of Denning, at Sloan's command, had revealed the man's homosexuality. Joe's plan of seduction got him close enough to Denning to discover that his knowledge of his stepbrother's murder, knowledge Sloan had feared he might have carried with him from prison, really existed. The written document of details Denning had ferreted out after his release, the document that Joe had stolen from Denning's house, had long since been destroyed by Sloan.

So without real fuel, the investigation into Denning's death and his killer would eventually disappear.

The link Thomas had with Denning would die with Thomas, and Sloan's aspirations to the summit of the political high life would atrophy, too. Life would return to an even keel, and after Sloan got over the disappointment of it all, he would see that everything Joe had done was for the best.

As usual, Sloan would come back to him.

Joe wrapped his hand around the small caliber pistol in his pocket and smiled with real satisfaction. For the first time in weeks his heart was light. He nodded affably to one of Thomas's visitors knowing either he or several like him would provide the police with a pool of possible suspects for a while. All Joe had to do was wait for Thomas's room to clear for a moment—it was all the time he'd need to wipe the man out of his life.

Joe turned the corner and quickened his step, his thoughts on Sloan and the imminent return to their comfortable life.

Chapter 22

Gil waited impatiently to get past the hospital's torturously slow electronic doors. As soon as they opened, he squeezed through and bumped hard against someone going the other way.

"Sorry," he said, and kept moving. He could see Adam out of the corner of his eye, right beside him. They took the elevator to Thomas's floor, not speaking as the car rose. Gil knew there was every possibility they would encounter nothing, but his gut was telling him such an easy outcome was a dream.

The elevator doors opened, and Gil and Adam quickly stepped out. Gil caught the eye of one of the nurses at the floor station just as she looked up. She broke off her conversation with a doctor as she watched Gil and Adam quickly approach.

"Lieutenant, what's wrong?"

Gil gripped the edge of the counter. "I want all of Senator Thomas's visitors cut off until I give word otherwise. I want—" Gil's head swung around. "O'Connor!" Gil darted around the station and took off.

O'Connor jerked around and saw the cop. He slowed, indecisive, then he saw the hardness in Stewart's eyes. He ran.

Gil took off after him. One of the police guards at the end of the floor came away from the wall. "Gil?—"

"Stop him!" Gil shouted.

The patrolman lunged as O'Connor passed—and never had a chance. O'Connor pulled a gun from his coat pocket and fired at close range.

Pandemonium erupted. Confused bystanders screamed. Gil shouted, "Get down, dammit, get *down!*" He pulled his own weapon. O'Connor was at the end of the corridor, skidding into a turn.

"Hold it right there, O'Connor, you've got nowhere to go!" Gil cried. O'Connor came to a sudden stop. Gil watched the other man's back, his own gun braced, his adrenaline pumping.

The surrounding cacophony of raised voices and panicked whispers behind Gil faded away. In his awareness, time slowed and isolated him and O'Connor. Their standoff and the tension around it became excruciatingly clear. Gil's voice was just as clear. "I said turn around. Drop the gun, and do it *slowly.*"

After the longest moment, O'Connor moved. Gil was ready—and still stunned by what happened. In the midst of his turn, O'Connor's hand suddenly lifted toward Gil. The gun he was holding went off.

Gil fired almost simultaneously. Only when O'Connor's body crumpled did Gil realize that he, himself, was unharmed and that his shot had killed O'Connor.

The screaming started anew as Gil lowered his gun and approached the body. Adam was at his side by the time he kneeled down.

Adam looked at Gil then back at O'Connor. Gil held his silence as other police guards clustered around him. Reaction would come later. Right now, despite the fact that he had taken a life, he could feel only the coolest dispassion because a darker fear was building inside.

"Maggie . . ." Gil didn't know he'd actually said anything until Adam's eyes lifted to his.

"What?" Adam said before comprehension dawned. "Oh, shit."

Gil stood and shouldered the surrounding cops and spectators out of the way. He spied a wall phone, headed for it, and grabbed the receiver. It seemed to take an eternity to complete his dial.

"*New Horizons*, can I help you?"

"Jerry, Stewart. Let me talk to Maggie."

"Sorry, Gil, she's not here. She's gone for the day."

"Alone?" Gil demanded.

"Yes, I'm pretty sure. What's wrong?"

Gil ignored Jerry's concern. "Did she go home? I told her to wait for me before she goes home."

"No, she said she had business elsewhere, that she would be back later tomorrow—"

"And? *What*?" Gil demanded at Jerry's hesitation.

"She said you knew about it."

Goddammit. Gil hung his head and slammed the receiver down, thinking. Where could she go that would keep her away all night?"

"Gil?" Adam tapped Gil's shoulder.

Gil shook his head. "She's gone. Where? *Where*?"

Adam suddenly looked energized. "Isn't Manderly due back this afternoon? Isn't that what his secretary said?"

That's when Gil knew. She had gone to Blake Manderly. Hadn't she convinced herself that she needed to long ago? He'd seen it often in her eyes, during the quietest moments when they were together. And the other night, when she'd calmly asked him when Blake Manderly was coming home, she'd become very still after he'd answered her. And he'd let it go.

He'd underestimated her again. When would he ever learn?

"I'm going to Manderly's estate," Gil said, already moving away. "Tell Myer."

"Wait," Adam grabbed his arm. "What about Michaels, what if he's heading for Manderly, too?"

"What the hell do you think? Go talk to his wife. Lean on her if you have to. We have valid assumptions and a dozen reasons to support them, but we still need a distinct probable cause to arrest Sloan. Maybe she can give it to us."

"All right." Adam reached out. "Gil?"

Gil looked down at the hand on his arm again, impatient to be gone.

"Don't be stupid, man."

Gil shook Adam off. "You just get to Michaels's wife so that we can get what we need on the bastard to take care of him." He tugged his arm loose and walked swiftly away.

Maggie administered a final touch of lipstick, put the tube back in her purse and got out of her car. Blake Manderly's estate sprawled beautifully across twenty rolling acres of prime Georgia land.

She'd called his office this morning to tell him she wanted to do a profile of him to include in the next issue of her magazine. Manderly, as she had anticipated, had accepted her request with alacrity, knowing that a spread in *New Horizons Magazine* was an instant dose of credibility the public wouldn't second-guess.

At some point during their discussion, she intended to bring up Blundon, her father, Jeff, and Sam. Though she could only guess what his reaction would be, she knew she couldn't go another day without learning something definitive. A man had been murdered more than thirty years ago. Another one curious about that death had been brutally cut down all these years later. If her father and the men she had called her friends were integral to that crime . . .

Maggie walked along Manderly's flagstone walk, noticing the abundance of cars and limousines parked along the curving drive. Manderly had agreed to talk to her, yes, but he'd neglected to tell her that they would not be doing the interview alone. She rang the doorbell.

"Yes, ma'am?" The butler stepped aside for Maggie after she introduced herself and her purpose. Inside, she saw that guests were sparse. She could tell, nevertheless, by snippets of conversation that she had walked into a fund-raiser.

"Maggie!"

Maggie turned to the man who had come up behind her. "Hello, Blake. Thanks for agreeing to the story."

"You know very well that I should be thanking you. How about a drink?"

"No, thanks. I really don't have a lot of extra time to spare today."

"Of course. This is just a little gathering some of my staff decided might be good."

Maggie looked around. "It appears to be going well."

Manderly smiled. "We'll know after we tally up the proceeds and see how much is left after the bills are subtracted. Let's talk in the study. It's right through there." He gestured to Maggie's right. "You go on in; I'll join you in a minute."

"Thanks." Maggie snagged a glass of club soda from a waiter who passed before the closed study door, then she went inside.

Very tasteful, Maggie decided, looking around. It was all a tad conservative, but saved from austerity by flashes of Blake's personal life. The flashes were revealed through a collection of mementos stashed here and there.

A wedding picture, freezing the carefree smiles of him and his wife, sat on an end table by the sofa. Maggie remembered it was only last year that Tricia Manderly had died. A group of snapshots, capturing the toddling antics of their three children sat to the side of the table, its gilt frame slightly chipped. The scars struck Maggie as lovingly worn.

On the mantel over the fireplace sat two trophies Blake had won for community service recognition. On the wall above those was a mounted plaque recognizing his contributions to youth education and disabled child care. All of it recorded a man who had distinguished his life with selfless giving.

Maggie felt unsettled all over again. Was she going to instigate a sad epilogue because of her mission here?

"Sorry to keep you waiting," Blake said, closing the study door. He walked over to the sofa and sat down. "Let's do it over here."

"Fine." Maggie joined him. "Do you mind if I use a recorder?" She was already reaching inside her purse.

"Not at all, dear. How's your father? It's been a week or so since I've visited the hospital. My hectic schedule, you understand."

"Don't apologize to the daughter of a politician. I do understand." She checked the volume control on the recorder and set it down between them. "He's good. Thanks for asking."

Blake's brow creased a little. "You sound a little down."

"No, I just meant what I said." She started the tape. "Let's begin."

For the next forty-five minutes, they talked. Manderly told Maggie about his Southern childhood, during which poverty was never very far away. His determination to break away from a grim cycle of destitution and despair he had been born into was a story of inspiration, ambition, and drive.

That Blake had eventually made his mark in education had been a particular source of pride for his family. Both his parents had been functionally illiterate when they had died. That Blake had parlayed his success into the nationally respected status of multi-published historian and professor emeritus was a distinction they never could have envisioned. The honor continued to grant him entrée into the very finest teaching institutions across the country.

"My desire, nowadays, is to translate my academic success into public service," he told Maggie. "I've always found a way to give back to the country's kids. Now I want to tackle a bigger arena, and see what changes, if any, I can make there."

"Sounds pretty idealistic."

Blake smiled. "That's exactly what I mean. That we live in a time when one man's desire to make a difference, to clean up a little of the mess our society has made of things is considered idealistic, well, it's a sad time.

"I don't have anything to risk, politically. I have three wonderful children and a passel of grandchildren. In short, I'm not looking for any self-gain at this stage in my life. I just want a shot at helping the government make things a little better for myself and my community, if I can."

"And with any luck, the electorate will decide to vote you into state office so that you can have a long-lasting shot at it."

Blake chuckled. "Win, lose, or draw, this campaigning business is already turning into one hell of a ride."

The more Maggie listened to him, the more she admired him. She hated to ruin the pleasant mood of the interview, but the hour was getting late and it was time to make her move. She switched off the recorder.

"Blake, there's something I have to ask you."

"Ah," Blake said, sitting back, "finally, here's what's put the shadows in your lovely eyes."

Maggie squarely met the gaze of her father's very dear friend and took the plunge.

"Detective, I have nothing to say to you." Monica Michaels attempted to shut her front door in Adam's face.

"Wrong, Mrs. Michaels." Adam pushed back. Sloan Michaels's wife was forced to step aside. "I think you have plenty to say to me, and I think all if it has to do with some interesting facts about your husband." When her eyes dropped, Adam knew he was right.

"Whatever it is you think you know—"

"Why don't we start with Joseph O'Connor for starters."

"What?"

Adam almost smiled at her startled expression. "You heard me. Are we going to talk?" Apparently, they were, Adam concluded, when all of the indignation suddenly seemed to drain out of Monica Michaels.

"You'd better come with me," she said, stepping aside.

Adam was led to a graciously appointed living room, heavy with floral accents splashed against primaries and whites. Elegant with a flair, just like the woman. When they were seated, Adam sat back, silently inviting her to begin.

"It was on television," her voice was almost detached. "The news commentators broke in about fifteen minutes ago. Joe O'Connor is dead." She looked away from Adam, studied the toe of her shoe. "I thought he'd slinked out of our lives for good sixteen years ago."

"I know the particulars, Mrs. Michaels."

"Monica," she responded. "That's who I've been for a long time now in my mind."

Adam inclined his head. "Monica. What I want to know is, what was the relationship between your husband and Joseph O'Connor most recently?"

Monica brushed a tear aside. "I think perhaps they were still lovers," she said very quietly.

"For how long?" Monica started to speak, then just shook her head.

One night about two years ago, she told Adam, Sloan told her a tale. His employer, Paul Thomas, had confided something incredible to him. Sloan had asked Thomas early on in their association for all of the skeletons that could potentially sabotage Thomas's political career. What Thomas had given him, the facts of the Parsons incident, was something Sloan had never dreamed of.

"Why would Thomas risk confiding that information to anyone?" Adam wondered aloud.

"You mean, why now? I wondered the same. But I think the answer is simple, Sergeant. These last few years, Paul Thomas has been a man in turmoil. For whatever reasons, since they were never made public, he had a huge falling out with his daughter. The fact that there was a rift did go public and was obviously very painful for them both. Perhaps more so because that break came on the heels of the other major upheaval in their personal lives."

"The controversy over Sidney Brooker, highlighted by Thomas's public dissension and showdown with Gil Stewart."

Monica nodded. "Added to all that, Paul Thomas isn't getting any younger. I think he's a very lonely man feeling sorely adrift. And into that vulnerability walked Sloan."

Adam wondered if he'd ever seen a smile so bitter.

"To understand what that means, you have to understand how very persuasive my husband is."

"What did he persuade Paul Thomas to do?"

"To look beyond his exterior as an adviser, to catch a very enticing glimpse of the man Sloan wanted him to see. From what Sloan told me, Thomas slowly started to regard him as something of a godson. It's got to be the only explanation for why Thomas would ever confide to Sloan something so deeply buried and explosive."

"But it all went beyond Thomas's telling and Sloan's listening, didn't it, Monica? Once he had that information, what did your husband do?"

"He panicked at first, but then shortly after that response, he grew very calm. I thought he'd reasoned that it was so old that, carefully concealed, it probably was still unable to touch Thomas's career. But about a year ago, Sloan started talking to me about things that made me afraid." Monica leaned her head back against the sofa and closed her eyes. "I wouldn't listen, and now two men are dead."

"Sloan killed them?"

"Had them killed. He used Joe O'Connor. After the scandal in California, I caught odd glimpses of O'Connor here and there. He hovered around the edges of Sloan's life like some devoted puppy. It was pitiful."

"You allowed it?"

"Sloan had convinced me a long time ago that getting tangled up with O'Connor had been a terrible mistake. He said that incident had been O'Connor's fault, that O'Connor had tricked him into getting high. He promised me it was the only way O'Connor or anyone ever could have taken sexual advantage of him."

"You believed him."

"I loved him, Sergeant. I still do. That's why I wanted to believe him. That's how from that point until this, I could listen to his lies and keep my eyes shut."

Adam couldn't keep the disgust from his voice. "Then help me out, Monica. Why precisely have you decided to open them now?"

She lifted her head and focused on him. "Because no matter what Sloan's past failings have been, no matter what they continued to be, I never believed him capable of actual murder. When he talked about all of the Blundon principals needing to be eliminated so that there would be no possibility of Paul's involvement coming to light, I dismissed it as idle chatter."

"But when Paul Thomas was hurt and the men involved started dying—

"Yes. I confronted Sloan. I even conjured a little extra courage from somewhere to call and write to Maggie"—she smiled without humor—"anonymously. I tried to warn her that perhaps she was in danger. But then, soon after, Sloan distracted me from my fears. He started pampering me like he used to, started reminding me of how well he'd always taken care of me. He told me that with Paul our ship was really sailing in.

"He told me when it was all over, he'd engineer a way to pin the blame on O'Connor. He'd claim, when O'Connor tried to implicate him in the crimes he'd committed, that O'connor was involving him because he was obsessed with him. Sloan would tell the police

O'Connor had intermittently stalked him during all the years since their past encounter.

"Sloan assured me nobody would believe the word of a sociopath like O'Connor over his. And once Sloan succeeded in disassociating himself from the entire unhappy episode, our lives would go on. With Paul Thomas in our corner, we'd both live better than we ever had before."

"You realize I could haul you in as an accessory to murder?"

"Of course I realize that. I may be unforgivably blind, Sergeant, but I'm not stupid. The point is, I admit I have no defense on my behalf, and beyond what I've just told you I have nothing more to say."

"Oh, yes you do. You're going to repeat that story to my superiors. In return, we may be able to swing some kind of deal for immunity."

Monica thought about it for a very long while before finally saying, "Sergeant, for what I've allowed to happen, I can never be immune." She folded her hands in her lap. "If you want my husband, the least I can do at this stage is to help you get him."

Blake had gone absolutely still. Maggie watched his bent head, pleading silently for him to say something. But when he finally looked at her fully in the face, she knew.

"Oh, God," she whispered. "Oh, my God."

Blake just shook his head. "I can't believe this has come back."

Maggie found it devastating that a man who had sounded as if the world was in his hand one moment could sound so utterly broken the next. She could hardly bear to ask what she had to know. "My father, you, Jeff, Sam—you killed that man?"

"No, Maggie," Blake Manderly's voice sounded unaturally bleak. "I did. I killed Owen Parsons."

"And your friends covered up for you, Manderly."

Maggie and Blake started violently, their attention pulled to the man who had silently entered the room and just as quietly shut the door behind him. Now that he was standing inside, Sloan Michaels continued to hold their attention with the gun he held on them.

Maggie managed to speak. "Sloan, what the *hell* are you doing?"

"Protecting my interests. If that's not enough for your puritanical conscience, I'm bringing a murderer to justice, just as I did his fellow murderers.

"The only thing in your father's life that could sabotage his political future and mine is this dirty little secret he and his friends have been living with for all these years. As long as it existed, someone was bound to dig it up sooner or later. I've just taken pains to erase that eventuality."

"You killed the others?" Maggie was still having trouble comprehending what Sloan was telling her. And then Sloan's expression turned dark.

"No, I didn't pull the trigger on the others, but it doesn't matter because the one who did is dead, too." He smiled. "I'm not lying, Maggie. Your lieutenant will tell you, or rather, he would have had you not had to die, too."

"Sloan, listen to me—"

"Get up!" Sloan gestured with the gun.

Maggie felt suffocated, her heart was pounding so hard. "What are you going to do?"

"I've already told you, finish it." He was suddenly impatient. "You two are going to precede me, and I'll follow you out past the guests. Remember, even though my gun will be concealed, it's going to stay aimed at your backs."

Maggie stood close to Blake. "You can't really hope to get out of this clean, Sloan. If you try, the police will track you down wherever you are."

"Maybe. But then there's still the outside chance they'll never know. Everyone who could incriminate me is dead, or will be. That means you, too. However, I won't even have a hope of getting out of this safely if I let you live."

"Blake hasn't spoken of this for nearly forty years, in doing so now he has everything to lose. And even if you were to kill him, as you said, with everybody else dead it would be only my word against yours. Why do we have to die?"

"That cop of yours. He'll keep pursuing it because of you."

Maggie flinched at Sloan's cold eyes.

"Don't think I can't tell you've been screwing him again. I've seen the way you look when you talk about him, and when he mentions your name he gets that same look in his eyes. The simple truth is, you'll run to him the first chance you get if you live."

"He'll hunt you down until the day you die if I don't."

"An eventuality I'll just have to chance. Besides," he added enigmatically, "none of us can live forever, not even Gil Stewart. Now let's move."

All the way across the foyer, in the wake of short glances and polite smiles, Maggie wanted to cry out, say something, end this deadly game by calling Sloan's bluff. But she didn't want to die, and she knew that making Sloan's perfidy public would ensure her death.

Sloan Michaels was desperate. Desperate men had little to lose.

At the door of Blake's Seville, Sloan forced Blake to take the wheel. He directed Maggie to take the front passenger's seat, and then he scooted himself inside the back.

"This gun is still aimed at you both," Sloan said. "I want you to drive about five miles south of here, Manderly."

Blake froze. "There's nothing in that direction but Ollier's Bluff."

"Precisely. I've decided you're going to have a very untimely accident. Perhaps you were traveling to some casual destination with Maggie along for the ride. Your staff knows she arrived at your house with the intention of conducting an interview. That's exactly what they'll tell the police."

Maggie tried again. "Sloan, you can't get away with this. Let us go and cut your losses now."

"Shut up, Maggie. Manderly, let's go."

Blake sat unmoving with his hands stubbornly on the wheel.

Sloan raised his pistol a little and tapped Blake's ear. Blake jumped.

"I said drive, you murdering son of a bitch."

Blake started the engine, put the car into gear, and drove.

As Sloan forced Maggie and Blake from Blake's house, Gil was less than ten minutes behind them. A curious guest, having observed Manderly's car leave, had directed Gil in the same southernly direction the scholar had taken.

Gil's cellular beeped, and he snatched it to his ear. Adam's message was concise, exactly what Gil had hoped to hear. "Thanks man. Round up some back-up." He told Adam his location and the general direction in which he was traveling.

"You got it."

Gil slammed the phone back in its cradle and

accelerated. Though Sloan Michaels didn't know it, the nail was already in his hide. Unfortunately, he also probably had in his clutches the very thing Gil found even more important.

He and Maggie had lost each other once. The eight years it had taken them to find their way back together had been much too long.

He'd be damned if he'd lose her again.

Ollier's Bluff came into sight. "Pull up to that embankment and stop," Sloan told Blake.

Blake did as he was told.

Maggie sat rigid, desperately trying to think of something to do. She jumped and gasped in surprise when Blake tried something first.

Manderly whipped around so quickly that Sloan was taken temporarily off guard. The back of Blake's fist hit Sloan squarely on the jaw. Sloan's recovery was deadly and fast.

Maggie screamed when the popping discharge of the pistol filled the car. Her ears were ringing even as Blake Manderly's blood splattered on the windshield and the metallic smell of it filled the close confines of the car. Maggie didn't even know her hand was hitting the door handle until she almost fell out of the car in her desperation to get out.

When she hit the dirt, it registered that despite the murder he'd just committed, Sloan, too, must have been a little stunned because he didn't follow immediately on her heels. Even so, she knew her advantage could only be measured in seconds. She ran for a copse of trees to her right.

The slam of Sloan's car door was the first clear sound she heard as she reached what she hoped would be a concealing stand of evergreens.

"Maggie! You can't outrun me. Give it up and I'll make it quick!"

Her lungs were bursting. All she was aware of was the sound of his taunting voice coming closer. That and the vision of Blake's vicious death.

"Maggie, I can see you! Stop, or I'll shoot you now."

Again, Maggie hit the dirt. The report of Sloan's gun followed an instant behind her. She knew she was crying, but she couldn't stop, and she couldn't get her footing on the loamy ground. She almost had it when she felt herself sliding. An incline she hadn't seen was right behind her, and the loose sticks she was standing on were giving way. It was only her desperate clutch at a tree trunk that saved her fall.

God, help me, she prayed.

"Maggie!"

It was *Gil*. "Gil! I'm here, I'm over here." There was another pop of gunfire, and then two more in rapid succession.

Maggie was still sobbing when Gil's arms closed around her.

"Jesus Christ, honey. When I heard that shot back there where he killed Manderly, I thought it was you." He held her away from him. "Are you hurt? Look at me, Maggie, are you *hurt*?"

Maggie followed Gil's horrified gaze and searching hands. The side of her shirt was saturated with blood. She started shaking all over when she realized it wasn't hers.

"He killed him, Gil. Sloan killed Blake right in front of me. I couldn't help, I couldn't get away . . . oh, *God*."

Reassured that her response was due only to shock, Gil wrapped his arms around her again. "Now, listen to me. He can't hurt you anymore. I took him down. He's wounded, and he won't hurt you."

Maggie shook harder even as Gil's voice grew calmer.

"I'm going to take you away from here now, okay? Can you walk?"

"Yes!" Maggie gasped. "Yes." She let Gil pull her away from what had, in this short time, become her safety zone. As she did, she heard sirens approaching from the distance.

When they got back to the scene of Blake's murder, a platoon of squad cars had converged. Maggie got one look at Sloan. His shoulder was bloody, but that didn't stop the cops who surrounded him from slapping him in cuffs.

The next thing she knew, Gil was exchanging a few words with Adam and a couple of other officers. Then she was in Gil's car, his hand resting on hers, as he drove them away.

Epilogue

Maggie and Gil walked down the hospital corridor together. Nearly two months since the day of his injury, Paul Thomas had regained consciousness. It was the first full week after his awakening, and Maggie couldn't bear to put off the talk any longer.

The two officers guarding Thomas's door moved aside when Maggie and Gil approached. "Lieutenant," one of them said.

"Hi, Dale. Is he sleeping?"

"No, sir. He's awake."

"We won't be long."

"We'll be here," the other officer responded.

Yes, Maggie thought, they would be. The question was, would they be there to ensure her father's safety for the rest of his stay, or would they be standing on hand to take him away? Too many important answers to this tragedy were still maddeningly unclear.

Paul Thomas sat in the visitor's chair beside his hospital bed. He was wearing his bathrobe and the shirt of his pajamas peeked from beneath the collar. Maggie let go of Gil's hand and walked across the room until she was standing at her father's side. She'd visited constantly since his latest recovery, but in the wake of his weakness, conversation had been kept to a minimum.

Now he was able to talk, and Maggie knew that she still wasn't prepared for this discussion. She felt like a frightened little girl. "Hi, Daddy."

Paul Thomas seemed to rouse himself slowly from a deep contemplation. His features were stern, his eyes wary when he looked up at his daughter.

"How are you feeling?" she asked hesitantly.

Thomas's eyes moved past Maggie to Gil. "Why am I not surprised that you're here. I guess I always knew deep down in my heart you'd have to come back."

Gil nodded from across the room, studying this man who had meant so much to him. Paul Thomas was definitely on his guard, but nevertheless seemed . . . defeated.

Gil considered how Thomas had been updated on the passage of events, from the real elements at work behind his own accident to Sloan's arrest. He'd had a week to digest the consequences, and now Gil was just as restless as Maggie to see his response.

Thomas looked away from Gil and pursed his mouth, seemingly content to study the floor. Then he surprised his child. "Maggie, come here." He reached out a hand to her.

Maggie caught it and sank to her knees. Her father pulled her close, and her head was in his lap beneath his stroking hand before she knew it.

"How can you ever forgive me," he asked. "I've been so wrong . . . so wrong."

For the second time, Thomas looked up, and Gil saw that his face had softened as if he were trying to draw the man he watched into the same embrace. "To you both, I've been wrong."

The words unsettled Gil, threw him off balance. He folded his arms and braced a shoulder against the wall. "I survived, Paul. I think right now your daughter needs you." Paul Thomas looked unutterably sad, then he glanced down at his own hand as he continued to stroke Maggie.

"I can never make things up to you," Maggie heard him say. "I can only try to explain Blundon, why—how the things that came to pass could have happened. Will you let me, baby? Will you at least let me try to make that much up to you?"

Maggie raised her head. "We'll both try, Daddy. But for now, I have to know."

Paul Thomas held his daughter and stared over her head, off into the distance. "You can't understand how strongly racism and all its hate can affect you unless you've lived through it. You were very, very young when Dr. King founded the movement, even later when others like myself dedicated our lives to preserving it.

"We found great peace in his message because it was a message that actually demonstrated how nonviolence could work. But that was after, Maggie. Before . . . oh, before that the South was a turmoil for black people. For black men like me, like us—Jeff, Sam, and Blake—living our lives day after day could be an unbelievable . . . trial. We all found our individual ways out of it, ways that gave us enough distance to cultivate what was best in us so that we could give back to our people, so that we could use our reason and intellect to fight the good fight. But that awareness only came fully to us as men. We were still children when we passed through Blundon and made the fateful decision to stop at that diner that night.

"We were on our way back to school. We'd just come off a college break and were a little tired but feeling good. We'd rented a cottage up North and ended up heading for home pretty late the weekend before classes resumed. When we stopped at that diner for gas and encountered Parsons, all of us were brought back with a vengeance to the segregation and racism we had left behind for a week.

"We just planned to get in and get out. We wouldn't have stopped at all, but the gas tank was nearly empty and we were desperate. We were also surrounded when we pulled in. That diner was obviously a favorite haunt for the reddest of rednecks, good ole boys from around the town. Parsons came outside and tried to start something, cause trouble. We just kept to ourselves and let the older station attendant pump our gas."

Gil listened from where he stood, wondering at the replay of that tense reality, at how vivid it still must be to cause the bleakness that shadowed Thomas's eyes.

"We were just pulling away when Blake turned his head and looked back. He saw Parsons kick that old man, kick him in the back of the knees, kick him after he was down on the ground. We stopped the car, trying to decide whether or not to go back. That's when the diner door opened and two more bastards stepped outside. They had shotguns in their hands. They kept their eyes on us while we sat there. And then they started to laugh."

Thomas's hand had stilled. Maggie drew away a little so that she could take that hand in her own. He lapsed into silence, and Maggie let him sit, knowing that the trauma of what he was remembering was gripping him now as it had gripped him then. At length, she asked, "What happened then, Daddy?"

Thomas shook his head a little, as if he were trying to shake the moodiness away. "We drove off. I was at the wheel; I was the one who drove us away. The last thing that I heard was those bigots' laughter. The last thing I saw in my mind's eyes was that old man's tears."

Gil slowly pushed away from the wall. He walked

over to the bed and circled it until he was very close to this man who, until this moment, he hadn't really been sure he wanted to listen to. He sat down and waited for Thomas to collect himself from the pain that had haunted him for nearly forty years.

"Sam was shaking. Blake and Jeff sat in that car like stone. I could feel their rage. I remember very clearly the next thing that happened. Blake said just one word. He said, 'Stop.'

"We were on a two-lane road. The diner was at the end of the road, so we knew anyone leaving would have to pass us."

"None of us asked why, but I think we all knew what Blake was up to. So without saying a word in response, I pulled over, cut the engine and headlights, and the four of us waited by the side of the road.

"Thirty minutes passed, maybe an hour, I don't know. Finally, we heard a truck coming. He so easily might not have been alone, but even knowing that, we didn't care. The moment had become unreal, completely unreal. All we knew was that that old man hadn't gotten any justice, and we'd done nothing, *nothing* to even try to help him while we were there.

"When the truck got close, I eased the car out into the road to block it. His headlights picked us up, and he stopped." Thomas paused again. His eyes were closed when he resumed his story.

"Even when he got out of the truck, he was cocky. He said he wasn't scared of 'no educated niggers,' told us if he had his way, he'd line us all up and shoot us. That's when Blake hit him. He just charged right up to Parsons and hit him in the face. Parsons went down hard and couldn't get up, because by the time he tried Jeff had rushed forward and joined in.

"They beat him and beat him. Sam and I looked at each other before we got the nerve to step forward.

Blake was standing back by then. Even in the moonlight, I could see Parsons's blood on him. 'Go ahead,' Blake told me, 'go ahead and get your lick.' Parsons was severely wounded, but even as I saw that, I saw that old man again. I leaned down and hit Parsons. I only meant to do it once, but the hate in his face . . . my rage took over.

"Somehow, Parsons struggled to his knees. He was swaying, and a part of me felt sick to my stomach. But a deeper part kept telling me that all four of us were doing right."

"What about Blake?" Gil gently asked.

"I don't know why none of us were paying attention to Blake. Maybe it was just destiny, maybe it was just part of what was supposed to happen all along on that strange, awful night. I was the one who heard him come up behind us. 'Move over,' he said, and I remember jumping because his voice was so close, so hard.

"I think I moved to stop him, but I was too late. He raised the gun we found out later he kept in his glove compartment, and while Sam, Jeff, and I stood frozen, watching, Blake calmly shot Owen Parsons in the head."

Maggie held onto her father's hand, but her own fingers had long since grown cold. She could only whisper, "The four of you lived with that murder all these years."

"Yes, we lived with it. Somehow. After we got Parsons's body back inside the truck where it was later discovered, we drove out of Blundon, Georgia, forever, and our lives went on.

"We graduated from college and over the years, we stayed in touch. But the truly incredible thing about the aftermath of that killing is, not once in nearly forty years did any of us ever speak of it, not one utterance.

Maybe we rehashed it to ourselves in our more private moments, but we never did with each other."

"Then, why did you tell Sloan?" Gil wanted to know.

"Ah, Gil." Paul Thomas turned his head Gil's way and opened his eyes. "To understand that, you have to understand this. I was lost. I'd pushed you out of my life because the anger and racial bias that consumed you then reminded me unbearably of my own when I'd been young and rash like you. The reminder started to loom out of proportion until every time I looked at you I saw myself as I'd been, as we'd been when we'd killed Owen Parsons.

"I couldn't bear it, and eventually I couldn't bear you. I used my own child and the magazine close to her heart to engineer your destruction. I wanted you to leave her, leave me. When you did, I thought I'd be able to reclaim some peace."

"Oh, Daddy." Maggie dropped his hand, but she held his eyes with hers. "You still didn't find your peace."

"No. Every time I looked at you and saw the accusation in your eyes, I hated myself. Maggie, I just kept hating for so long that eventually it became easier to absolve the tangled guilt and regret of that hate by transferring it to you. *You* were the one pushing me away, *you* were the one declaring your independence, rejecting my guidance and love.

"By the time I'd succeeded in driving you from me, I had no one and I was lonely. But I'd pushed you both too hard to ever be able to make it up, so I pretended the separation didn't matter to me because I didn't know what else to do.

"Then Sloan came along. I saw in him all the bright possibilities I'd cherished and tried to nurture in you both. It was easy for me to let him into my heart, to allow him to take the place of the children I had lost."

Thomas sighed. "Perhaps our union was another piece of fate because retribution has come full circle. Maybe now, the ultimate price of what we did in Blundon can be called even. Maybe now I'll stop feeling the awful repercussions of the violence from that night."

They had all come full circle, Gil thought. Each of their lives had been marked by struggle and pain. But they had survived it, and maybe that was what really counted for something in the end. He sensed Maggie looking at him and lifted his hand. Their fingers touched and meshed over Paul Thomas's lap, and Gil knew in that moment that despite the pain she'd suffered and despite his, the two of them were going to make it this time. The two of them, together, were going to be all right.

"Full circle," Thomas murmured. "He's good for you, Maggie. In fact, at this moment, I'm very sure that he's a much better man than I ever was. Stay with him. And you stay with her, Gil, because the one thing I couldn't destroy despite everything is the purest truth in all of our lives."

"Daddy—"

"You two have found a love that all the ugliness and weakness and hatred in this world can't destroy or even deny."

"Daddy, I love you," Maggie cried, letting Gil go to press herself into her father's arms. "I love you so much. That's another love that won't ever die."

Thomas looked at Gil over his daughter's head . . . and again shut his eyes when the hand he extended to the only man he'd ever been really proud to call son was clasped in a grip that was cool and strong.

"Whatever happens in the future," Paul Thomas said "will only be right and fitting. But until that moment comes and even beyond, this is the start of my real future. I have my children back, I have all I need. I love you both completely."

Gil knelt beside Maggie and finally closed the circle that he knew, at last in his heart, would last forever.

Dear Reader,

I hope you enjoyed Maggie and Gil's story as much as I enjoyed writing it and tapping into some serious issues that shaped their lives.

Racism is perhaps the most insidious social disease affecting us today. It continues to take tolls that wound us because its negativity collectively lessens the quality of all our lives. Maggie and Gil found their way to a place where, together, they could begin to heal their scars through the timeless power of love. Perhaps that power is the most important element to their story; as a writer, it is certainly one whose complexities I never tire of exploring.

I hope you'll keep me company as I embark on the journey again and again.

In fact, my newest novel, *The Final Act*, will venture into newly textured territory, just as compelling yet a little different.

It's the story of Shannon LaCrosse, a woman who is maneuvered into a crime she is horrified to commit. She survives the hell of prison, only to realize that her best chance at restitution—and retribution—lies in the hands of David Courtney, the ex-cop who helped imprison her.

They begin their ill-fated journey together searching for a criminal mastermind still on the loose. What they find is the key to a conspiracy, and the opportunity to unlock their hearts to a second chance at love.

Look for *The Final Act* in winter 1996.

I'd love to hear from you. Drop me a line at: P.O. Box 44378, Indianapolis, IN 46244-0378.

Until next time, peace and love.

—Tracey Tillis